‘Oh, heavens!’

The exclamation of [illegible]
woman in the pool. She had just seen him.

‘I mean you no harm,’ John assured her. ‘I came upon you by accident. Where are your clothes?’

‘No! I don’t want you to… I don’t need my clothes.’

‘You don’t?’ John had caught sight of a bundle of clothing tucked into a bush. Ignoring her protests, he picked it up. A towel, a black dress…and a cap and widow’s veil. He frowned. ‘But these aren’t yours. What are Mrs Duval’s clothes doing on this path?’

Caroline choked with laughter. ‘Throw me my towel and yours, and I’ll come out.’ Standing before him, swathed in towels, she said humbly, ‘You see before you, Colonel Ancroft, a penitent. I’m afraid I’ve been playing a dreadful trick on you.’

‘Indeed, ma’am?’ he said coldly. ‘I’m afraid I do not find any of this amusing. I suggest that we return to the inn, where I shall listen to your explanation with interest.’

Dear Reader

The Duchess of Richmond's ball in Brussels, on June 15th 1815, is one of the great dramatic occasions in history. But what makes the ball noteworthy isn't the brilliance of the guest list—it is the poignancy of what happened in the three days that followed. The young men who danced so light-heartedly in their uniforms of scarlet, blue, green and gold on the night of June 15th, dazzling the beau monde with their gaiety and charm, left the ballroom, some of them still in their dress uniforms, to ride straight into one of the hardest-fought battles in European history—the Battle of Waterloo. By 18th June the Duke of Wellington had triumphed over Napoleon Bonaparte. But the cost in lives was huge, and many of those young men were never to return.

Firm friends, Adam Calthorpe, Ivo Trenchard and their commanding officer Colonel Ancroft, do survive the battlefield to return to London Society's opulent drawing rooms. Three soldiers, skilled at war, but not nearly as adept as they think when it comes to the ways of women. How will they fare? *Lord Calthorpe's Promise* and *Lord Trenchard's Choice* introduced the first two of these soldier heroes, and their exploits are continued in *Colonel Ancroft's Love.*

Sylvia Andrew

COLONEL ANCROFT'S LOVE

Sylvia Andrew

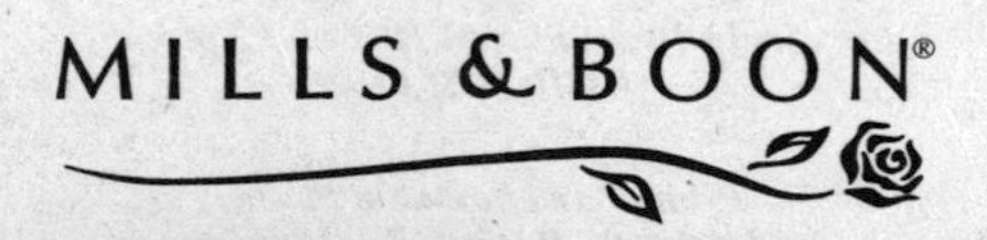

All the characters in this book have no existence outside the imagination of the author, and have no relation whatsoever to anyone bearing the same name or names. They are not even distantly inspired by any individual known or unknown to the author, and all the incidents are pure invention.

First published in Great Britain 2003
Harlequin Mills & Boon Limited,
Eton House, 18-24 Paradise Road, Richmond, Surrey TW9 1SR

ISBN 0 263 83526 X

Set in Times Roman 10½ on 12 pt.
04-1003-85115

Printed and bound in Spain
by Litografia Rosés S.A., Barcelona

Sylvia Andrew taught modern languages for a number of years, ultimately becoming Vice-Principal of a sixth-form college. She lives in Somerset with two cats, a dog, and a husband who has a very necessary sense of humour and a stern approach to punctuation. Sylvia has one daughter living in London, and they share a lively interest in the theatre. She describes herself as an 'unrepentant romantic'.

Recent titles by the same author:

LORD CALTHORPE'S PROMISE
LORD TRENCHARD'S CHOICE

and in the Regency series *The Steepwood Scandal:*

AN UNREASONABLE MATCH
AN INESCAPABLE MATCH

Prologue

Brussels, June 15th 1815

Colonel John Ancroft watched from the gallery as his two best officers joined the throng in the Duchess of Richmond's ballroom. He didn't envy them. The evening was stiflingly hot and the room was crowded. He saw with approval that Adam Calthorpe was talking to the Countess Karnska, doing his best to reassure her after the rumours of the French advance. Ivo Trenchard was, of course, making for the loveliest woman in the room. Tom Payne was whirling some poor girl round the ballroom with more energy than style. The Colonel nodded. The situation was normal—that is, as normal as it could be in these extraordinary circumstances. He went back into the small room and fingered the papers lying there. Reports, none of them precise, none reassuring. Where the devil was Bonaparte? Some of the scouts put him just a few miles away on the border, but everything was vague, nothing clear. One thing, however, was quite certain. The two greatest generals in Europe, Wellington and Napoleon Bonaparte, would very soon come face to face in battle.

Possibly as early as tomorrow. Even now, while the cream of European society was dancing and laughing below in the Duchess of Richmond's ballroom, Wellington was closeted in the Duke of Richmond's library, together with his corps commanders, his generals, and his senior Staff Officers, drawing up battle plans. When they were ready and the situation made clear, it would be up to him, Colonel Ancroft, to see that Calthorpe, Trenchard and the rest of the men under his command carried the marching orders to the regiments stationed outside Brussels. Till then he had nothing to do but cool his heels in this cramped little room in the Duchess's house, listening to the music drifting up from the ballroom.

The Colonel was a severely disciplined man. He seldom let himself dwell on the past, or think of the future. The past was too painful, the future too uncertain. But tonight he allowed his thoughts to wander. If he, John Ancroft, survived the coming battle, what would he do with his life? Where would he go? It would have to be London. He would buy a house in London. There was certainly no home for him in Yorkshire. While his uncle lived, still nursing the implacable hatred that had taken possession of him after the death of his only son, Marrick Castle was closed to him.

He frowned. Marrick… He had avoided even thinking about Marrick for years, had deliberately shut out the sunny memories of his childhood, playing with Philip, riding with Philip, wrestling with Philip, of being second only to Philip in his uncle's regard and affection. He had been very young when his own parents had died within months of each other, and he and Philip had been brought up together at Marrick like brothers. As they grew older there had been rivalry, of course. Two lusty young men, anxious to prove their manhood, were bound to cross each other from time to time. But before Gabriella Ainderby made her appearance it had all been basically good-natured. It was love for Gabriella which had brought about the fatal change in the cousins' relationship, and since that time he had almost forgotten what love was… Fourteen years ago, but the memory still had so much power to hurt…

This wouldn't do! He suddenly got up and went back on to the gallery, staring down at the mass of people, willing himself to think only of the present. Trenchard was nowhere to be seen—he was probably out in the garden with Madame de Menkelen. No, the lovely Isabel de Menkelen was down there, dancing with someone else. Ivo must be losing his touch… Calthorpe was now with Tom Payne. A nice boy, Lieutenant Payne, but wayward. He would make a good soldier when he learned to submit to discipline…

'Colonel Ancroft!'

He turned. One of the Duke's aides was standing respectfully behind him. 'His Grace wishes to see you, sir. In the library.'

So the summons had come, the action was about to begin. And not a moment too soon. He followed the young man down the stairs and disappeared into the library.

In the great battle of Waterloo that followed, Colonel Ancroft fought with courage and daring. Twice he was wounded and twice he went back to stay with his men. In the end he was carried off the field half conscious and weak from loss of blood with a dangerously deep sabre cut in his thigh. He was more fortunate than Tom Payne and thousands of others. He was one of the survivors, but it was two years before the surgeons finally pronounced him fit. By the beginning of 1818 he was living, as he had planned, in London.

Chapter One

London, May 1818

Colonel Ancroft stood at the window of his house in Mount Street, contemplating the scene. Two street vendors were having a lively discussion in the street below. He watched them for a few minutes to see if they would come to blows, and wasn't sure whether he was relieved or disappointed when they settled their difference and went on their way without incident. He sighed, turned, and surveyed the room. What should he do next for entertainment? Count the stripes on the wallpaper? He walked restlessly about the room, finally coming to a halt at the writing table. After staring at it for a moment he sat down with a gesture of impatience, poured himself a glass of wine, and took up his pen. He would catch up on his correspondence.

By the time his man came into the room the Colonel was absorbed. He eventually turned and said irritably, 'Well, don't just stand there, Betts. What is it?'

'Mr Fennybright is here, Colonel.'

There was a short silence during which the Colonel got

up and straightened himself. He took a breath, then said, 'Very well. You'd better show him up.' As Betts turned to go he added, 'And fetch more wine. That decanter is almost empty.'

A minute or two later Betts returned, accompanied by an elderly gentleman whose dress and demeanour made it obvious that this was a lawyer. The lines on his face showed humour and benevolence, though at the moment the expression on it was solemn enough.

'So, Fenny! I take it that you have some news for me.'

'Your uncle passed away three days ago, my lord. I arrived in London early this morning and have come straight here.'

After a short silence John Ancroft said, 'So that's it. It's over.' He walked to the window and stared out. Without turning, he asked, 'Were you there at the end? Did… did my uncle leave any message, send any word?'

The lawyer shook his head. 'None, my lord.'

'Did he mention me at all?'

Mr Fennybright hesitated. 'Not…not anything to the point.'

'Come, Fenny, come! You needn't be discreet—I can guess what the gist was. Someone will tell me, why not you? There was no relenting, no word of forgiveness, I take it.'

'Lord Coverdale was old and ill, my lord. He…he was not himself.'

'Damn it, tell me, Fenny!'

'His lordship never became reconciled to the tragic death of his son, not even on his deathbed.'

'What did he say?' Then, as the lawyer hesitated again, John Ancroft turned to him and said brusquely, 'I intend to know, Fenny! His exact words, if you please!'

'Forgive me,' said the lawyer in troubled tones. 'You

will not enjoy what you hear.' In response to a gesture of impatience, he took a breath and said, 'Very well, my lord, since you insist... In spite of anything we could say, his late lordship remained implacable. His exact words were that he...he cursed his misfortune that not all of Napoleon's armies had managed to rid the world of the villain who had murdered his son. That his sole regret in quitting this life was that you had survived him to inherit the title for which you had killed your cousin.' John Ancroft turned back abruptly to face the window. After a lengthy silence, the lawyer added earnestly, 'It was a shocking scene, my lord. No one present believed anything of the sort. Indeed, there isn't another soul in Yorkshire or anywhere else who believes that Lord Philip Ancroft's death was anything but an accident. But none of our remonstrations—not even those of his chaplain—could persuade Lord Coverdale to withdraw his words. He died soon after. I'm...I'm deeply sorry, my lord.'

John said harshly, 'You needn't be. My uncle was wrong in one thing—I never thought of or wished for the title. But there was some truth in the rest. I *was* responsible for Philip's death. For two deaths—Philip's and... and Gabriella's. And then Rose died, too...'

'No, really, my lord! You must not say such things! You ought not even to think them! Your wife had been ill for years before she died. And I remember, if you do not, your kindness and generosity to her. Even though—'

'Even though she hated the sight of me? No, that's wrong. Hatred was too strong an emotion for poor, gentle Rose. But she saw as little of me as she could. God knows, I wasn't there very often, but she couldn't disguise her unease in my company, even for half an hour! Towards the end she had hysterics whenever she saw me. And she brought little Harriet up to feel the same. It was no wonder that the child regarded me with such horror. Between them, my wife and my uncle convinced her that I was a murderer.'

'That was very wrong of them,' said the lawyer gravely. 'Wickedly wrong. You would never have wished your cousin Philip any real harm. How can anyone talk of murder? You weren't even near him when he wrecked his curricle and killed himself and Miss Ainderby!'

'I drove him to it. No! Don't try to say anything, Fenny. The truth is that Philip and I were both in a fury when he got into that curricle, and, instead of stopping him, I goaded him further. There's no excuse for my behaviour. I was older than he was and should have had more control.'

'You are too hard on yourself, my lord. No one, not you, not even his father, could control Philip Ancroft when he was in a rage. And as for Miss Gabriella Ainderby… A lovely young lady, but—'

'No!' The sudden exclamation stopped Mr Fennybright. 'Leave it, Fenny, leave it!' After a pause John went on, 'You've been a good friend to me, Fenny. You have never wavered in your support of my case, I know. But I have always understood my uncle's reaction. He had good reason to hate me. In the end it was all he had left—his hatred of me. It's what kept him alive—that and his desire to outlive me.'

'I'm afraid that might well be true and I am sorry for it. I think the death of his only son turned his mind. May God now give him rest.'

'Amen to that,' said John sombrely, as Betts came into the room with a decanter and glasses. 'You'll take some wine with me?'

The two men sat down and sipped their wine in silence. After a moment John said thoughtfully, 'You know, there was a time in the early years when I hated myself as much as my uncle hated me. Nothing would have pleased me more than to satisfy his hopes.'

'My lord?'

'Don't pretend you don't know what I'm talking about. We've known each other too long. You know as well as I do that I never wanted to succeed to this damned title! In those early days in the army I would have been only too happy to oblige my uncle by getting killed in action. But the French failed us both.' There was a touch of self-mocking humour in his voice as he went on, 'He was bitterly disappointed, and all I got for my pains was swift promotion for what they called my admirable disregard for personal safety!'

'Was that why you stayed on the field at Waterloo? Even after being so severely wounded?'

'Curiously enough, no. By that time, I had begun to value life a little more. No, I stayed with the action at Waterloo because Wellington needed every man. It was a very tight thing, Fenny. But we survived. And won.'

'Are you now fully recovered?'

'Yes, yes! A slight touch of fever now and then, but otherwise perfectly sound. I wish now I had not sold out of the army. Last year I saw no future in a military career, but now… Apart from the odd occasion when I act as aide to the Duke when he is in England I'm at a loss.'

'That will fortunately no longer be a problem, my lord,' said Mr Fennybright briskly. 'You now have a large number of responsibilities waiting for you up in Yorkshire, for which a strong hand is needed. The sooner you take charge the better.'

John stared down at his wine. 'What makes you think I want to take charge at all?'

Mr Fennybright was so shocked that for a moment he

could not speak. 'But, you must!' he exclaimed finally. 'My lord, you must!'

'*Must*, Fennybright?' asked the Colonel, a touch coldly.

The lawyer took a breath and said firmly, 'Yes. Must, my lord. Forgive me, I have no desire to offend you, but I've looked after the interests of the Ancrofts, here and in Yorkshire, all my working life, as my father did before me, and his father before that, and I would be failing in my duty if I did not remind you of your obligations. You are now the fourth Marquess of Coverdale and a considerable landowner. You have responsibilities, which an honourable man, such as I know you are, would never avoid.'

'A *considerable* landowner, Fenny? I should have thought my uncle would have left me very little!'

'He was not able to dispossess you! Most of the Ancroft property is entailed. My lord, as one of Wellington's most highly regarded officers, you know the meaning of duty. You have now inherited large estates in Yorkshire, together with property in London and elsewhere in the country. You have hundreds of people dependent on you for their continued fortunes. And then there's your daughter Harriet, too. I cannot believe you mean to fail them!'

John got up and walked like a caged tiger about the room. 'Dammit, I swore I would never go back again after that last visit! My uncle's point-blank refusal to receive me, my wife's hysterics when I insisted that we met, the fear on the child's face when I approached her… Call me a coward if you wish, Fenny, but I cannot face a return.'

The lawyer put down his glass and said firmly, 'But you must! Lady Harriet would soon get to know you better. And she needs someone who is more than a father in name alone.' He paused. 'The rest of the people up there would give you the heartiest of welcomes. Your uncle was a recluse and deeply suspicious of change. The estate has been managed well enough, but time has moved on, and change is *needed*. Only you can see to that.'

John gave him a hard look. 'I don't know…' he said slowly. 'I never thought—not for one moment—of ever living in Yorkshire again.'

'I beg you to reconsider. It…it would give your life the direction you said it lacked.'

'You may be right,' said John slowly. He sat in thought for a moment, then said decisively, 'Thank you for coming, Fenny. I can't answer you at the moment. You must give me time.' As the lawyer got up to go, the Colonel added, 'By the way, I'd be obliged if you kept this news to yourself for the moment. For the past seventeen years I never acknowledged my connection with the Coverdales. The Honourable John Matthew Ancroft, heir to the Coverdale title, didn't exist as far as the army was concerned. My family history has been my own affair, and, with very few exceptions, I have not talked to anyone about it.' He added with a bitter smile, 'Hardly surprising, is it? So, until I give you the word, I will continue to be known as plain Colonel Ancroft. Understood?'

'As you wish, my l—Colonel. I am at your disposal. Will you call in at my chambers at Lincoln's Inn? Or would you prefer me to come here in a few days' time? There are business matters to discuss, whatever your decision.' Betts appeared at the door, and the lawyer bowed. He paused and said, 'My lord—'

'Colonel, Fenny, *Colonel*!'

'Colonel Ancroft, I have known you, as you say, all your life. I have been proud that the firm of Fennybright and Turner has continued to serve the Ancroft family with loyalty and discretion, even during the last seventeen difficult years. I have always looked forward to your return.

Not just to England, but to Yorkshire—to Marrick. That's why I have always kept you informed of events up there. I am not the only one who would be bitterly disappointed not to see you take your proper place.'

John did not reply to this, but said merely, 'See Mr Fennybright out, Betts. Then bring up a bottle of brandy.'

Betts returned after a few minutes, carrying a salver on which was a bottle of brandy and two glasses.

'Two? Are you thinking of joining me, Sergeant?'

'No, sir. Captain Trenchard called while you were with Mr Fennybright. The Captain said he would come back later. Shall I pour out some brandy, Colonel? Or will you wait for the Captain?'

'There's no need to look like that, Betts. If I want a drink now, I'll have one and be damned to you!'

'As you wish, Colonel. Doctor Hulme won't be best pleased, though. He said—'

'I know what the confounded doctor said, Betts! When I want a nanny I'll send for one. Meanwhile, you can do your duty and pour me out a brandy. There's too strong a taste of the past in my gullet. I need to drink to the future, though at the moment I have no idea what it will hold!'

Falmouth, May 1818

At the same time as the Colonel was receiving his lawyer, the landlord of the Green Bank Hotel at Falmouth, three hundred miles to the west, was reverently receiving his latest guest and promising her the best parlour his inn could provide. The inn was a popular one with travellers from the West Indies, but it had seldom seen a more striking, or, what was more to the point, a more clearly wealthy one. The lady was tall, generously built, with hair the colour of burnished chestnuts. Her dark green pelisse was cut with style, and her shoes, gloves and the fall of lace at her throat were all of the highest quality. A dashing hat worn to the side was trimmed with a beautifully curled ostrich plume. She was accompanied by her maid and a retinue of porters carrying a large trunk and numerous bandboxes and valises. Ignoring the curious and admiring glances that followed her, the lady walked with perfect self-possession through the hallway, up the stairs and into the parlour.

The landlord watched anxiously as her green eyes passed over the room, and breathed a sigh of relief when she sank gracefully into the settle by the empty fireplace. Her voice when she spoke was perfectly modulated—warm, husky, with an unmistakable air of authority.

'Thank you, landlord. A fire, please, as soon as possible, and then you can show the bedrooms to my servants here. Oh, and send up a bottle of brandy, if you please.'

'Brandy, ma'am?'

She surveyed him coolly. 'That was what I said, I believe. Your best.'

For a few moments all was bustle—the servants from the inn made up the fire, stored boxes and cases in the bedrooms under the guidance of the lady's maid, while the lady herself took off her hat and pelisse and settled by the hearth.

Presently the travellers were left to themselves, and the lady's maid, a buxom lady in her late forties, was back in the parlour with her mistress. A second servant who had just appeared, a man a few years older than the maid, was standing in silence by the door. Burly, thickset, with powerful shoulders and a decidedly pugnacious air, it would have been hard to decide what his role in the household was. He had none of the polish of a footman or major-domo, but at the same time appeared to be more at ease in the parlour with the two women than any ordinary groom would have been. There was nothing remotely servile in his manner.

The maid bustled about the room like a small whirlwind, scolding all the while.

'No wonder that landlord stared, Miss Caro! Sending for a bottle of brandy! You're in England now, miss, and proper ladies in England don't drink brandy. Not unless they're ill.'

The lady laughed. '*Proper* ladies don't in Jamaica, either, Maggie. What makes you think I should become proper just because I've crossed the Atlantic? Don't be such a killjoy! We've arrived! I want to celebrate!' She jumped up, spread her arms wide and laughed again. Then she said to the man at the door, 'Bring two more glasses over here, Joseph. We'll all celebrate!'

As she poured out the brandy she looked at her companions and said, '*Smile*, you two! Here we are in England at last, and my villainous cousin and his men have been left behind, four thousand miles away on the other side of the Atlantic! There isn't another boat for two weeks. We're safe!'

Maggie shook her head. 'We've not finished our journey yet, not by a long chalk. They were telling me on the ship that it's three hundred miles to London, and we've a long way to go after that.'

'Yes, yes, I know. But the roads must be better over here. I believe the mails can reach London from here in less than three days, so even travelling at a comfortable pace it shouldn't take us more than a week. Joseph, drink up! You must set about hiring a suitable carriage and horses for us. A post chaise, I believe it's called. If there isn't one to be had here, try the King's Arms.'

'*Hiring* a carriage, Miss Caro?'

'Yes. We must get to London as soon as we can. Once we are there we can take the time to look for our own equipage. I have my directions, Joseph! Off you go!' Joseph turned. 'Wait! I almost forgot. There's something else. Take this letter to a Mr Trewarthen at the address on the envelope. If the lawyer back in Jamaica has done his job properly, there'll be money to pay our shot here and have something in hand.'

'Will that be all now, Miss Caro?'

'Of course. And, Joseph! I'd like to set off tomorrow, so do what you can.' The man nodded and went out and the lady turned to her maid. 'Maggie, you can go along to the bedroom to pack a couple of the bags with clothes for a week. Leave the trunk and the rest of the luggage locked. We won't need them on the journey. I shall keep the small case with me, as usual.' She gave her maid a sharp look. 'What the devil's wrong with you, Maggie? Do cheer up! Aren't you pleased to be back in your native land again?'

'This isn't my native land, Miss Caro! This is Cornwall. I was born in Derbyshire! And it's over thirty years since I left England. I'm not sure whether I'm pleased or sorry to be back.' She rallied and said in her former scolding tone, 'But one thing I *am* sure of—and that is that you'd better watch your language when you're in England. No "confoundeds" or "devils", if you please! And none of the scandalous words you picked up in New Orleans, either! You don't want to set people's backs up, the way you did in Kingston. You haven't got your grandfather now to silence the critics.'

The lady's face changed. 'No,' she said briefly. 'No, I

haven't. Very well, Maggie. I know you mean well, and I'll try, I'll try. Don't say any more. Go and deal with the luggage.'

When the maid had gone out, the life and vitality drained from Caroline Duval's face. She sank onto the settle and leaned back, closing her eyes. After a moment she rallied and murmured, 'My apologies, Grandfather! A moment of weakness, I'm afraid. But don't worry. I'm doing my best. I don't intend to let you down.'

She got up purposefully, walked over to the door and locked it. Then she went to the table, and pulled towards her a worn leather case something like a small hatbox. She opened it, using a key that hung on a chain round her neck. At first sight the contents consisted of two very stylish headdresses, frivolous confections of net, lace and feathers. These she put to one side. Then she took out two sealed envelopes. And then, very carefully, she lifted out a leather pouch that had lain hidden on a bed of soft wool underneath. She opened it, unwound a length of fine linen, then slowly held up a richly jewelled cup, a chalice. It was not large—a mere five or six inches tall—but when it caught the light from the window streaks of blue, red and green fire flashed out from it, almost hurting her eyes with the intensity of their light. She gazed at it for a moment, marvelling again at its beauty, its air of mystery. The cup was old and very beautiful. It had been an object of veneration for centuries. And now, after an absence of over sixty years, it was on its way back to where it belonged…

Then she gave a sigh and, after removing a small purse which lay at the bottom of the case, carefully re-wrapped the treasure and set it back in its nest. The envelopes and hats were replaced, the case securely locked, and the purse slipped inside her reticule. Then she unlocked the door and sat down again to wait for Joseph's return. The first stage in the fulfilment of her beloved grandfather's last orders had been achieved. She had brought the Ainderby Chalice back to England, as Peter Leyburn had wished.

Now for the second stage, the journey to London and a place called Lincoln's Inn, where she was to look for the chambers of Fennybright and Turner. One of the partners, Samuel Turner, was the son of an old friend and ally of her grandfather. He would help her with the third and most difficult stage—the safe restoration of the chalice to its former home in the wilds of Yorkshire.

Chapter Two

Joseph returned after half an hour and reported that a well-sprung post chaise would be waiting for them at whatever time they chose to leave the next morning.

'Good! You've done well, Joseph. What's this?' 'This' was a note from Mr Trewarthen, the lawyer, inviting Mrs Duval to dine with him and his wife that evening.

Caroline frowned. 'Confound it, I shall have to set Maggie to shaking out one of my evening dresses! I hoped not to have to unpack them! But I'll have to go—it would be uncivil not to. Tell her, would you, Joseph?'

'Aye. And then I'll take a walk round the town, Miss Caro. I might hear a thing or two.'

'Such as what?'

'Where the villains are—there's always one or two. They're not all at home in Jamaica, missy. And there was a character outside this inn when I came back... I'll just take a little stroll.'

'You think it necessary?'

'That's what I'm here for, isn't it? To look after you?'

'And I'm glad of it.' Caro Duval smiled warmly at the man. 'After all, it's what you've done most of my life.'

'Aye, nigh on. I'll see Maggie, shall I?'

'Yes, do that, Joseph. Tell her I'll be along in a few minutes.'

Joseph left and Caroline turned her attention to what she should wear that evening. Though it was only an invitation to dine from a small country town lawyer, it would be her first encounter with society in England, and she was not yet sure of the local customs. Would the Trewarthens be shocked if they saw she was not in mourning for her grandfather? Then, with a totally characteristic toss of her chestnut locks, she laughed and said, 'Oh, devil take it! I'll wear whatever comes out first!'

In the event Caroline tried after all to conform to notions of propriety. The dress she wore to the Trewarthens' dinner party was of plain white silk. True, it had been imported from Paris just a few months before, and was somewhat daringly cut, but then so were most of her dresses for the evening. Maggie produced a shawl of black lace which she draped carefully round Caroline's neck and shoulders. But when she stood back, she frowned.

'I'm not sure that's any better,' she said doubtfully. She was right. Caroline's shapely form and creamy skin were enhanced rather than concealed by the lace.

'Stop fussing, Maggie! I haven't anything more suitable. And what does it matter anyway? I shall never see these people again.'

'All the same, Miss Caro. You behave properly! There's no point in offending people unnecessarily. Not here in England.'

Mindful of Maggie's words, Caroline kept her manner and her conversation polite to the point of insipidity that evening. The company was naturally curious about her life in Jamaica, and she answered their questions as best she could, though she was sometimes forced to use discretion rather than strict truth.

It wasn't always easy, for she and her grandfather had behaved pretty much as they chose in their little world on Jamaica. Those ladies on the island who regarded themselves as the arbiters of taste and behaviour might disapprove of the Leyburns, but they knew better than to be critical in public. Peter Leyburn's position as one of the island's foremost citizens was secure. It was based not only on a huge personal fortune, but even more on his connection through his wife, Caroline's grandmother, with the Willoughbys, one of the oldest and most respected families in the West Indies. It would be brave, not to say foolhardy, to risk antagonising someone so influential, and no wife or mother with the interests of her family at heart would risk it.

Without her grandfather's support and protection Caroline would have been much less fortunately placed. Always beautiful, high-spirited and strong willed, she had committed the ultimate social sin of running away with a handsome adventurer at the age of seventeen. She had returned a penniless widow just eighteen months later. There was talk of scandalous company she had kept in New Orleans—but this was never confirmed, and Caroline never spoke of it herself.

The ladies of Kingston would have ostracised Caroline Duval from decent society forever if they had dared, but Peter Leyburn, proud of his granddaughter's stubborn refusal to let the episode break her spirit, saw to it that she was once again accepted by the world as his granddaughter and heir, and the ladies were eventually forced to give in. However, they neither forgave nor truly welcomed Caroline. In their opinion she was too bold, too unrepentant…and far too attractive. What eligible young man would look twice at their own carefully brought up daughters when Caro Duval was there with her slow smile, her air of mystery, her graceful, swaying walk and the hint of danger in her green, green eyes? And they were right. Most of the men in Kingston, eligible or not, had sooner or later fallen victim to Caro Duval's spell.

Nothing of this featured in Caroline's account to the Trewarthens' guests of life on the island of Jamaica. In reply to their eager questions, the history of the island, its agreeable climate, the beauty of its mountains were all carefully described. Even the liveliness of its social life was briefly given its due. But no mention was made of Caroline's own determination to ignore the gossip, to maintain a pose of mocking indifference to sly snubs and cold sideways looks from the ladies. She had only laughed when she heard them calling her the Widow Duval behind her back, and though she was sometimes forced to put gentlemen, who should have known better, back in their place, she never lost her temper.

In truth, her looks and manner were deceptive. After that first mad escapade, she had never felt the slightest temptation to stray. She had fallen in love once, and the lesson had been short, swift and severe. It had been enough to cure her for life. Behind the charming façade, the delightful laugh, the challenge in her green eyes, lay a cynical scorn for most of society. Her adored grandfather had been the only man in the world for whom she had any real respect. With very few exceptions, she regarded all other men as fools or knaves.

But none of this showed in her manner at the Trewarthens. As she returned to the inn, accompanied as ever by the faithful Joseph, she congratulated herself on behaving exactly as a stranger, a widow and newcomer to

England would be expected to behave—with modesty, decorum and courtesy.

She would have been surprised and, being Caroline, highly amused, if she had heard the conversation which took place afterwards in the Trewarthens' bedchamber.

'A very fine woman!' said Mr Trewarthen. 'A real lady and very well informed. I found her account of Jamaica most interesting.'

Mrs Trewarthen sniffed. 'You are mistaken, Mr Trewarthen! In my opinion that woman is a hussy if ever I saw one! Did you see the neckline of that dress? Why, half an inch lower and you could have seen down to her waist!'

'Oh, come! You exaggerate, Mrs Trewarthen! Mrs Duval is certainly...er...well endowed, but the dress was perfectly modest.'

'I dare say you have a better idea of that than I have,' said Mrs Trewarthen tartly. 'You didn't seem able to keep your eyes off it. But her hair, too! You must agree that her hair is a most extraordinary colour. It has to be dyed!'

'You are not usually so uncharitable, my dear,' said Mr Trewarthen mildly. 'I thought her manners and appearance perfectly ladylike. Whatever has she done to offend you?'

Mrs Trewarthen stopped and thought. Then she said slowly, 'Nothing, I suppose. She was polite enough. But there's something about her. I didn't like her. It was as if...as if she was secretly laughing at us all.'

'You are talking nonsense, Henrietta! Mrs Duval is a widow who has just lost her grandfather, and is over here on the mournful task of carrying out his last wishes. She never met us before tonight. How could she *possibly* be laughing at us?' He looked at his wife sternly. 'I think we should stop this. It is not for us to criticise or question the affairs of a valued client. Mr Peter Leyburn's letter asked us to assist his granddaughter in any way we can, and that is what I have tried to do. Now, shall we go to bed, my love?'

The next morning the party from Jamaica was all set and ready to go at an early hour. Before following Maggie into the carriage, Caroline had a word with Joseph.

'Do we need so many men? Driver, postilions *and* a groom?'

'I thought it best, Miss Caro. We have to cross Bodmin Moor, and they say that's a terrible lonely road. Too many men is better than too few, to my way of thinkin'.'

'You're being very cautious, Joseph. Are you suspicious? What about the man you saw last night? Have you seen him again?'

'I can't say I have, Miss Caro. But all the same…'

'All the same, what?'

'I think someone was keeping an eye on me down at the stables.'

'Oh, come! Who could it possibly be? I'm quite positive that none of the other passengers on the boat was in league with my dear cousin Edmund. Respectable people, the lot of them. And Edmund himself, and all his men, were left behind in Jamaica. We saw them standing on the quay as the boat left Kingston.'

'That fellow Trewarthen knew you would be coming,' said Joseph obstinately. 'Why couldn't someone else have been forewarned, too?'

Caroline stared at him for a moment. Then she shook her head. 'I don't believe Mr Trewarthen has been indiscreet. And anything else would mean that Edmund had unbelievable foresight. No! I cannot think that is so. You're being over-cautious, Joseph.'

Joseph was persistent. 'Well, what about the crew of the ship we came on? Shall I ask around at the quay? If one o' them wanted to follow us, he'd have to leave the ship. Someone might know—'

'We haven't time,' said Caroline firmly. 'I wish to be in London as soon as possible. In any case I think it would be a waste of effort. No, don't argue! It's highly unlikely that we are being followed, and I intend to set off straight away. This carriage is so heavily laden we shall have difficulty in keeping up anything like a decent pace. Help me in, then on to the box with you.'

The carriage lumbered out of the yard of the inn and on to the high road. Caroline sat back and breathed a sigh of relief. They were on their way. Five or six days and they would be in London.

But progress on the journey was slow. The roads in this part of the West Country were not particularly good, and though the coach was comfortable it was not built for speed. By the time they were crossing Bodmin Moor they were all weary, and Caroline began to long for a warm fire, a good meal and a comfortable bed. She decided to abandon her intention of making for Launceston, and when the driver drew up at a small posting inn, she got out and inspected it. She was reassured to see this was a stopping place for the mail coach, so the place must be respectable. It had a good menu and several rooms. The inn, small as it was, would do.

'Don't bother changing the horses! We'll stay here for the night,' she said with decision.

Joseph looked doubtful. 'It's a lonely place, this. Better to stay in a town, Miss Caro.'

'It can't be all that bad if the mail calls here,' said Caroline impatiently. 'We all need a rest, Joseph. Maggie has a bad head, and I am stiff and tired myself. I see that there's a good stable behind the inn with accommodation for postboys and grooms. We'll leave the trunk and valises in the coach—they'll be safe enough with you and the men sleeping above—and with an early start tomorrow we can easily make up the distance. Maggie will tell you which bags to bring in.' Refusing to listen to any further protests, she entered the inn.

The landlord and his wife were obviously respectable, with rosy, country faces and smiles for their unexpected windfall. There were no other guests, and Caroline was shown two rooms that were cramped, but clean. After a moderate meal and a glass of excellent brandy she retired for the night and the rest of the party did the same.

But in the early hours of the morning they were all woken by shouts and the sound of scuffles in the stable yard. Caroline jumped out of bed and opened her door. Maggie was on the landing with the landlady. The lamp in the landlady's hand revealed a face full of distress.

'Oh, ma'am! I don't know how to tell you, that I don't! It's never happened before, I swear! Not like this. Them villains off the moor—you never know what they'll do next, and that's a fact!'

'What is it? What has happened?'

'Your carriage, ma'am! It's been broken into! All your lovely things—all thrown everywhere, all over the yard. Oh, ma'am!'

'What? Maggie, fetch Joseph!'

'Your man is already there, ma'am. He gave the alarm.'

Caroline put on some clothes and hurried down. The landlord, looking as distressed as his wife, led her through to the yard. She stopped in shock. Every trunk and valise had been taken out of the carriage and their contents strewn over the yard. Dresses, shifts, stays, fans, shoes, shawls lay in the dirt and dust in hopeless confusion.

'It's that Burnett family, ma'am,' said the landlord grimly. 'I helped to get one o' 'em transported last year and they've borne a grudge ever since. This is their revenge, I suppose.'

'Are you sure?' asked Joseph.

The landlord nodded. 'I'm sure,' he said. 'Who else would do such a thing? Wanton destruction, that's what it is.' He looked at Caroline. 'What can I do to put things right, ma'am?'

Caroline was looking at the mess with growing anger. 'I take it that the culprits are well away? Have you sent anyone after them?'

'I have. But once they're on the moor it's not easy to find them. It might take a week or two. But we'll catch them, though, sooner or later and when we do...'

'I trust they'll be adequately punished. But I don't have time to wait to see it, landlord. Meanwhile...'

'What shall I do about this?' He turned to look at the mess in the stable yard, and burst out, 'Dang it, if I had those miscreants in front o' me now...' He smacked one fist into the other in fury.

Caroline felt much the same, but said briskly 'You can tell your people to gather my garments up out of public view, as quickly as possible, then have them brought to my room. My own maid will sort out what can be saved. The rest can go on the rubbish heap. Come, Maggie! Goodnight.' Caroline was so angry she could not have said another word. The clothes were not important, but the thought of strangers, rough men, having handled them was intolerable. She would probably throw most of them away. The inconvenience and delay would be considerable. Why on *earth* had she not followed Joseph's advice and stuck to staying in the towns?

By the time dawn was breaking Caroline and Maggie had put aside those garments that could be laundered, and had rejected most of the rest. A number of delicate things, such as fans, sandals and parasols, had been so trampled on in the fight that they were ruined. Fortunately she still had the contents of the valises they had brought into their rooms with them, so they were not totally without a change of clothing.

'Well, this is a fine welcome to England, I must say!' said Maggie as they sat down, exhausted, to take some refreshment provided by an anxious landlady. 'What shall we do now?'

Caroline drew a breath. 'The people here can appease their consciences by washing and pressing this lot,' she said, touching one bundle with her foot. 'They can do what they like with the rest.'

'But, Miss Caro! Are you going to wait here until that's all done? I thought you wanted to be in London before the week was out?'

'I do. We shall leave this morning as planned. As soon as the clothes have been properly dealt with, the landlord can put them in my trunk and send it all by carrier to London. It shouldn't take very long. The trunk will probably arrive before I've completed my arrangements with Mr Turner. Don't look so doubtful, Maggie. We can always buy new things if necessary. Now, finish your chocolate—it's time we were off!'

The landlord was only too glad to promise whatever Mrs Duval wished, and by eight o'clock they were on their way again.

* * *

In spite of the landlord's belief that the attack had been prompted by his enemies, the experience at the inn had made them cautious. They decided only to travel in daylight, and always to stay in large towns. The roads improved as they drove towards the capital, and though Joseph still kept a close watch he saw nothing to worry him. As they pulled up at the Star and Garter in Andover on the next to last night of their journey, Caroline was in better spirits. Hounslow, where they were to spend the following night, was the largest coaching centre in England and only ten miles from London. She would soon make the acquaintance of Samuel Turner, and some of the burden of this long journey would be taken from her.

But Joseph returned with a long face from a walk round the town. 'I can't swear to it, Miss Caro, but it's my opinion there's a character in town I've seen before.'

'When? Where?'

'On the quay at Falmouth. I think I saw him the night the carriage was broken into, too.'

'So you think the landlord was wrong? It wasn't the Burnett gang?'

'I never thought it was. No use saying anything, though. No evidence.'

'Joseph, what do you think we should do?'

'Well… The road isn't the best for us. There's a bit of a deserted stretch just before we get to Hounslow. Three or four miles of it and it's lonely. They say here it's the haunt of highwaymen.'

'It's not highwaymen I'm afraid of! But surely the road is busier than the roads in Cornwall? And if we take care to use it in daylight?'

'Aye. We'll do that. But we'd best take a few other precautions. I'll have my pistols close at hand.'

'I'll make sure mine are within reach, too, but don't

tell Maggie. I don't want to listen to another of her lectures on what is ladylike. And there's something else I shall do, too... Right, Joseph. Now for a good dinner, a night's sleep and an early start.'

They reached the edge of Hounslow Heath by late afternoon when it was still quite light. Caroline took heart. The road led in a reasonably straight line across bracken-clad heathland. Surely nothing could happen here! But they had hardly gone a mile when she heard Joseph give a warning shout and when she looked out she saw a band of six or seven mounted men thundering up behind them. They swept past, there was the sound of shots, and the carriage came to a sudden halt. The doors on each side were flung open and two men jumped in. It all happened so quickly that there was no time to get out her pistol to defend herself.

'There's the case!' said one of the men. 'Get it!'

One of the men made a lunge for the leather case that never left Caroline's side. She kicked out at him and he gave a shout of pain as he lost his balance and fell through the open door. 'Joseph!' she yelled. 'Where are you? Come and help me! *Merde, alors!* Where are the *confounded* men I hired?'

The second villain made to snatch the case from her arms. Maggie dragged him back valiantly, but he turned and slapped her and she fell back with a cry on to the seat.

'Maggie! Maggie, are you all right? Where the *hell* are those men?' Caroline turned on Maggie's attacker, but this time he was ready. He gave her a violent chop on the forearm and she involuntarily released her grasp on the case. In a flash he had snatched it up and had disappeared out of the carriage. Caroline scrambled out after him, but she was too late. Her attacker had thrown the leather case up to one of his accomplices and was already mounting his horse.

'Right! Away! Let's be off before anyone comes! We have what we want,' he called. In a flash they were all away over the heath. She turned to urge someone to follow, but saw Joseph sitting on the ground swearing, while the groom bound up his arm with a rather dirty handkerchief.

'Joseph!' Caroline ran to her servant's side. 'What's wrong?'

'My arm, missy! They got me in the arm.'

'He didn't ought t'have tried to stop them,' said one of the postboys gloomily. 'Always best to let 'em 'ave wot they want. They don't hurt you then. He shot one o' 'em, y'see. Winged 'im. That made the others real angry and they shot back.'

'Give me your kerchief! Come on, hand it over!' She passed it to the groom, who added it to the bandage on Joseph's arm. 'Why the devil didn't you come when I called?' she went on. 'And why didn't anyone chase after those men? What did we hire you for?'

'Beggin' your pardon, ma'am. We're just postboys. We're not bloomin' 'eroes. We wouldn't last long if we objected to all the coves trying to make a dishonest livin' on the 'igh road. It's company policy to stand aside, see? If you want protection, you travel with the mail!'

Caroline looked at them, seeing them properly for the first time. In spite of their name, there wasn't a boy among them. Wizened old men, the lot of them. Even the groom. She and Joseph had made a serious mistake.

'Can you get into the carriage, Joseph? You must see a surgeon. I suppose there's one in Hounslow?' she said, turning to the men. They nodded rather doubtfully.

'Right, then we'll set off again. Don't look so worried! Those men won't be back. They've taken what they wanted.'

Joseph, looking ghastly, was helped into the carriage, and in a short while they were travelling on towards Hounslow. Maggie had fully recovered, but Joseph lay back against the squabs, his lips tightly compressed. Blood was seeping through the makeshift bandage the groom had applied, in spite of all Maggie's attempts to stem it with more cloths.

Caroline drew the folds of her cloak around her and shivered. Edmund must have an accomplice on this side of the Atlantic. Those men were no ordinary bandits. They had taken nothing but the leather case. And Joseph, her old friend and staunch protector, had been injured, perhaps badly. Her heart stopped for a moment. Joseph mustn't die! Not Joseph! She leaned forward and put her hand on his knee. He opened his eyes and nodded faintly.

'Nothing fatal, missy. Don't worry.' Then he shut his eyes again.

Caroline was not reassured. As they drew into Hounslow she was desperately considering what she should do.

Hounslow was noisy, chaotic and, apart from coaching requirements, had very limited resources. The place consisted of a large number of posting inns strung along the road and little else. But the groom proved himself of some use by finding them rooms in one of the quieter places, run by a Mrs Hopkins, a widow whose heart was as large as her anatomy. She instantly took them under her wing.

'That poor man!' she said, gazing at Joseph. 'Fancy being attacked like that in broad daylight! I can't understand it!'

'I was hoping to find a surgeon,' said Caroline. 'I think the bullet is still lodged in his arm.'

'You won't find that here!' said Mrs Hopkins roundly. 'There isn't a surgeon in Hounslow I'd trust with my dog! Drunken sots, the lot o' 'em. If you'll take my advice, you'll take him to London.'

Joseph had been put to bed in one of the ground floor rooms and the groom was in the process of re-binding the arm when Caroline went in.

'I've stopped the bleeding for the moment, ma'am,' he said. 'But he needs a surgeon. The bullet is still there.'

'Could he travel? I'd like to take him to London.'

'Tomorrow? Yes.'

'Then would you please reserve places for three on the first coach to leave Hounslow in the morning? Ask Mrs Hopkins if you can book them in her name.'

'That'll be the Bristol Mail. I'll do my best, ma'am.'

As soon as the groom left Joseph woke and tried to sit up. 'I don't need a surgeon!'

She pushed him back against the pillows. 'Don't be a fool, Joseph. Of course you do!' She looked at him remorsefully. 'I owe you an apology. You were right.'

'It's not for you to say anything, Miss Caro. The master trusted me to get you and that case safely to Yorkshire. And I failed at the first hurdle!' Joseph turned his head away.

'No, no! You haven't failed! We're not dead yet!' Caroline leaned forward and whispered. 'They didn't get what they wanted.'

'You needn't try to comfort me! I saw them riding away with it!'

Caroline smiled mischievously. 'They took the case. And they took what was in it. Two hats, and a pewter tankard from the Star and Garter at Andover. I don't think they'll be happy with any of those, do you?'

'Is that right?' Joseph's worn face broke into a grin. 'Where's the other?'

'Well, Joseph, haven't you noticed? Look at me!'

She stood up and removed the large shawl she had been wearing. In spite of his discomfort Joseph began to laugh. 'Miss Caro! What a lass you are!'

Caroline appeared to have changed overnight. The face was the same, but her shapely figure and slender waist had quite disappeared. The lady who stood before Joseph looked ten years older and three or four stone heavier.

'How did you do it?'

'Petticoats—Maggie's, as well as my own. And part of the bedding from Andover. I left a very handsome tip for the landlady there. You needn't worry, Joseph. My grandfather's bequest is safer than ever.' She patted her middle.

'What happens when they find out?'

'That will take some time. The case was locked, and I doubt the men who stole it will stop to open it before they hand it over. By that time I hope we shall be safely hidden in London.'

'You must go on without me, Miss Caro. Take one of the mails that pass through here. Go tomorrow. Find Mr Turner.' Joseph had been sitting up again, speaking feverishly, but now he slumped back. 'But who'll look after you?' he groaned.

'Don't think for one moment that I shall leave you here. We'll all go together. Listen to what I've decided...'

The groom had done well. He had managed somehow or other to book the places Caroline had asked for and early the following morning she joined the overnight mail from Bristol to London. No one could have recognised the elegant creature who had arrived at Falmouth six days before in the stout lady who, together with her 'sister' and 'brother-in-law', was to attend a funeral in London. The morning was chilly and all three were well wrapped up. Caroline was dressed in a voluminous black cloak, her glorious hair hidden under a cap and bonnet, all acquired from Mrs Hopkins. Joseph was wearing a black coat that had belonged to the late Mr Hopkins, his arm easily accommodated in its ample width, and Maggie had managed to find a cloak in her own luggage which was suitably drab. No one in the stable yard took the slightest bit of notice of them as they left.

Just over two hours later they were in the Swan with Two Necks in the centre of London. Caroline saw Joseph comfortably settled with Maggie in charge, then she sat down to write a message to the lawyer. She sealed it and gave it to one of the grooms to take to Mr Turner in the chambers of Fennybright and Turner at Lincoln's Inn as quickly as possible.

They had barely finished breakfast when Mr Turner appeared. After introducing himself, he said, 'All is arranged as you asked, Mrs Duval. A room is being prepared for your man in my own house. The chaise waiting below will take him there immediately, and a surgeon will call on him as soon as it arrives.'

'You're very kind, sir. Maggie, you go with Joseph.' She went over to Joseph and took his hand. 'I shall follow very soon. I have to explain things to Mr Turner before I leave the inn, but Maggie will take good care of you.'

After Joseph and Maggie had gone Caroline turned to the lawyer. 'First I must give you a letter from my grandfather. May I ask you to read it?'

Peter Leyburn first thanked the lawyer formally for his services since taking over from his father ten years before. He then went on,

'You may sometimes have asked yourself how I came to know your father. We met in Yorkshire many years ago, long before I came to Jamaica. He knew my history, he knew my real name—which is not Leyburn. In return for a small favour I once did him he kept my secrets and gave me help whenever I needed it. I think you could say we were friends. But he is dead and I am now dying…

In the past ten years I have found you to be as trustworthy and as discreet as your father, Samuel, so I am asking for your help in paying one final debt. My granddaughter has agreed to take my last bequest to my family home in Yorkshire. I did them a great wrong, and am now doing my utmost to put it right.

Caroline is a courageous and resourceful woman, and Joseph Bellerby a loyal servant. He will protect her to the death. But England is strange to her, and the journey to Yorkshire is a long one. I ask you to see that she has everything she needs. I cannot think there is any real danger, but if she needs extra servants, extra guards, then make sure she has them.

I know my granddaughter. She understands how important it is to me that what she has is delivered safely to Yorkshire. You see? I will not even now write down the true nature of what she carries, nor its exact destination. Only she knows that. You, and anyone else who is curious, may call it my "remains", for it is all I have left to do in this life.

Do this and you will earn my eternal gratitude—wherever I am. I rather think my ultimate destination is not a happy one. But perhaps if Caroline succeeds in her task there may be some hope of intercession for me.

You will also earn a large sum of money, which has been set aside for the purpose. Otherwise, apart from one or two trivial sums, Caroline has inherited everything. I leave her affairs in your care. If she marries, her husband will take over from you. But since I doubt that my granddaughter will ever risk a second marriage, your commission may prove to be a long one.

Look after her, Samuel. In memory of your father, if not of me. With my thanks and my regards,

Peter Leyburn'

The lawyer laid down the letter. 'Your grandfather pays me a great compliment.'

'I think it may prove to be a great burden!' said Caroline with a wry smile. 'Especially in view of what has happened.'

'No, I assure you. I regard it a privilege to help you in any way I can. Your grandfather's "small favour" saved my father from ruin. I could never repay that debt.'

Caroline nodded, then went on. 'I'm afraid he was mistaken in one thing—there *is* danger.' She got up. 'Mr Turner, I would like to tell you more about this, but these are not very suitable surroundings, and I'm worried about my servant Joseph. His injury was caused by men who are determined to stop me from carrying out my grandfather's wishes. So far they've been on our track wherever we've gone. I *must not* be seen leaving this inn in your company. My disguise was good enough for an early morning coach journey, but not for London in broad daylight.'

'You're disguised?' asked Mr Turner in astonishment.

Caroline stared at him, then burst into laughter. 'It must be better than I thought! Yes, Mr Turner, I'm in disguise.' Still laughing, she pulled off her bonnet and cap.

'Good God!' Then the lawyer said, covered in confusion, 'Oh, I beg pardon, Mrs Duval! What must you think of me? But... But... The difference!' He gazed in fascination at the riot of chestnut hair tumbling down Caroline's back.

'Good! I seem to have succeeded. So, if you agree, we shall now part company. If you permit me, I shall call at your house to see Joseph. Can you warn your people to expect me?'

'Of course,' said Mr Turner, still looking slightly stunned. 'I'll send a boy to Mrs Turner immediately. She will be delighted to welcome you.' He looked doubtfully at Caroline's hair.

'Ask her to expect a Mrs Hopkins. And never fear! I'll tidy myself and be back in disguise before I venture out. May I call on you at your chambers this afternoon? ''Mrs Hopkins'' will come to consult you about her husband's estate.'

'Of course. Is there anything else I can do?'

Caroline grew sober. 'I can see that you are somewhat overwhelmed, Mr Turner. Perhaps you even think me mad to act like this?'

'No, no! I am sure you have the best of reasons...'

'I assure you I have. Those men on Hounslow Heath weren't ordinary thieves. They knew what they were looking for, and it's only by the merest chance that they didn't get it.'

'Then I'll help you all I can. Shall we say three this afternoon?'

'Three o'clock it is. Mrs Hopkins, remember. I'll tell you more then about the man who is trying to prevent me from reaching Yorkshire. If you could meanwhile think of a way in which I could go north with adequate protection, I should be most grateful. Joseph's arm will, I fear, take some time to heal.'

Mr Turner took his leave of this extraordinary client and returned to his chambers. After sending a message to his wife, he sat down to ponder. This was a strange coincidence! His partner, Edward Fennybright, was at this very moment strongly urging John Ancroft, the new Marquess of Coverdale, and another of the firm's most important clients, to take up his duties in Yorkshire. If he succeeded, then there would an escort for Peter Leyburn's granddaughter that could hardly be bettered... Colonel Ancroft was one of the Duke of Wellington's aides, and a notably brave and resourceful officer. He pulled a face. He was now also a peer of the realm, a Marquess, with huge estates in the north of England. How on earth could one persuade such a man to take on an escort's duties? The idea was preposterous...

But after his interview with Caroline that afternoon he decided that he would try. Without wishing to go an inch beyond a perfectly professional relationship, he had found her totally captivating. She was as her grandfather had described her—resourceful and courageous. And, with him at least, she had been frank. He had not been put off by an undercurrent of cynical amusement in her conversation. He had seen her concern for Joseph Bellerby, and heard the change in her voice when she talked of her grandfather.

But from her account of the events since her grandfather's death there was real danger in her mission. It would not be long before this cousin of hers made his way over to England to join his accomplices. From all accounts he was determined to capture whatever it was Caroline Duval was carrying. She would need all the protection he could find for her on her journey up the Great North Road.

In the meantime, she would need somewhere safe to stay until Joseph Bellerby could travel, somewhere not far away, but outside London, perhaps. There was a house in Barnet…

Chapter Three

'Have you gone mad, Fenny? It's quite out of the question. The journey to Marrick would be tedious enough without adding a sorrowing widow to the party. What the devil are you thinking of?'

Mr Fennybright sighed. Colonel Ancroft's reaction to Sam Turner's suggestion was very much as he had predicted. 'I beg pardon, Colonel. I should never have mentioned it, and indeed would not have done if Mr Turner had not been so concerned for the lady.'

'Who is she, anyway?'

'At the moment she is known as Mrs Hopkins,' said Mr Fennybright carefully.

'"Known as"? "At the moment"? What does *that* mean?'

'It is for her own protection. The lady is under some threat. She…she believes she is being pursued.'

'Worse and worse! A *nervous* sorrowing widow!'

'It is true that her own groom was shot on their road to London.'

Colonel Ancroft stared at him and said slowly, 'So she has some reason to be anxious. Is he dead?'

'No, but badly injured. She is waiting for him to recover a little before she takes the road north. She is determined to take him with her.'

'I don't believe it! You are actually asking me to undertake a journey of over two hundred miles, which you know I'm reluctant enough to take, in the company of a nervous widow and a fellow who hasn't the sense to avoid being shot by some highwayman or other. Is that it?'

'The lady has a maidservant, too, of course...' said Mr Fennybright, scrupulously exact as ever.

'What is wrong with the maid? Smallpox?'

'You are pleased to jest, my lor—Colonel. As far as I know there is nothing wrong with the maid. And Joseph Bellerby, the groom—'

Colonel Ancroft sat up. '*What* did you call him?'

'Joseph Bellerby, Colonel.'

'Bellerby... The Bellerbys were a large family on the Marrick estate—and it's not all that common a name. Tell me, why does the mysterious Mrs Hopkins wish to travel north?'

'I concluded from the little Mr Turner told me that she is taking her husband's remains to the family home.'

Colonel Ancroft regarded him sardonically. 'This gets better and better! A nervous widow, a wounded man, a maid with smallpox—oh, no, the maid is perfectly fit—and now a corpse! What devilish rigmarole *is* all this?'

'There's no corpse, my l—Colonel. I suppose there must be ashes,' faltered Mr Fennybright, wishing he had never mentioned Sam Turner's wretched client. But he went on bravely, 'The lady is perfectly genuine, and so are her difficulties. I've seldom seen Mr Turner so concerned.'

The Colonel thought for a moment. Then he sighed and said, 'I make no promises. But I'll listen to what Mr Turner has to say.'

* * *

In the following meeting Mr Turner used his considerable powers of persuasion. No one who knew dashing Caro Duval would have recognised her in the picture he drew of a nervous, vulnerable woman on a mournful mission, in a strange country, with only an elderly maid and a wounded man for company. He gave the Colonel a most affecting description of the lady's shock when the men she had hired to protect them on the road to London had let her down, and her reluctance now to trust strangers. He ended by appealing, in the most respectful manner possible, to the Colonel's chivalrous instincts as an officer and a gentleman.

Indeed, he was so convincing that Colonel Ancroft found it impossible to refuse him.

'Excellent! You are very kind, Colonel Ancroft.'

'May I now know her real name? And her final destination?'

'Er…as I have told you, my client is convinced that she is in danger. She wishes to keep her assumed name and a measure of disguise, until she is safely outside London.'

'Come, come! My tongue won't wag. Is this theatre really necessary?' said the Colonel impatiently.

'So the lady believes. But in strict confidence, Colonel, she is Mrs Caroline Duval of Kingston, Jamaica. Her goal is somewhere within twenty miles of Richmond in Yorkshire. I am unable to be more accurate—that is as much as I know of her precise destination.'

He saw that the Colonel was beginning to look doubtful once again and hastily added, 'Mrs Duval is the granddaughter of the late Mr Peter Leyburn, who was a highly respected member of Jamaican society and one of my firm's oldest clients. I can vouch for her respectability.'

'Very well, very well. I've said I shall do it and I shall.

I have engagements in London till the middle of July, but wish to leave soon after that.'

'That would suit very well, I am sure. The groom will hardly be fit to travel much before then. Do you wish me to make arrangements for you to meet her? It would need some notice—she is not living in London at the moment.'

'Please do.'

In the event, the Colonel did not meet Mrs Duval till shortly before they were due to leave. But they corresponded—to the satisfaction of neither. The Colonel was happier writing reports or lists of commands to his officers, rather than composing letters to a lady of quality. His style was courteous but stiff, and he found it impossible to avoid a distinct flavour of command. Caroline was anxious not to antagonize someone who had said he was ready to help her, but she found the old-fashioned formality of his tone a rich source of amusement. At the same time the assumption of authority, which it did not disguise, caused some resentment. She said as much to Mr Turner when he visited her in Barnet.

'What a block of wood your Colonel is, Mr Turner! It's quite obvious he has no idea how to handle the female sex! Perhaps I can amuse myself on the journey north by teaching him some graces. He certainly needs them!'

'I am sorry you're disappointed in Colonel Ancroft, ma'am. It's true he has been little in society, but he is a capable man, and one of great courage. Surely in your present situation these qualities are more use to you than an ability to please the ladies?'

'You're right, of course. Still, I suppose his career as a soldier has led him to expect unquestioning acceptance of all his suggestions, too. Well, I'm sorry, but that I cannot do. I've been too used to ordering my own life to leave everything to someone else. He writes to me as if I'm in my dotage, unable even to think for myself.'

'Mrs Duval, please, I beg you to be careful. The Colonel is not an easy man, but that is understandable. He has some consequence in the world, and is used to exercising authority. He will not take kindly to argument. And in order to persuade him to accept your company I had to present you to him as being older, rather more timid, and certainly more helpless than I think you are. Try not to spoil my picture before you have even met him!'

But, try as she might, Caroline was quite incapable of leaving matters completely in the Colonel's hands, however capable he might be. And just as much as she resented his commands, did *he* resent her attempts to interfere.

'Who the devil does the woman think she is, Fenny?' demanded the Colonel. 'Anyone would think *she* was doing *me* the favour! She has already questioned my decision to use my own horses. She doesn't wish to waste any time, if you please! Can't she see that I planned it so for her sake? Has she any idea how demanding it is to be constantly on the move for over two hundred miles? And just as I thought we had agreed on that, she now wishes to know how well sprung my carriage is and what accommodation it provides. She's anxious for her groom. A confounded *groom*! One might have expected a servant to travel in a wagon if he wasn't fit to ride!'

'I understand that the groom has looked after Mrs Duval since she was a child,' said Mr Fennybright soothingly. 'He means a lot to her. Shall I ask Mr Turner to arrange for some other conveyance for the groom?'

'No, there's no need. As it happens, there will be no shortage of room, though she's damned lucky that it is so. I intend to ride most of the way. I hate to be inside when the weather is warm. There'll be enough room in the carriage for luggage, *and* maids *and* grooms—*and* widows, too! At least she has finally stopped questioning the route I intend to take. Tell me, Fenny, was I foxed when I agreed to all this?'

'Mrs Duval was not questioning the route so much as wishing to learn what it was, Colonel Ancroft.'

'Why does she need to know? Confound it, there wasn't a man in my command who would have raised so many questions. I'd have had him in irons if he had! And the obstinate woman still won't tell me where she wishes to finish!'

Some spirit of mischief inspired Caroline to act and dress the part when she and the Colonel finally met. She would have gone in disguise anyway, the chalice, as always, in a specially designed cradle round her middle. But if the Colonel expected an elderly widow, then an elderly widow he would get! Basing her impersonation on a very tiresome woman back home in Jamaica, Caroline walked with the aid of a stick. Under her cap and bonnet her face was half hidden by a fringe of pathetic grey curls. And she practised talking like Mrs Jameson, whose plaintive voice had an irritating habit of fading away at the end of every sentence. When she demonstrated all this to Maggie before they set out to meet the Colonel for the first time, the maid shrieked with laughter. Even Joseph smiled.

'You're wicked, Miss Caro!' Maggie cried. 'That's Mrs Jameson to the life! But it's too much! You won't deceive the Colonel!'

'Oh, yes, I will, Maggie. I know his type. Our Colonel is a man of fixed ideas. He's expecting a tiresome, melancholy, elderly frump, and that's what he'll see. I don't expect to deceive him for long. Even Colonel Ancroft will eventually penetrate my disguise. But I hope that won't be before we are a good few miles along the road to Yorkshire. Now, if you will pass me those spectacles and the veil I'm ready.' Since the spectacles Maggie had acquired for her had such strong lenses that she could hardly see anything at all when wearing them, she slid them into her reticule, ready to put them on just before meeting the Colonel.

But at the last minute they were very nearly overtaken by disaster. Outside the lawyer's chambers Caroline had to lift up her heavy skirts to get out of the carriage. She realised her mistake when she met the boldly appreciative eye of a gentleman standing nearby. She hadn't been able to disguise her ankles! Unusually flustered, she looked away and turned towards the entrance, but a sudden gust of wind blew her veil high into the air. She dropped her stick during the subsequent struggles to put it back in place. Hot and exasperated, she forgot herself so far as to swear roundly in some of the more lurid language she had picked up in New Orleans. Then she called angrily, 'Maggie! Come and fix this damned veil for me!'

Startled out of his lazy appreciation of her charms, the gentleman's jaw dropped and his eyes opened wide. This was too much for Caroline's ever-ready sense of the ridiculous. She started to laugh. When an answering gleam of amusement appeared on his handsome face, she gave him a conspiratorial look, then lowered her veil with a sigh of relief. He wasn't about to denounce her. He picked up the stick, gave it to her with a bow, then went away, still laughing.

Her escape was even narrower than she could have

dreamed. The handsome gentleman was one of Colonel Ancroft's closest friends in London. Captain Lord Trenchard had in fact only just taken his leave of his former commanding officer. But Caroline was undeservedly lucky. Though the Captain had guessed who she was, and what she was doing in that particular spot, he decided for reasons of his own not to unmask her.

After the formalities had been completed inside the lawyer's chambers, Caroline sat with her back to the light and covertly studied Colonel Ancroft. He was not at all what she had imagined. She wondered if London had more than its fair share of interesting men. The one outside had been quite startlingly handsome, and though this man here was not his equal in looks his appearance was very distinguished. In his late thirties, she guessed, with silver wings in his coal-black hair and cool, silver-grey eyes. He was broad-shouldered, if a little thin, but as tall and as upright as her grandfather, and he had the same look about him, too—as if he wouldn't tolerate what her grandfather had called shufflers and shirkers. Indeed, this man's whole aspect was unbendingly severe. A cold man, she guessed, without much humour. *He* wouldn't have laughed at her lapse outside. She sighed. Colonel Ancroft might be younger and better looking than she had imagined, but he didn't look like much of a kindred spirit. The journey was going to be very long!

She had been so busy examining her escort that she had missed some of the conversation, and when she started listening again she was surprised to hear the Colonel say with quite a bite to his voice,

'*Colonel* Ancroft, Mr Turner. *Colonel!*'

So our friend is sensitive about his rank? she thought. Well, well, well! Who would have thought it? There's some fun to be had, after all! She then applied her mind to the discussion and was pleased to see that, though the Colonel might be severe, he appeared to be efficient. When the chance arose, she said tentatively,

'I am so grateful to you for taking so much trouble, Captain Ancroft. You have no idea what a comfort it is to me to have a man in charge. I've been so long alone...' Her voice trailed away and she put a lace handkerchief to her eyes. Then with a little sniff she whispered, 'Thank you so much!'

'Not at all, Mrs...Hopkins. I am...delighted to be of assistance. But if you will forgive me—it is *Colonel* Ancroft. Not Captain.'

'Oh, I'm so sorry! What must you think of me—'

'It is perfectly all right, Mrs...er...Hopkins—'

'No, no! It isn't! I'm so stupid, you see. I have never had much to do with the military. Before my loss I lived a very sheltered life, Captain Ancroft.'

The Colonel looked grim. 'So it would appear, ma'am,' he murmured. He turned abruptly to Caroline's lawyer. 'Well, Turner? Are the details clear? I shall call for Mrs Hopkins on Tuesday at twelve noon. We shall set off as soon as the carriage has been loaded.' He turned to Caroline. 'Unless noon is too early an hour for you, ma'am?'

'Well...' she said doubtfully. 'I think I could be ready. Yes. Twelve noon. On Wednesday.'

'Tuesday, ma'am, Tuesday!'

'Are you sure? I thought you said Wednesday...' Caroline sounded worried, but behind her veil she was grinning.

He controlled his obvious annoyance and said patiently, 'No, it was Tuesday. I shall call for you on Tuesday. But pray do not trouble yourself, Mrs Hopkins. I shall send a groom to Barnet on Monday to remind you.'

'You are very thoughtful,' said Caroline. Then she added kindly, 'Er...I see you do not like addressing me as Mrs Hopkins, Captain Ancroft. Once I feel we are safely clear of London, you may call me Mrs Duval.'

The Colonel had obviously had enough. 'And you, ma'am, may call me Colonel!' he snapped.

In spite of her teasing Caroline was ready for the Colonel the following Tuesday, as, true to form, his carriage drew up at noon precisely. A coachman was on the box, and two grooms sat behind, all in dark green livery. The inside of the carriage was empty, for the Colonel was riding a superb bay with his groom at his side. The Colonel, his carriage and his servants all standing at the gate made an impressive display.

The servants began to load the carriage. Caroline invited Colonel Ancroft into the house to wait. He stopped when he saw Joseph standing by the door.

'I guess this is Joseph Bellerby. Are you fit again, man?'

Joseph held himself as upright as he dared. His arm had become infected and had taken longer than they had expected to heal. Even now it was often more painful than he would admit. But he was as anxious as Caroline to see their mission over. 'Pretty much, Colonel,' he said. 'I think I'd be of some use in a fight.'

'I'm sure you would, Bellerby. But let's hope it doesn't come to that! I should like to hear more from you about the attacks on the road from Falmouth. Are you quite certain it was not just a strange coincidence?'

'As certain as a man may be, sir.'

Colonel Ancroft nodded. Then, seeing Joseph's pallor, he said brusquely, 'Into the carriage with you. My man will see you comfortably installed. We shall speak another time. It's time the loading was finished. Are you ready to start, Mrs…Hopkins?'

'Of course, Captain.' Caroline let a nervous titter escape her. 'Oh, I'm sorry, do forgive me! *Colonel* Ancroft!'

It suited Caroline very well that the Colonel rode alongside. The day was warm and her heavy veil and widow's black outfit, not to mention the padding round her middle, were causing her some discomfort. Once in the carriage with Joseph and Maggie, she took off her veil and the cape she wore over her dress and sat back with a sigh of relief. She looked out of the window. Colonel Ancroft was riding some distance ahead.

'So, Joseph, what do you think of our Colonel Ancroft?' she asked.

'I've not yet seen enough of him to judge, Miss Caro. But he's not a man I'd care to cross. I shouldn't play too many games with him if I were you.'

'Oh, I'm safe enough! Colonel Ancroft has too low an opinion of the female sex and too high an opinion of himself to believe that any woman could make game of him.'

Maggie shook her head. 'I'm not so sure. Joseph's right, Miss Caro! There's more to the Colonel than you think! Those lawyers, even Mr Turner, treated him with a lot of respect. And it's clear that he's a man of wealth. Look at this carriage! Your grandfather didn't have a better one.'

'Aye, and the horses, too,' Joseph added. 'They're prime cattle, every one.'

'That's not to say anything! Kingston was full of men who were rich and flattered by the lawyers, but it didn't mean that they were particularly clever. I've known only one man whom I couldn't take in when I tried, and that was my grandfather. I don't doubt that the Colonel is highly respectable and very worthy, but he's too solemn for my taste. Teasing him is quite irresistible! If only this damned disguise wasn't so uncomfortable!'

'And when are you thinking to discard it?' asked Maggie.

'Tomorrow or the next day. When I've thought of somewhere safe to keep this.' She tapped the bundle round her waist.

'If you'll take my advice, you won't leave it a moment longer than you have to,' Maggie warned. 'That gentleman is by no means as stupid as you think him. You can always tell a man by the way his servants behave, and Colonel Ancroft's servants treat him with great respect. What's more, they like him, too.'

When they stopped at Hatfield, Caroline was surprised to see one of the Colonel's grooms leading his horses away and an ostler from the inn coming out with a different team.

She only just remembered to speak in her adopted voice as she called out, 'What's happening, Colonel Ancroft? I thought you wished to travel with your own horses?'

'I decided that it would make the journey too tedious, Mrs...Hopkins. To use the same horses for every stage would mean long delays. Your man is more fit to travel than I had feared, and, as I understand it, you are in some haste to be in Yorkshire, I believe. We shall use post horses.'

'But this was not what was arranged!'

'Are you now saying that you wish to take four or five days longer than necessary on the road, after all?'

'No. But I wish you had informed me beforehand of your change of mind!'

'Why? What would you have done differently?'

'Why, nothing, I suppose. But I should like to have known in advance, all the same!'

The Colonel regarded her thoughtfully. Then, with a sort of patient indulgence which set Caroline's teeth on edge, he said, 'I apologise. But I really didn't see the necessity. You have asked me to see you safely to Yorkshire, and that I will do. Why should you be worried with the details? Now, with your permission, we shall continue. I've sent ahead to book rooms at Buckden for the night. We really shouldn't waste any more time.'

Once in the carriage again Caroline sat fuming. It did not pacify her to know that the Colonel was in fact merely doing what she had wanted all along. He had no right to make a change in their plans without telling her. None at all!

'I don't understand, Miss Caro,' said Joseph, observing her obvious annoyance. 'The Colonel has decided to oblige you. Why are you so put out?'

'He should have consulted me first!' said Caroline angrily.

'But what would you have said if he had?' Maggie asked, looking puzzled.

Caroline looked at her two companions, started to speak, stopped, then suddenly laughed. 'Yes, yes, yes. You're quite right, both of you. I'm being unreasonable. All the same…'

'If you don't mind my saying so, Miss Caro, you have only yourself to blame. The sort of ninny you pretended to be would have been very happy to leave all the decisions to someone else. The poor Colonel was only doing what he thought best. He doesn't know what you are really like.'

'*Poor* Colonel? What's this, Maggie? What has the Colonel done to arouse your sympathy?'

'Well, it might have escaped your notice, but it hasn't escaped mine. That poor man is not looking at all well. From what Mr Fennybright's clerk told me, he's only just recovered from the wounds he received at Waterloo. Two years it took! They must have been terrible. Riding in this heat can't be good for him, and he looks as if he's paying for it.'

'Nonsense! You're imagining things! Colonel Ancroft is an iron man, nothing would affect him. He wouldn't permit it!'

Maggie pursed her lips and said no more.

It was getting late when they reached Buckden. Joseph was looking exhausted and Caroline was relieved when the Colonel oversaw his transfer to a small room off the stables with a comfortable bed in it.

'Thank you,' she said. 'I'm surprised the inn can provide such a suitable room.'

'Normally they don't,' he said briefly.

'You arranged for it in advance?' she asked in astonishment.

'All the inns where we shall be staying have been warned to make similar arrangements. Bellerby isn't young, and that wound of his has obviously not yet healed. He's a good man and deserves your concern.' He stopped and wiped his forehead. Caroline looked at him properly for the first time. He had not sounded as incisive as usual.

'I believe you're not well yourself, Colonel,' she said.

'Nonsense. I'm perfectly fit, ma'am. I've arranged for

supper to be served in your room in half an hour. Now, if you'll excuse me, I shall bid you goodnight.'

'Wait! Are you not to have any supper?'

'Thank you, no. I'm not at all hungry. Goodnight.' Before she could say any more he had bowed and turned away.

Maggie took some supper to Joseph, then she and Caroline ate together in the small parlour which had been reserved for them. After the meal they went upstairs. Caroline looked doubtfully at the door of the Colonel's room, which was just along the landing.

'I wish he had eaten something,' she said. 'I think you might be right, Maggie. He isn't well.'

'He has his man to look after him, Miss Caro. He'll be all right. I'm more concerned about Joseph at the moment. He seemed a bit feverish when I took him his food. I'll just go down to see him again after we've taken those things off you.'

Maggie removed the bonnet and cap, then helped her mistress out of her widow's stiff black dress.

'Oh,' Caroline sighed. 'That's better! My head was aching under that bonnet. And the air is so cool on my arms! Now, help me to unwind this, but be careful!'

The bindings round her waist were taken off, and the pouch with its precious contents was put carefully on the table. Caroline took a deep breath, then stretched like a cat. 'Is that what women feel like when they are carrying a child? So misshapen, so heavy and awkward? And so hot!'

'They have their reward at the end,' said Maggie with a smile.

'You're right, of course.' Caroline walked over to the

window and gazed out. It was rapidly getting dark. 'I don't expect I shall ever have a child, Maggie.'

'Why shouldn't you?'

'Because a child needs a father! Preferably one who is married to its mother. And unless I go stark, staring mad, I shall never again put my head in that particular noose.' Maggie nodded sympathetically. She knew more about Caroline Duval's marriage than anyone other than the girl's grandfather.

Caroline returned from the window and sat down. Still in silence Maggie prepared her for bed, brushing the grey powder out of her hair, both of them thinking of the past.

Except for the period of Caroline's disastrous marriage, Maggie had looked after her all her life. After her own baby had died, she had been asked to nurse little Caroline and in her grief she had taken the child to her heart. For the first seventeen years she had been both confidante and nurse. She had listened to her childish secrets, had comforted her when, not quite nine years old, she had lost her father, mother and only brother in a freak storm at sea. And as her charge slowly grew into a young woman, a bright future had beckoned. Caroline Leyburn was one of nature's darlings. She was rich, beautiful, and intelligent. But more than this she had a warm heart, an enchanting openness, an ability to infect everyone who met her with her own vivid zest for life.

But then, at seventeen, Caroline had fallen headlong in love, and no one could persuade her that the man she had chosen was unworthy. Neither Maggie nor anyone else had been able to protect the girl against the practised charms of Laurent Duval. She believed everything Duval told her. And he, a gambling adventurer, had seen in Peter Leyburn's heiress a golden opportunity.

Of course, thought Maggie sadly, they had all handled

the situation with sinful stupidity. She had remonstrated in vain. Peter Leyburn had threatened to cut his granddaughter off without a penny, forecasting that Duval would desert her if he did. When Caroline simply refused to believe him, he had lost his temper and made the biggest mistake of all. Without warning, he had had Duval summarily shipped out of Jamaica and back to New Orleans. Caroline, in love, and intensely loyal, had packed her bag in a fury, filled her purse with gold, and had left in the middle of the night, heaven knew how, to follow her lover. They hadn't heard a thing from her for eighteen long months. Nor had they ever again heard from Duval.

Maggie was one of the few who had seen Caroline Duval's condition, both physical and mental, when she first arrived back. Duval was dead, the money had disappeared long before, and Caroline was destitute. It took months to restore her spirits and health, and over a year of her grandfather's energetic encouragement before she was ready to face the world again. Then, confident and defiant, she took her place in society, hiding her cynical contempt for most of those in it behind a curtain of laughing mockery. Her great love for her grandfather and her affectionate concern for her two servants were the only signs that were left of the delightfully open, lovingly trustful child she had once been.

Maggie sighed. Surely there must be someone somewhere who could find that child again. Caroline had so much to offer. But even if the right man appeared, Caroline herself would be his greatest enemy in his attempts to unlock her heart. Maggie sighed again and returned to the present.

'There, that's done,' she said. 'I'll just go to take a look at Joseph. I won't be long.'

But in fact she was back within minutes, looking very

worried. 'He's very restless. And he has a fever. I think he's in pain, though he'll never admit it.'

'I'll come,' said Caroline with decision. 'Where's the medicine chest?' She got up and put on her wrapper.

'You can't leave the room dressed like that!' said Maggie, scandalised.

'Why not? Who will see me? It's quite late—there's practically no one about. And it's dark. I haven't time to put on all those black clothes again!'

'But your hair!'

'Damn my hair!' said Caroline forcefully, shaking her mane of hair back over her shoulder. 'Are you coming or not, Maggie?'

Together they descended the stairs, each with a candle. The inn was silent.

They spent some time making Joseph comfortable until he was nearly asleep. Maggie, who had remained uneasy, suggested that Caroline should go back to her room. 'I'll just stay till he's fast asleep,' she said. 'But you go. I shan't be happy till you are out of sight, Miss Caro.'

Caroline looked at Joseph. He seemed peaceful enough. 'Very well. Don't be long.'

She crept out of the stable and went quietly up the stairs. At the door of her room she paused. Muffled cries could be heard coming from the Colonel's room. Then sounds of stumbling. Suddenly the door was flung open and Colonel Ancroft appeared in the doorway. He was still in his shirtsleeves, but without a cravat and with his shirt open to the waist. In the dim candlelight Caroline could see a forehead gleaming with sweat, flushed cheeks, and eyes which were black hollows in a pale face. The hand clutching the doorpost was trembling.

She forgot her lack of disguise. 'Colonel!' she exclaimed. 'What's wrong?' She hastily put her candle down on the table nearby and came towards him.

Chapter Four

Colonel Ancroft didn't appear to have heard her. After a moment of stunned disbelief, his face was suffused with a look of ineffable tenderness. Before she could stop him he had come towards her and taken her gently in his arms. 'Gabriella!' he said huskily, gazing down at her. 'I can't believe it! My love! You're here again! I thought I'd lost you forever. Where have you been? Oh, sweetheart, I've missed you so much!'

Caroline gazed up in amazement. The Colonel's face was transformed. The discipline, the strong jaw, the firm mouth were all there still, but no trace of severity, no coldness. He was smiling, his eyes glowing with feeling. Suddenly she saw a younger, less forbidding, Colonel Ancroft, his soul in his eyes, a young man deeply, overwhelmingly, in love. Her heart twisted. Lucky, lucky Gabriella!

He stroked her cheek, then with a deep sigh of contentment, bent his head and kissed her, almost tentatively at first, as if he wasn't sure that she was real. Then, as she stood unprotesting in his arms, his kiss grew deeper, more passionate.

'Come, Gabriella,' he whispered. 'Come, my dearest!'

Slowly he drew her into his room and shut the door. Caroline moved with him as if in a trance. She found herself in the grip of feelings she thought she had banished forever, a slow stirring of the senses, a warmth in her blood, a leaping response to a man's touch on her body. What was happening to her?

She murmured incoherently against his lips, but when he kissed her again, this time with more assurance, she was lost. Still clasped together, still locked in a kiss, they moved slowly towards the bed. Her wrapper fell to the ground and her shift followed it as he pushed them both off her shoulders. When they reached the side of the bed he sat down, holding her so that she stood between his knees. 'Such a slender waist,' he said, worshipping her with his eyes, hands and lips. 'Such beautiful... perfect...breasts.' He drew her closer and rested his head against her. 'Oh God, Gabriella, I want you so. It's been so long. Let me show you again how much I love you, my bride.' Putting his arms around her, he pulled her slowly but irresistibly down on to the bed beside him till their bodies were closely entwined. He kissed her hungrily, his hands pulling her ever closer till they were almost one. For a moment Caroline felt happier than she had felt for many years, lost in pure sensation... But she came suddenly to her senses as she realised with a shock that the Colonel was so burnt up with fever that he was hardly aware of what he was doing. This mustn't go any further!

She pulled back. 'No! Let me go! You're making a mistake!' she cried, struggling to free herself. 'I'm not your bride. I'm not Gabriella. Please let me go!'

He held her for a moment desperately trying to focus his eyes on her face. 'Not...not Gabriella?' he said incredulously. 'But you must be! Who else could look so much like her, and *not* be Gabriella? Oh, no! Now that I've found you again I shall never let you go, never!' He stroked her cheek and murmured, 'You've no need to be afraid, my love. I want to cherish you, live with you, spend the rest of my life with you, just as I promised all those years ago. You have no reason to be afraid. But don't try to tell me you're not Gabriella—I couldn't feel like this about anyone else in the world.' He started to kiss her again.

'Confound it, I am *not* your Gabriella! Let me go, sir! Let me go, I say!' Caroline wrenched herself free and leapt up. She picked up her shift and wrapper, then, still holding them against her, she turned to him. Making an effort to speak calmly, she said, 'You're ill, Colonel Ancroft. Let me fetch your man.'

The man on the bed lay rigid for a moment. Then he nodded painfully 'I think I must be. The sun was so hot…I…I'm sorry… I thought you were someone I knew. You look so like her… But now I hear you, you don't *sound* like Gabriella. I must have been dreaming… Or in a delirium. I'm sorry!' Then he turned his head away and said with a groan of despair, 'And, indeed, I know that Gabriella is dead. I saw her die. She and Philip together…'

Stifling an impulse to comfort him, Caroline hurriedly dressed herself. When she turned to face him again his eyes were closed, his face ghastly in the candlelight. It was as Maggie had said. The long ride in the hot sun had taken its toll of a body only just out of convalescence. He had probably woken out of a dream, a nightmare, even, and in his sickness had mistaken her for Gabriella. She wondered fleetingly who the girl was and what had happened to her. She had clearly meant everything to him.

Caroline would never have imagined John Ancroft capable of such intense feeling, such passionate love.

He opened his eyes and looked at her as if seeing her for the first time. He seemed more sensible. She bent over him. 'Where is Betts?' she asked.

'I sent him away. He…he's in the stables… With… with… *Who are you?*' he asked desperately.

For the first time Caroline saw the danger she had put herself in. Colonel Ancroft mustn't find out like this what sort of game she had been playing with him… She thought, then said, nervously backing away, 'One o' the maids, sir. If you'll excuse me, oi'll just fetch yore servant.'

When she went to her own room Maggie was there, looking shocked. Caroline shook her head and gave the maid a rueful grin. 'It's not what you think, Maggie, dear! Joseph isn't the only one who is suffering tonight. Colonel Ancroft has a fever as well.'

'I'm not at all surprised. I told you.'

'We have to find his manservant.'

'I know where he is,' said Maggie. 'He's sleeping in the stable rooms. It seems the Colonel asked him to keep an eye on Joseph. I'll fetch him, shall I?'

She went to the door, then turned. 'The Colonel didn't see you like that, did he, Miss Caro?' Caroline was silent. *'Did he?'* Maggie looked appalled. 'He *did*! Oh, heavens! What did he say? What are you going to do?'

Caroline gathered her wits together, and said as calmly as she could, 'Go and fetch Betts, Maggie. It's all right. Colonel Ancroft didn't recognise me. I told him I was one of the servants. Make haste. I suspect this is not the first time he's been ill like this. Betts will know what to give him.'

* * *

Betts was not unduly worried by the Colonel's attack. Caroline heard him talking to Maggie as he came up the stairs. 'You needn't worry about the Colonel, Miss Maggie. He'll be as right as rain in the morning, you'll see. A dose of 'is medicine and a good night's sleep—they'll fix 'im. Strong as an ox, the Colonel. Mind you, I thought 'e was gettin' over these attacks. 'E 'asn't 'ad one for months. It must've been the sun.'

Betts's voice died and the door of Colonel Ancroft's room was opened and shut. Caroline breathed a sigh and prepared to go to bed.

But she found sleep impossible. Her mind was filled with the extraordinary events of the night. John Ancroft had suddenly revealed himself to be a man of feeling, a man who had suffered greatly, still suffered. The man she had dismissed as a wooden block had tonight become a vulnerable and passionate human being. What was his story? Had Gabriella been his wife? Caroline doubted that. It had sounded more as if she had been betrothed to him rather than married. How had she died? And what part had this Philip played in the tragedy? That there had been a tragedy of some kind she had no doubt.

For the first time she began to consider John Ancroft seriously, and she came to the conclusion that he was more of a mystery than she had realised. He was obviously very wealthy, though he hadn't appeared so when she first met him. He dressed simply enough, yet his carriage, his horses and his servants' livery were all of the highest quality. He was severe, a disciplinarian, one would have said, yet his servants' respect was mixed with liking, and Mr Fennybright had seemed fond of him! Then again, he clearly knew this Great North Road well, but had not travelled it for some time. And tonight... Well, that was something altogether astonishing, a revelation indeed! A world away from the man she had dismissed as a simple, rather unimaginative soldier.

All of which brought her to herself. However hard she tried, she simply could not account for her wanton behaviour tonight. Somehow or other this new John Ancroft had broken through the shell that she had built to protect herself from any further humiliation and despair. The Widow Duval had had no heart. In the years since Laurent Duval's betrayal there had been many men who had begged in vain for her kisses. She had driven them mad, laughed at them and secretly despised them for it. But tonight… It was unaccountable! What spell had caught her? Tonight she had been helpless in John Ancroft's arms, had met passion with passion, given rein to feelings she had long since forgotten, been eager to lose herself in a man's caresses. She had damned nearly given herself to him! This was danger of the highest degree, she told herself. Had she not sworn that she would never again place her self-respect, her emotions, her body at the mercy of another being? How could she have forgotten? How had it happened? Caroline tossed restlessly in her bed, unable to find an answer.

But after a while her ability to treat herself and others with mocking irony came to her rescue. It was unlikely she would be put to any further test. Tonight's situation was one that was most unlikely ever to be repeated. She grinned as she thought over the more intimate moments of her encounter with the Colonel. Betts had said his fever would have gone by the morning. But how would he behave? Would he try to seek the 'servant girl' out or would he do his best to avoid her? Would he have a guilty conscience, or would he regret that the situation had come to an early end? Or was it perhaps possible that he would remember nothing at all? Caroline was not in the slightest afraid that she would be unmasked. The candlelight had been dim, her appearance had been so different from what he knew of her, even her voice was several tones deeper than the one she normally used in speaking to him. No, she was safe.

She finally went to sleep with a smile on her face. But she dreamt of a man's strong arms holding her with such tenderness, and his deep voice telling her how much he loved her, and calling her his bride. And when she woke she had tears on her cheeks.

If Caroline had not known the truth of the matter, she would have said the next day that the Colonel had a hang-over. His manner was even stiffer than usual, his voice more peremptory, and he held himself carefully as if he ached all over. She was concerned for him, but said nothing. Betts had approached Maggie as soon as he saw her. 'Best not say anything to 'is nibs,' he said. 'The Colonel's as fit as a flea this morning, 'cept for being a mite short-tempered. But 'e's very touchy about 'is illness. He don't like people to know about it, see? So, mum's the word.' As the Colonel looked suspiciously his way, he raised his voice and said cheerfully, 'Mr Bellerby seems better this morning, miss. 'E'll be fit to move on, never fear.'

When Caroline appeared the Colonel gave her a brief bow. 'Today's journey will not be so strenuous,' he said. 'We are travelling the same distance, but if we can get away in the next hour we should have two or three hours in hand over yesterday. We'll take a more leisurely break at midday. Your man should be able to cope.'

From the safety of her veil Caroline looked at him closely and marvelled. It was difficult to see the passionate lover of the night before in the man standing before her. Except for the fact that he was paler than usual, and a small frown creased his forehead, this was all Colonel Ancroft, her wooden soldier! She restrained a sudden desire to smooth his brow, and said in the high, light tone she used for 'Mrs Hopkins', 'Thank you, Colonel. I believe we are going to Grantham, are we not?'

'Yes,' he said curtly. 'The inn there is excellent.'

The little party moved off. Caroline took one last look at the inn as the carriage drove out of the yard. It was hard to believe that she had not imagined it all...

The day promised to be warm again, and John Ancroft hoped to heaven that he would manage better than he had on the previous day. Fifty miles to Grantham should be a reasonable day's stint, especially if they could take an hour's break in the middle. If his memory served him correctly, the road was bordered with trees for a good stretch of the way. He gritted his teeth and climbed into the saddle.

Betts was looking concerned, damn him! Betts was an old woman. The Colonel would be travelling in the carriage if Betts had had his way, and that was something John Ancroft refused to contemplate! The ride might be uncomfortable at first until his head cleared, but anything was better than travelling in a closed carriage with the Duval woman! He needed to do some thinking, and the less he heard of that whining voice the better he'd be pleased!

The day was still young, a soft breeze kept the air fresh, and the trees along the roadside gave plenty of shade. Today's ride would be pleasanter than the one from Barnet to Buckden. For the first half-hour John concentrated on staying upright in the saddle, but after a while his head cleared and his mind began to work again. What the devil had been going on the previous night? Had it all been a nightmare brought on by his fever? He had been a fool to ride so far in yesterday's unbroken sunshine. The bouts of fever that had plagued him ever since his spell in the marshes of southern France had been growing less frequent and less severe, and he had begun to hope they had gone forever. Yesterday's attack had taken him by surprise.

Things might have been better if he could have fallen straight into bed after reaching Buckden, but because of his idiotic commitment to Mrs Duval, he had first had to see that the ladies and Joseph Bellerby were suitably accommodated. Mrs Duval had seemed fit enough after the journey, though she had looked hot. That was much her own fault. She'd do better to lose some weight! And it was surely not necessary for her to wear that absurd veil whenever she was in public? He had little sympathy for such a woman, and why he had given in to Fennybright and agreed to see her to Yorkshire he could not imagine.

But Joseph Bellerby had looked exhausted. Why couldn't his mistress have left him in London where he could have been comfortably looked after? All the fuss about danger, and pursuers and God knew what else. What nonsense it was! The woman had a grossly overactive imagination.

As a result it had been far too late by the time he had escaped to his room. Betts was seeing to Bellerby, so he had been alone. He remembered taking his cravat off, and undoing his shirt, feeling worse and worse all the while. His memory of what followed was unclear, but he supposed he must have collapsed. John Ancroft frowned. What *had* happened afterwards? Had he dreamed it all or had it been real? That servant girl… No, not a girl. A woman. A beautiful woman with full breasts and lovely limbs… There had been no one like her in the inn this morning, though he had searched for her as discreetly as he could. If she *had* been real, then she must have thought him either mad or an unprincipled villain.

Ever since Fenny had convinced him that he ought to go back to Yorkshire he had been having dreams, but never one as vivid as this. Even now in broad daylight he could feel his body tightening as he remembered... God damn it, he hadn't felt so unsettled, so frustrated for years! She *must* have been real! He could still remember the feel of her body against his, the long legs, the deep bosom, a waist so slender that he could circle it with his hands... And that glorious hair... Or had the hair been part of his dream, part of his conviction that she was Gabriella?

She had been holding a candle when he first saw her. No wonder he had gone mad—the shock had been almost more than he could take. Her hair—Gabriella's hair—had flamed in the candlelight, the dark, red-brown tresses surrounding the loveliest face he had ever seen or ever wished to see. Gabriella's face, with Gabriella's eyes. Had that been just an illusion? A figment of his fevered imagination? She had seemed enough of a living creature afterwards...

But if she had indeed been a real person and not a ghost, why had she allowed him to make love to her without a word? No false protestations of modesty, no haggling, none of the usual hesitation before money was exchanged. Her response had been silent, immediate and total. There had been not the slightest demur before they had very nearly reached the point of no return. She *must* have been one of the serving wenches. Was she a trollop or was she a tease? She hadn't looked like either. Perhaps he had offended her by mistaking her for Gabriella? Surely not! In his experience serving wenches of that sort were not so nice in their feelings—they couldn't afford to be. On the other hand, she hadn't stayed for a reward either, but had been concerned for him, had promised to send his man to look after him. He would ask Betts who had come to tell him that he was needed.

But Betts could only say that Mrs Duval's maid had come to see to Joseph and had told him the Colonel seemed to be ill. There hadn't been any mention of a servant from the inn. One thing was sure. It certainly wasn't Miss Maggie in his bedroom last night. She was almost as unlikely a candidate as Mrs Duval! For the first time that morning John Ancroft smiled. Now there would be a substantial armful!

Cheered by the absurdity of such a thought, John sat up straighter and started to enjoy the ride. The inn at Buckden was behind them. He might never know the truth of what had happened there, and he must dismiss it. He resolved one thing more. If he was to live at Marrick and survive, then he must lay Gabriella's ghost for good, along with all the other poor ghosts.

They passed the monumental milepost at Alconbury where the road through Huntingdon joined them, paused for a while in Stilton, then stopped for quite a time in the town of Stamford. Colonel Ancroft found a comfortable seat in the shade for Joseph Bellerby, then suggested that the ladies might care to take a stroll round the town.

'Oh, Captain! Is it safe?' asked Caroline.

Colonel Ancroft gave her a hard look. 'I would correct you yet again, if I didn't suspect you mean to tease, ma'am. I am quite sure it is safe. We are now something like ninety miles from London, and there has so far been no sign whatsoever of pursuit. Are you quite certain you have not made a mistake? It is my opinion that the previous attacks on you were unfortunate, but unconnected. In fact, I would say that disguise is really no longer necessary—I suggest that I now call you by your proper name, and though I must respect your feelings, I think you would be cooler if you removed your veil. Is it really necessary?'

With a touch of genuine panic Caroline said, 'Quite necessary. Absolutely necessary, Colonel. But you may call me Mrs Duval.'

The Colonel gave a slight shrug of the shoulders, then said politely, 'As you wish. Shall we walk, Mrs Duval?'

'You mean to come with us?'

'Of course. After half a day in the saddle, I need to exercise my legs a little! And do you think me so churlish as to leave you to walk unescorted round a strange town?'

'Oh, no, Colonel!'

'Then shall we set off?'

Their tour of the town proved very pleasant. Caroline was impressed with the Colonel's knowledge and said so.

'I have travelled this road many times before, ma'am.'

'Oh? Are you a native of Yorkshire, then, Colonel Ancroft?'

'Yes, Mrs Duval.' The Colonel's tone was not encouraging, but Caroline persisted. Since the night before she had developed a healthy curiosity about her wooden soldier.

'I suppose you have many friends there.'

'I have been away from the area for some years.'

'Why is that? Has the army been so demanding?'

'That and the fact that I…I had a disagreement with my uncle, which made it awkward for both of us if I was anywhere near him.'

'Do you have any other family?'

'One daughter.' This time there was a warning in the

Colonel's voice which said her questions had gone far enough, and Caroline was silenced. In truth, she could hardly have said anything more. Her breath had been taken away by this startling revelation. So her wooden soldier *had* been married to Gabriella. His 'bride' had been his wife, and the mother of his child!

They said little during the rest of the walk. The Colonel pointed out one or two items of interest, but the enjoyment had gone. They were all glad to get back to the inn, where an excellent meal was waiting for them.

They stayed the night at Grantham as planned, but nothing untoward occurred. Joseph needed no attention—he was feeling and looking considerably better. The Colonel excused himself early, and Caroline and Maggie retired to their room before nine o'clock.

'So, Mrs Duval,' said Maggie as she helped Caroline out of her heavy clothes. 'No need for further disguise, eh?'

'Don't be absurd, Maggie. Of course there is! The Colonel is not so stupid that he wouldn't recognise his servant girl if he saw me as I really am. There's no help for it. I'll have to keep this confounded disguise for the rest of the journey. I shall probably die of the heat!'

'You're in a right pickle, Miss Caro. It wouldn't be so bad if you hadn't made fun of him with your ''Captains'' and your silly voice. He might forgive the servant girl trick, if it weren't for the rest.'

'Oh, no, he wouldn't! You don't know the half, Maggie.'

Maggie was now engaged in her nightly task of brushing the powder out of Caroline's hair, but at these words she stopped, brush in mid-air. Her eyes met Caroline's in the looking glass. 'Why wouldn't he?'

A slow blush began in Caroline's cheeks and spread down over her neck and shoulders. Her whole body seemed to be on fire.

'Miss Caro! You said that nothing had happened last night!'

'No, I didn't!' said Caroline with a touch of defiance. 'I said the Colonel was ill, and that he hadn't recognised me. But you needn't look so shocked, Maggie. Nothing of any consequence happened.'

Maggie put the brush down. 'Now you just tell me exactly what went on! Did he...did he attack you?'

'Of course not! He's a gentleman.'

'Hmph! From what I've seen, being a gentlemen wouldn't have stopped him. But in this case I believe you. The Colonel seems a very honourable man. Are you going to tell me what happened or not?'

Caroline gave Maggie a carefully edited version of the events in Colonel Ancroft's bedchamber the night before. It seemed unnecessary to go into detail about her own behaviour...

'So you see, Maggie,' she concluded, 'our Colonel has a tragic past. There's a mystery about it which I would dearly love to solve.'

'I'd talk to Mr Betts if I thought it would do any good, but it wouldn't. He's as close as an oyster about his master. If I hadn't actually had to fetch him last night, he would never have told me about the fever attacks. In any case, I don't think he knew the Colonel before their army days.' Maggie looked severely at Caroline. 'What is more, Miss Caro, if I were you I'd stop wondering about him. You need to concentrate on your own problems, not go borrowing trouble from others. Yours are big enough, heaven knows!'

'Don't be such a Job's comforter! If this heat continues,

it is quite likely that wearing these clothes will carry me off with an apoplexy—then you'd be sorry! If only I could think of something to do... But I cannot, cannot confess all to the Colonel. What *would* he think of me.'

'Why should he think ill of you, if, as you say, nothing happened? I'm beginning to think you've been less circumspect than you've given me to understand, Miss Caro!'

'I let him kiss me.'

There was a short silence. Then Maggie said slowly, 'I don't understand. You've never so much as hinted that you found the Colonel attractive. You've even made fun of him, called him your wooden soldier. What has caused such a change? Why, you've hardly let any man get close enough to hold your hand, let alone kiss you, ever since—'

'Yes, yes, ever since I came back from New Orleans. And I can't answer your question. I don't know. I don't know, Maggie. It wasn't just that I felt sorry for him. He...he seemed...he seemed different. Not Colonel Ancroft at all.' She paused, then said with a return to her normal manner, 'Still, it won't happen again. No one was hurt, Maggie. Let's forget it.'

'As long as the Colonel does, too,' Maggie said soberly.

'Yes, well as long as he doesn't see me as I really am he won't dream of connecting me with that girl. Now, since I am condemned to wearing them for the remainder of the journey, what can we do about these clothes?'

'I suppose you could leave off the heavier petticoats,' Maggie suggested. 'I doubt anyone will notice.'

'Well, I will! After all, I'm now Mrs Duval. She has more courage than "Mrs Hopkins". And who knows? It may get cooler as we go further north.'

* * *

But Caroline's optimism was unfounded. The weather seemed to get warmer with every day that passed. By the time they reached the inn just beyond Doncaster she was in serious trouble. Maggie did her best to cool her down with the limited facilities the landlord could provide, but the bath the servants brought up to the room was too small, and no amount of sponging could reduce Caroline's discomfort to any real extent. That night she lay limply on the bed, still feeling dirty, sticky and hot, wondering if she could survive the journey. Yet to reveal herself to John Ancroft was a step she still could not contemplate...

She slept fitfully, and woke ridiculously early, long before anyone, even a servant, was stirring. The sun was streaming through the cracks in the shutters—it would be another hot day.

She sat up in bed. Maggie was still sound asleep at the other side of the room. From outside the window Caroline could hear the sound of water, and she remembered that the night before they had driven alongside a laughing, gurgling stream for the last mile or two. The sound had driven her mad. Now temptation was too strong. She must seek it out!

Mindful of an extra need for caution, she decided to wear her black widow's dress and to take her cap and veil with her to put on if necessary. The cumbersome bindings which made her dress so very uncomfortable could be left behind, though. If anyone saw her she could manage somehow or other to bulk her appearance out. She wrapped the chalice carefully and hid it under Maggie's bed, taking care not to wake her. Then, picking up a cake of soap, a towel, and her cap and veil, she slipped out of the room and down the stairs like a shadow. She was soon outside, running through the field at the back of the inn in search of the stream.

After a minute or two she found the perfect place, where a small waterfall was splashing on to a platform of rock above a deep pool. A scent of summer hung in the air from the flowers and shrubs edging the pool, and overhanging trees and tall plants hid the spot from general view. She hid her bundle of clothes in a bush, and then in rapturous delight she walked slowly, testing the ground, feeling every ripple, into the clear, cool, scented water. It was sheer heaven! She swam about for a few moments, then climbed up and stood under the waterfall. After a moment she fetched her soap and washed her hair, twisting and turning in the stream of water, loving the feel of it as it poured through her hair and over her body. She stretched her arms in the air and laughed out loud for sheer joy…

The man picking his way carefully through thorns and spines heard the laughter and stopped short. He had remembered the pool with the waterfall from past visits, and after a sleepless night the temptation to enjoy the freshness of an early morning swim had been too great. Slipping on breeches and shirt for decency's sake, he had snatched up a towel and escaped. But for some minutes now he had been making his way slowly and painfully through an undergrowth of thistles and thorns! Either the path was more overgrown than it used to be, or he had missed it altogether.

When he heard the laughter he stopped and looked up. And caught his breath. Stones, thistles, thorns—all were forgotten in the enchantment of what he saw. It was an incarnation of every man's fantasies. A slender nymph under the waterfall, holding her head back to let the stream of water ripple over her mane of hair, her arms raised in sensuous delight.

Chapter Five

John Ancroft stood spellbound for a moment, then with an effort he turned his eyes away. This was no nymph, no creature of legend. This was a young woman who had come to this secret place to bathe. And he was no peeping Tom to indulge in lascivious enjoyment of her nudity. He would have to forgo his own bathe and leave like the gentleman he claimed to be. With a last, regretful glance he turned to go…and stopped.

The girl was now lifting her wet hair to shake it dry. Dark chestnut tresses glowed like fire in the early morning sun… Memory flooded back and with amazement John saw in her the servant who had been with him in the inn at Buckden. Was he going mad? Had his memories of Gabriella so distorted his mind that he saw her image in every red-haired female he met? This girl could not possibly be the same, Buckden was a hundred miles to the south. No, this was some local village maiden, and he was a fool with an obsession. He must get away from here. Quickly. He flung a last glance at her…

'Oh!'

The exclamation of dismay came from the girl in the

pool. She had finished with the waterfall and was starting to wade towards the bank. She had just seen him.

'Oh, heavens!'

The horror in her voice shamed him. 'I mean you no harm,' he assured her. 'I came upon you by accident—' He was unable to go on. Now he saw her better he realised that the long legs, and slender waist and hips seen under the waterfall had deceived him. This wasn't a young girl. This was a mature woman—all woman, too, just like the Buckden female. Unless he really was going mad, there really couldn't be two so alike, and so like Gabriella! This *must* be the woman from Buckden! But how had she got here, and why? He took a step forward, then stopped to consider. Was it possible that Mrs Duval had been right, after all, to be afraid? Was someone keeping track of their movements? And, absurd as it might seem, was this woman part of the plot? He saw her again in his mind's eye, stretching and twisting under the waterfall in such spontaneous, innocent enjoyment. No, that wasn't possible! But he owed it to Mrs Duval to make certain.

'Just a moment,' he said sternly.

'Stay away!' she said. '*Please*, stay away!'

'I mean you no harm. But I want to talk to you. Just to be sure. Where are your clothes?'

'No! I don't want you to… I don't need my clothes.'

'You don't?' John smiled grimly, more than ever convinced that there was more to this than he had thought. 'So you mean to talk to me as you are?'

She pulled her hair forward over her shoulders. 'Why not?' she asked. 'I can talk to you from here, though I should prefer you to go away. What do you want, sir?'

'This is absurd! I'll get your clothes and then—'

'No! I don't want you to! Stop! Stop, I tell you!'

John had caught sight of a bundle of clothing tucked into a bush. Ignoring her protests he went towards it. 'Here, I'll pass them to you and you can dry yourself and put them on. Don't worry. I'll stay well clear. I won't ask you to talk to me until you're decently clad.' He bent down, picked the bundle up and held the clothes out to her. A towel, a black, ungainly dress...and a cap and widow's veil. 'But these aren't yours—' he began. He looked back at the girl and frowned. 'Just what is going on?' he asked sternly. 'And what are Mrs Duval's clothes doing on this path?'

The situation was potentially catastrophic. Any moment now the bubble of deceit would burst. But none the less Caroline felt laughter welling up inside. It might well be hysteria, but the sight of John Ancroft in breeches and half-open shirt, holding out that dreadful dress, the veil and the streamers from the cap hanging down limply below his knees, was testing her gravity to its limits. Did he think she had somehow got rid of Mrs Duval? Was he about to arrest her forthwith on suspicion of abduction, or even murder? Before he did anything he'd have to find some other clothes for her first!

It was no use. She burst into a rich laugh. And the expression on the Colonel's face, astounded, outraged, angry, only made things worse. She choked again with laughter. He made a sudden move towards her.

'No, no,' she spluttered. 'You don't have to fetch me. Throw me my towel and yours and I'll come out without your help.'

But in spite of her laughter Caroline was facing some unpleasant facts. Her little game was very nearly over. Indeed, the moment John Ancroft had seen her in the pool her charade was doomed. She cursed the misfortune that had brought him to this very spot at this particular time. Her only hope was that he would not altogether abandon their journey north when he heard the truth.

He passed her the towels, and then drew back a little, though it was clear he did not trust her enough to let her out of his sight. Ignoring the silent observer, Caroline waded nearer and covered herself without undue haste. Then she stepped out of the pool. She was sober again. Standing before him, swathed in the towels, bare legs showing beneath, she said humbly, 'You see before you, Colonel Ancroft, a penitent. I'm afraid I have been playing a dreadful trick on you.'

'Indeed, ma'am?' he said coldly.

'Yes. Though I did not start out with the intention of deceiving you, I assure you. Mr Turner—'

'Excuse me a moment. Am I to understand that I have the honour of addressing Mrs Duval? The *real* Mrs Duval?'

Caroline's ever-ready sense of the ridiculous was roused once again. What would an onlooker make of this excessive formality between two people who, to say the least, were much less than formally dressed? She was practically naked, and he wore only breeches and shirt. Her wet hair was hanging halfway down her back, and his was standing on end, as if he had not combed it but dragged it through the bushes. Any impartial onlooker would swear that they must be escaped Bedlamites! She forced herself to rise to the occasion, however, and replied gravely, 'You have, sir.' Her voice shook as she went on, 'But the honour is mine, I assure you.'

It was no use. She could not stop herself. Laughter burst out again and rang across the pool.

He waited in icy silence till she was calm again, then said, 'I am afraid I do not find any of this amusing, Mrs

Duval. If you will put these things on, I suggest that we return to the inn. Then, after we are both more suitably dressed, I shall listen to your explanation with interest. In an hour's time?'

He turned away. Caroline put on the black dress and wound her hair into a knot. She followed the Colonel back towards the inn in silence.

The inn was stirring when they returned, and they received several curious glances, but neither paid any attention to them. Caroline went swiftly up to her room, and was met by Maggie at the door.

'Miss Caro! I was just about to come to look for you. Where have you been?' She held Caroline away from her and studied her dress. 'What's this? And your hair is wet, too!' Her voice changed. 'Miss Caro! What have you been up to?'

'There's no time to explain properly. The Colonel caught me out, Maggie. He knows I was pretending. He wishes to see me in an hour, and I dare not be late. He is—'

'Angry?'

'Icily furious. I only hope I may not have turned him against us forever!'

Maggie did not waste time in 'I told you so's'. She said simply, 'Then you'd better be sure you are ready and looking your best. Take those things off.'

'With pleasure. There's one advantage at least in this business. Those clothes have had their day! They can be thrown away and burnt!'

'That's not much to rejoice in if the Colonel decides to abandon you.'

'Oh, I hope he does not! Somehow or other I must persuade him not to think too badly of me.'

Maggie glanced curiously at her mistress. There was more than simple anxiety at being stranded in Miss Caro's voice. What was going on? This concern for a man's opinion was not at all like her. She made no comment, however, but simply fetched one of her mistress's own dresses, one of the ones bought in London to replace those lost near Bodmin.

'Sit down and I'll do my best,' was all she said.

Caroline's hair was already drying. It was easy enough to wind it into a topknot and persuade some of the curls to form a frame round her face. The pale lemon-yellow muslin gown was a perfect setting for Caroline's colouring, and its simple cut flattered her magnificent figure. Maggie stood back and studied her work. 'You'll do,' she said.

'Let's hope the Colonel thinks so,' said Caroline with a wry smile. 'Pass me that bag, please.'

'This one? But it will ruin the look! It's far too heavy and big! Take the silk reticule, Miss Caro. Your grandfather's bequest will be safe enough with me.'

'I am sure it would. But I think I need to take it with me.'

Head held high, she went downstairs. John Ancroft was waiting for her at the bottom. He studied her in silence, but somewhat to Caroline's disappointment, he showed no sign of appreciation at her changed appearance.

Instead he said coolly, 'We shall take a walk, Mrs Duval. I am sure you would not wish the world to hear what we have to say to each other, though I assume your maid and Bellerby must be in your confidence. A pity. I had thought Bellerby an honest man.'

'He is! Colonel, I hope you will not blame either of my servants for this!' Caroline said. Her deep voice was calm, but quite firm. 'It would be unjust to think ill of them when they were doing their best to protect me.'

'Really? Well, you may try to convince me of that when we are more private.' The Colonel's tone was still very cold.

Yes, thought Caroline. You may listen to my reasons for the disguise, John Ancroft. I might even be able to persuade you that it really was necessary, and, in the end, you might even forgive me for it. But what you will *not* forgive is the business with the 'servant girl' in your room the other night. You will regard that as a betrayal. Proud, reserved John Ancroft cannot bear the thought that anyone, least of all Mrs Duval, has witnessed what he felt for Gabriella or seen his private agony. *That* is my real crime.

But nothing in her manner indicated that she was afraid. This was Caroline at her fighting best, the young girl who in the end had refused to let Laurent Duval defeat her, the Caroline who had roused her grandfather's support and admiration, and the woman who had ignored private condemnation and won back her place at the head of Kingston society.

They walked to the top of a small prominence where some kindly soul had placed a bench so that walkers could sit and enjoy the view. Here they stopped and she sat down.

'I'm waiting,' said Colonel Ancroft. Those who had been under his command in the Peninsula—those who still lived, that is—could have told Caroline that this was the Colonel's hanging voice. He regarded her without expression, his silver-grey eyes as cold as the Arctic in winter, his mouth a hard line, his manner one of someone who was prepared to listen and to judge. And afterwards to sentence.

Caroline decided to waste no effort in further pleas for forgiveness. What she had done had perhaps been ill advised, but it was not criminal. In any case, Colonel Ancroft was unlikely even to listen to apologies. So she drew a breath and plunged straight in.

'I dare say you concluded that I was merely suffering from an excess of nerves when I asked Mr Turner to find me an escort to Yorkshire. But I assure you, by the time I reached London I had every reason to think myself in danger. I have in my possession something which is badly wanted—fanatically desired—by a distant cousin of mine, a man called Edmund Willoughby. He pursued me in Jamaica for it, but I managed to escape him and believed myself to be safe when we reached England. The last I had seen of him was from the deck of the packet boat as it drew out of Kingston harbour. He and some of his men were standing on the quayside, unable, I believed, to harm us any more.'

'Harm you? How?'

'In Jamaica he had threatened me, killed one of my servants, and had ended up by imprisoning me in his villa outside Kingston. With Joseph's help I managed to fight my way out.' Caroline stopped. It had been such a near thing. She still could not think of it without feeling sick.

'What did this fellow want of you? A forced marriage?'

'No, indeed! He is already married. His object was more mercenary than that.' She regarded him thoughtfully. 'You look unconvinced. I think this is the moment when I have to trust you with a secret. I doubt you will continue to help me otherwise.'

'I think that's quite likely,' said the Colonel coldly. 'I enjoy being a dupe no more than the next man.'

'My cousin Edmund wants something my grandfather gave me before he died. Something which is worth a king's ransom, and which I promised to guard with my life. If you find that too dramatic, then I am sorry. It is so. Apart from…this morning, it has never been out of my sight since we left Jamaica.'

The Colonel cast a glance at the bag on her knee. 'I take it that you now have it in that bag? Why haven't I seen you carry anything like that before?'

Caroline's lips twitched. 'You saw evidence of it every time you looked at me, Colonel Ancroft. I had it round my middle. It was what made me so very…well built.' John Ancroft's expression changed slightly and a fleeting grin softened his mouth. A very faint ray of hope, the merest glimmer, awoke in Caroline's breast at these signs of amusement. The Colonel had a sense of humour, after all! She didn't comment, but carried on.

'We were wrong about having escaped Edmund. One of his men must have been on the ship with us, and as soon as he set foot in Falmouth he conscripted help on behalf of his master. The attack in Cornwall was a clumsy effort to search our luggage. The second attack, the one during which Joseph was wounded, was much better managed. The thieves knew what they wanted, and where it was kept. They left us, believing they had been successful. As they would have been, if Joseph had not seen someone acting suspiciously the night before. After that second attack we used the short time we had before they discovered their mistake to set up our defences. And so, I called myself Mrs Hopkins and put on her disguise.'

'At the same time finding a safe place for this.' He touched the bag. 'No doubt you will eventually explain where your husband comes into all this?'

'My husband?' Caroline said blankly. 'Why, nowhere, sir!'

'There is no husband?'

'There was. But he has been dead for years.'

'So where are his ashes?'

'What are you talking about, Colonel? I've no idea!'

'That was part of the deceit, too? I was told that you were bringing your husband's ashes back to his family home.'

'Not by me!'

'No, my lawyer, Mr Fennybright, told me. But I refuse to believe that Mr Fennybright would set out deliberately to deceive. Especially not me. So how did it happen? Perhaps he was misled? I've always believed Samuel Turner to be as honest a man as Fennybright, but did *you* persuade him to spin us the affecting story of an elderly widow, setting out on a mournful task of taking her husband's ashes back to his birthplace? If so, I congratulate you. It was a masterpiece. I would never have considered this exercise if Turner hadn't appealed to my instincts as a gentleman. So, Mrs Duval, did you manage to persuade Mr Turner to mislead both his partner and myself, or was he himself deceived?'

'But I didn't do anything of the kind! It's true that I'm a widow. It's true that I was nervous about the journey—with good reason, as you have heard. And it's true that Mr Turner was most anxious to help the granddaughter of one of his oldest clients and friends. Were you very reluctant when Mr Fennybright approached you?'

'Extremely so! In fact, at first I refused outright.'

'That must be it! I can only think that Mr Turner was told this, and embroidered the tale a little. Perhaps he thought a dead husband more affecting than a dead grandfather? But I promise you, Colonel Ancroft, the only deceit lay in pretending to be older than I was in order to disguise my identity from my enemies. I did not ask, much less persuade, Mr Turner to deceive his partner. I'm sorry if you think I did.'

'And the ashes? Are your grandfather's ashes in that bag you carry?'

Caroline stared at him, 'Most certainly not,' she said forcefully. Then her irrepressible sense of humour got the better of her and her lips quivered as she added, 'The last thing I would want to do is to travel round England with a bag of ashes round my middle! Very hazardous, I should imagine. And *most* disrespectful!'

This time the Colonel remained serious. He was still very angry, after all. What *could* Mr Turner possibly have said to give him such a false impression? No one knew what was inside her precious bag, but there had never ever been any mention of ashes! Ashes... Remains... Remains! 'Ah!' she exclaimed. 'I think I understand. Was the word used by your Mr Fennybright not "ashes" but "remains"?'

'It may have been.'

'I think Mr Turner may have deliberately obscured the truth—not exactly deception, but a lawyer's play with words. My grandfather wrote to Mr Turner that what I carry could be described as his "remains", since returning it to Yorkshire was all that was left for him to do in this life. That must be where Mr Turner got his idea. But it isn't anything like ashes. My grandfather was respectably buried in Kingston cemetery some months ago—with a great deal of ceremony, too.'

She felt a sharp pang at the memory and looked down, willing herself not to show what that death had meant to her.

'I'm sorry.' Briefly the Colonel's voice was gentle. But it soon hardened again as he said, 'So, you're travelling to Yorkshire for your grandfather's sake, not for that of your husband. And it appears that you were right to be nervous.' He paused. 'Was there no one else to do this? It seems a very odd thing for your grandfather to have asked of you, a woman.'

'I was the last of the Leyburns in Jamaica. There was no other he could trust. My grandfather and I... My grandfather and I were very close, Colonel Ancroft. I was willing to do anything for him, and he had good reason to believe me capable. I...I am not without experience in dealing with unscrupulous men.'

The Colonel looked her over. 'You do not surprise me,' he said drily. 'And I'm sure you have your own methods.'

Caroline was undisturbed. Worse things had been said to her in Kingston. She gave him a wicked smile as she replied, 'If you mean what I think you mean, Colonel Ancroft, then I have to tell you that a woman uses what weapons she can. Brute force is not often at her disposal.'

He nodded an acknowledgement, but didn't comment on this. Instead he went on, 'Why did you not trust me with the full story before we left London?'

Caroline hesitated. 'I wouldn't have trusted anyone. Even Mr Turner doesn't know the full story.' She looked him in the eye. 'Tell me what you would have done, Colonel. I was as near distraught as I can be. My servant, my *friend*, had been badly wounded, Edmund's men were very close, and I had come as close as I ever wish to losing my grandfather's most treasured possession, something I regarded as a sacred trust. I was a stranger in England, my only connection here my grandfather's lawyer. I was told you were a brave and honourable man, and can now believe it is true. But I didn't *know* then.'

There was a silence. Then Caroline added, 'I can't be sorry for my deception. But I do beg pardon for the smaller deceits I practised—calling you ''Captain'' and teasing you with my irritating voice and silly questions.'

The Colonel sat down beside her. 'Yes, why did you?'

Caroline hesitated, then shrugged and said with a touch of exasperation, 'You irritated me. Your letters were so patronising! As if I was a helpless idiot. I couldn't tell you what I really thought, so I teased you.'

'But dammit, from what I was told you *were* a helpless idiot! That was why I agreed to help in the first place! I didn't want to accept the commission, but could hardly refuse Turner, when he appealed to me as a gentleman to see you safe in Yorkshire!'

'I suppose you're right. I shouldn't have done it. Though…' she looked at him between her lashes '…it did enliven some dull moments.'

'I suppose it did.' He gazed at her and almost smiled again. But then he got up, walked a few paces to the edge of the slope and stood there contemplating the view. After a moment he turned round. 'When will you tell me where you wish to go?'

'You're still prepared to take me?' He nodded. Caroline felt such an enormous sense of relief that she was hard put to it not to hug the man standing before her. But she restrained herself. She must be careful not to do anything to remind him of the incident in the inn at Buckden. That had not been mentioned, and she had an idea the Colonel intended to forget it. It would not be wise to bring it to his mind.

He sat down again. 'Now, where?'

'A place called High Hutton. It is not far from Marrick Castle. In the next river valley, in fact. Why, what's wrong, Colonel Ancroft?' The Colonel had risen to his feet once more and was now staring down at her with a shocked look in those grey eyes.

'What game is this? You said your grandfather's name was Leyburn.'

'Yes,' said Caroline. 'Peter Leyburn.'

'And you said this was his family home, I believe?'

She nodded in bewilderment. Why was John Ancroft so upset?

'It may surprise you to know, Mrs Duval, that there are no Leyburns in that valley. Is this another of your tricks?'

Caroline stood up to face him. 'Colonel Ancroft, I've been as frank with you as I dared. I don't tell lies, nor have I made a mistake. My grandfather asked me to go to High Hutton. I'm sure he told me that he came from there. You can't know the area as well as you think!'

The Colonel gazed at her angrily. Once or twice he started to speak, then stopped. Finally he shrugged his shoulders and said, 'I'll take you to High Hutton, ma'am. You will discover for yourself that it's the only building of note for miles around. There are *no Leyburns* in the valley of the Alne! Certainly not at High Hutton. For the last three hundred years High Hutton has belonged to the Ainderby family.'

'Aind—!' Caroline closed her lips tight. The name had taken her unawares. This was the name of the chalice. It was the last secret of all, the one she had sworn to keep until the moment she put the Ainderby Chalice into the hands of its rightful heirs. She must not betray it by another syllable.

To her relief Colonel Ancroft's next words showed that he had mistaken what lay behind her involuntary exclamation. 'Yes, *Ainderby*,' he said. 'Not Leyburn.'

Very wary now, she said, 'Perhaps these Ainderbys were friends of my grandfather?'

'Perhaps. We shall see.' The Colonel's expression was

forbidding. 'And now, I think we should go back to the inn. We're making a very late start.' He turned towards the path down the hill.

Caroline sighed and looked at him in exasperation. Why would he not talk to her about his own affairs? It was clear to her that his feelings towards the Ainderbys were far from friendly. Perhaps his own family was at odds with them. Were they neighbours of his? So far she had no idea where the Colonel lived, or what he would do when he got there. He had a daughter somewhere. Was it to visit her that he was coming north? Or did he intend to live with her in Yorkshire from now on?

They went down back to the inn without speaking. Caroline was sad. For a moment she had felt close to John Ancroft, but he was now as remote as ever. What had she said? Though she racked her brains she could think of nothing. She had been honest and sincere in her apology. He had appeared to accept it. He had not mentioned the embarrassing question of the 'servant girl', preferring, it seemed, to put it behind him. So what had happened to make him angry again?

Humour came to her rescue. For a man who had twice been in very compromising circumstances with her, he was remarkably unfriendly! When she thought of all the gentlemen who would have given their left arm even to dream of being in a similar situation, she was quite put out! It was not at all what she was used to.

As a result of their walk on the hill they were indeed late setting out. Colonel Ancroft had reserved rooms at the Angel in Catterick, but he decided that a change of plan was necessary. There was some wild country in front of them, which meant that they would not be able to keep up the speed of previous stages. He sent a groom on ahead to cancel the rooms in Catterick and reserve others in Boroughbridge, which was some twenty miles nearer.

It was as well he did so. The weather, which had become increasingly sultry, suddenly degenerated and they were forced to take shelter more than once from severe thunderstorms.

In the middle of the day they decided to stop for a while at the Swan in Ferrybridge. Colonel Ancroft told her that it was reputed to be the most luxurious inn in England, and afterwards Caroline was of the opinion that this might well be so. They sat in comfort while the storm raged outside, enjoying an excellent meal. And when they came out afterwards they found that the weather had changed yet again. The sun was shining and the air smelt fresh, washed clean by the rain of the previous hour. Caroline decided that she had had enough of the carriage. The roads might well be muddy after the storm, but she would take advantage of the fact that she could now be seen as a comparatively young, energetic woman, and ride for a while. Besides, she hoped to learn more about Colonel Ancroft. Riding at his side must be more productive than sitting in a carriage with only Joseph and Maggie for company! So she went back into the inn, got Maggie to look out a change of clothing and appeared again, just as her escort was beginning to show some impatience. He frowned at her green habit, dashing hat and riding boots, his eyes lingering involuntarily on the chestnut curl hanging over her shoulder.

'Do I infer that you intend to ride, ma'am?'

'If you will permit, Colonel,' said Caroline demurely. But her air of submission was somewhat spoilt by the enchanting smile which followed.

The Colonel frowned. 'The roads will be dirty.'

'I'm not afraid of dirt, sir.'

He regarded her impassively for a moment, then said, 'I'll see if they have a suitable mount for you,' and wheeled away.

In a few minutes Caroline was riding alongside him on an elegant bay, rejoicing in her new found freedom, and admiring the view.

It was a weird, wild countryside with a strange beauty of its own. She had seen nothing like it in Jamaica. To the left was a sheer drop from the road into a wide valley, and now and then they could see coal mines in the distance. She asked the Colonel about them, and found him remarkably well informed for a man who had spent the previous seventeen years abroad in the army. She said so.

'Since I decided to come north, I've been reading about them, Mrs Duval. I thought it better to learn what has been happening since I was last here.'

'When was that?'

'Nine years ago.'

'Quite some time, then. Your daughter must have missed you.'

'She has been very well looked after. I doubt she has missed me at all. Do you see that ruin over on the horizon there, Mrs Duval? It was once an abbey.'

'That is something England has which Jamaica lacks. History, Colonel Ancroft. We're a very new country compared with yours. Are there many old buildings in Yorkshire?'

The Colonel took this subject up with obvious relief. He took a quarter of an hour to list some famous abbeys and priory churches to be found in the county, together with a brief history of each.

'Thank you, Colonel. My goodness! What an authority you are on your county. First coal mines, now abbeys! Is your own home anywhere near here?'

'No,' he said. 'It is more than fifty miles away. But there are coal mines and abbeys to be found all over the north.' He gave her a slightly amused look, then said blandly, 'I don't believe I mentioned the Cistercian abbey near Ripon. Fountains Abbey. It's particularly picturesque. It's a pity that our journey does not allow time to visit it. Are you interested in history, Mrs Duval?'

Caroline was forced to follow his lead. The Colonel, it appeared, did not wish to talk about his home. Nor anything else remotely personal. Just wait, my friend, she thought. We Leyburns do not give up so easily! I'll find out about you yet.

They rode in silence for a while. Then her companion said abruptly, 'You said that what you carry is valuable. Would it be safer with me? I'm very ready to look after it for you, Mrs Duval. These roads aren't always safe, even without pursuers! What is it? A necklace? Some other jewellery?'

'Thank you, but no. I'll look after it myself. I promised my grandfather, you see.'

'You were obviously very fond of him.'

'I adored him. My parents died when I was nine, and my grandfather and I were left behind to keep each other company. He was a wonderful man, though he could be ruthless when he chose. At one time in my life I...I made a catastrophic mistake. And afterwards, though he had been bitterly hurt by my behaviour, he took me back with not a single reproach. It's not too much to say that he saved me from destruction.'

'You were fortunate to have someone at hand.' He spoke harshly, bitterly even. Once again Caroline's interest was roused. But she knew better than to probe. It was not the moment. But with every hour that passed she was becoming more intrigued by Colonel John Ancroft. He was like no man she had ever met—except perhaps her grandfather. She had an idea that the Colonel was more scrupulous than her grandfather, who had occasionally revealed a devious side to his nature. But she was not at all sure that the Colonel would be less ruthless if and when he thought it necessary.

Chapter Six

John Ancroft stole an occasional glance at his companion as they trotted along in the sunshine. This was his first real opportunity to study her since he had discovered what she really looked like. He allowed his thoughts a free rein. She was very beautiful. In the clear light of day, he could see that she didn't in fact resemble Gabriella quite as closely as he had thought. It was true she had the same richly dark chestnut hair, the same pure green eyes, the same flawless skin. She was tall as Gabriella had been, and if Gabriella had lived to full womanhood he rather thought she too would have been a seductively full-bosomed, slender-hipped creature such as Caroline Duval.

But there were differences. Gabriella had had an innocence about her to which this woman was a stranger. Gabriella had given herself to him just once. She had shown such sweet abandon that he had been enraptured, especially as he knew that she had not done so lightly, or loosely, but because they were so in love that neither of them could have resisted. And because, as they both knew, she was so soon to be his wife.

But Caroline Duval... Why had she seemed so willing to join him in his bed at Buckden? *She* had not been suffering from a fever. And why had she then drawn back? Had he offended her in some way? Dammit, why couldn't he remember more clearly? What *had* happened that night...? But the memory remained obstinately elusive, and after a moment he gave up the struggle and returned to his musings.

They both had plenty of spirit, she and his Gabriella, but humour was not a part of Gabriella's make-up, whereas he suspected it was deeply ingrained in Caroline Duval. Gabriella had taken life seriously. She *might* have developed the same attractive little laughter lines round her eyes, but he doubted it. Besides, Gabriella, he thought with a pang, had always been so proud of her beauty, so anxious to preserve it, had stated her determination to stay young forever. As she had, of course. Eternally young in memory...

With determination he turned his thoughts back to the woman riding beside him. He had been amused by her efforts to question him, but he was damned if he would make it easy for her after the way she had teased him earlier! She was an intriguing mixture, all the same. Though she was obviously curious her questions had been basically harmless—such as any politely interested new acquaintance might have asked. After the scene at Buckden he wouldn't have been surprised if she had probed, been intrusive. But she had behaved honourably since that night, never showing by word or look that he had very nearly seduced her, nor that she had been a witness to his embarrassing parade of raw emotion. What other woman would have resisted the temptation to look conscious, or to give him sly looks, or significant nods? Or, worse still, to give herself the pleasure of offering advice or sympathy? But Caroline Duval had done none of these. If she had been a man, he would have called her a true gentleman.

Other qualities she had, too. Courage for example, and pride. When he had caught her under the waterfall she had been shocked, and frightened, of course. That wasn't surprising. But how quickly she had recovered, refusing to let herself be cowed, or show embarrassment or shame. Nor had she used the occasion to behave provocatively, either. Her laughter had been quite genuine, and clearly stemmed from a keen sense of the ridiculous. He grinned. She was right! It had been a bizarrely comic situation. Why hadn't he appreciated it at the time?

He rode on through the countryside considering this and his smile faded. Because he had been so angry, that was why. For a few moments he could have throttled her. It was many, many years since he had been in such a rage. Not since…not since Philip had died. It wasn't the simple fact of her deception. That would have annoyed him, but it would not have put him into such a fury that it had taken all his control not to give way to it. It was the thought that this woman had been privy to his passion and his pain, had witnessed feelings he had kept hidden from the world for years, that she had taken advantage of his weakness to deceive him into believing Gabriella had returned from the dead… That had been intolerable.

But had he been fair? *She* hadn't tried to persuade him she was Gabriella. He had persuaded himself. That much he could remember. But what sort of woman was she, to come into his bedchamber without protest? As far as he could remember he hadn't dragged her in. His memory of that night was fogged by the effects of fever, but he couldn't remember a struggle, only a sensation of overwhelming delight at rediscovering Gabriella, his love, followed by devastating grief at losing her all over again.

Strangely though, the remaining impression of the woman who had been in the room with him was not one of someone looking for excitement or sexual gratification of any kind, but someone who had treated him with dignity and compassion. And she had made no reference to the episode since. The woman was an enigma! He had never known anyone like her.

'You're frowning, Colonel Ancroft. Do you not approve of my riding with you like this? Is it "not done" in England?'

She was looking at him with that little air of mockery which seldom left her. Those green eyes seemed to hold an invitation to laugh with her at the world and its absurdities. She might *ask* about the rules of society, but he was not at all sure that she would allow them to *affect* her. If he were to tell her now that what she was doing would be severely frowned on by the *ton*, he was almost sure she would shrug her shoulders, and continue to ride with all the confidence and self-possession in the world.

Colonel Ancroft would have liked to test his supposition, but there was unfortunately nothing at all untoward in their riding together in full sight of the rest of the party. 'It is perfectly proper, Mrs Duval,' he said. 'Are the rules in Jamaica stricter, then?'

'I suppose they are. But my grandfather was somewhat scornful of the establishment, and I'm afraid he taught me to be the same. He used to say that one should abide by one's own code of conduct and be damned to the rest.' She added carefully, 'That was what my *grandfather* was used to say.'

For some reason Colonel Ancroft did not doubt that it was what Caroline Duval was used to say herself, too. But he merely remarked, '"To thine own self be true." Was that it? Make up your own rules. Didn't it make for difficulty in such a restricted world as I imagine Jamaican society must be?'

Caroline Duval laughed. 'Oh, yes! But then, I had everything to win and nothing to lose, you see.'

'I'm afraid I don't understand?'

'I was a black sheep, Colonel. The ladies of Kingston would have seen the Widow Duval drummed out of the regiment if they could have managed it. You're looking concerned. There's no need, I assure you. With my grandfather behind me, there was never any risk of it, and now... Now I'm a reformed character and *perfectly* acceptable anywhere.'

She gave him a wicked look. Reformed character, indeed! A sudden memory of this woman standing before him in the bedchamber, the perfection of her body, the feel of her skin against his cheek, took him by surprise. He looked away before she could read the flare of desire in his eyes. She was a witch! He fought to find something unexceptional to say.

'I'm sure you had many admirers, too.'

'Among the gentlemen, you mean? Oh, yes.'

'Were you... Have you never been tempted to remarry?'

This time Caroline Duval was not laughing. She said emphatically, 'Never! Not once! I make many mistakes, Colonel Ancroft, but I try very hard not to make the same mistake twice.'

He was surprised at her vehemence. The late Mr Duval, it seemed, had not been a success.

Then she said with a look of challenge in her eyes, 'Since I've satisfied some of your curiosity, Colonel Ancroft, won't you satisfy some of mine?'

He regarded her warily, but decided he would trust her

not to delve too deep. 'I might,' he said cautiously. 'What do you wish to know?'

'Where you live—and, before you say London, I mean here in Yorkshire.'

With only a fractional hesitation he said, 'Marrick.'

'Really? Grandfather described the castle there as something of a landmark.'

'He was right. It is quite large and prominently placed.'

'I see! So you *do* know the area! Have you been away long?'

'Seventeen years. Though I have been back briefly once or twice since then.'

'The last time nine years ago. You see, I do not forget what you have told me! Is your daughter at Marrick?'

'Yes, for the moment. She will go to London next year to be presented to society. She's seventeen next February.'

Caroline turned an astonished face towards him. 'Your daughter is sixteen?' When he nodded she said, 'You must have been ridiculously young when she was born?'

So she wanted to know how old he was? He didn't mind telling her. 'Thank you for the compliment. I was twenty-two.' With amusement he watched her working it out. 'I'm thirty-eight,' he added helpfully.

She laughed and blushed. 'I had already concluded as much,' she said. He was fascinated. He hadn't imagined Caroline Duval *could* blush, but she was damned attractive when she did.

'I shan't enquire how old you are, Mrs Duval. It isn't something a lady likes to be asked, I understand,' he said quirking an eyebrow at her.

'I'm twenty-six. And you may save any gallant exclamations of surprise, Colonel. The fact doesn't disconcert me in the slightest.'

He found himself saying, 'But then, from what I have observed, I think it would take a great deal to disconcert you, Mrs Duval.'

Once again colour rose in her cheeks. She raised an eyebrow and said quizzically, 'Are you reminding me of an episode...no, *two* episodes we would both rather forget, Colonel Ancroft?'

Her directness surprised him. He had made his comment without thinking, regretting what he had said as soon as the words were uttered. What the devil was it about this woman? After swearing to himself that he would never mention the incident at Buckden to anyone, least of all to Caroline Duval, here he was embarrassing them both by his words. He snatched a glance at her. The look in her eyes was mockery, not embarrassment! The wretched woman was laughing at his discomfiture! Well, he thought grimly, two can play at that game, my lovely one!

'You're surely omitting at least some aspects of those "episodes", if you think I would rather forget them, Mrs Duval. I have every man's appreciation of beauty,' he said smoothly. 'Especially natural beauty.'

He saw with some satisfaction that he had surprised her. Her face flamed, she sat upright in the saddle, and said hotly, 'Why, you *sal*—!' Then she stopped and bit her lip, nervously fingering her whip.

Colonel Ancroft laughed aloud at these signs of temper. He was willing to swear that Caroline Duval was not often caught off balance like this. She continued to gaze at him angrily for a moment, then a reluctant smile appeared and she nodded in acknowledgement.

'My congratulations, Colonel! I haven't often had a taste of my own medicine returned so quickly. I suppose I deserved it.' Her amusement this time was quite genuine with no trace of malice. 'But it was almost worth it just to see you laugh! Shall we now cry quits?'

He nodded, still chuckling. 'I must apologise. It was not a gentlemanly thing to do.'

'But irresistible, I'm sure,' she said drily.

They were just coming in to Aberford, their next stop.

'I think I must ride in the carriage for the next stretch,' said Caroline. 'More than my *amour propre* is hurting. It's months since I've been on a horse for such a long time. Thank you, Colonel Ancroft, for an instructive... and amusing ride.'

The Colonel helped her dismount, then watched her walk, somewhat stiffly, into the inn, the smile still lingering on his lips.

The decision to stay the night at Boroughbridge rather than to press on to Catterick turned out to be a good one. The inn was commodious and comfortable, and it served them with a delicious meal. The trout had been freshly caught in the river, the veal collops were done to a turn, and the pastry in the gooseberry tart melted in the mouth. In the interest of her own self-esteem Caroline had taken considerable pains with her appearance, and she felt she was looking her best. The evening was warm, but her short-sleeved dress of fine white lawn was elegantly cool. A Paisley shawl was draped over her arms.

Colonel Ancroft gave her a slight smile when she appeared, but once again made no comment. Caroline was slightly piqued. This was a man who didn't believe in empty compliments, it appeared! Over dinner they conversed on unexceptional matters, the scenery, the local activities, aspects of Jamaican life... It was all strictly impersonal. After the challenges of the journey it all seemed rather flat to Caroline. She would have enjoyed a further sparring match with the Colonel, but he was obviously not in the mood.

The inn had some old London newspapers and John spent some time after dinner perusing their columns. He gave a sudden exclamation.

'What is it, Colonel?'

He cleared his throat and said, 'I'll read it out. ''Mr Edmund Willoughby, one of Jamaica's most prominent citizens, has now left London after a disappointingly short stay. Mr Willoughby landed in Falmouth a month ago after a highly uncomfortable voyage from Kingston, during which the packet was delayed by violent storms in the Atlantic. He was forced to spend some time recuperating at the home of his English relatives in Kent, and had time for only one week in the capital. It is understood that he intends to see something of the countryside during his sojourn in England.''' He lowered the paper. 'Is this your cousin?'

Caroline nodded. 'English relatives—I wonder if Edmund found his ally among them?' Then she asked suddenly, 'But tell me, how old is that newspaper? When did Edmund leave London?'

'Several days ago, I should imagine. Does he know your destination?'

'He knew it was somewhere in the north, but that's all. My grandfather didn't really trust him, any more than I do. He knew very well that Edmund wanted what I am carrying, though I don't think he realised to what lengths my cousin was prepared to go to get it. But Grandfather was always cautious about this thing. He never discussed it.'

John respected her wish for secrecy, but he could not help wondering what it was she was taking to High Hutton. The whole affair was puzzling. She was always so careful not to give any clue as to what it might be. He had asked her whether it was jewellery, and offered to take care of it, but she had refused the offer without answering his question. What *was* her grandfather's connection with High Hutton? Was he a repentant thief? Had he been a pirate on the Caribbean in his early days, perhaps, and now wished to make amends by returning some valuable trinket to the Ainderbys? Or was it something of sentimental value, a souvenir of someone he had loved? He asked, 'Has it been in your family a long time?'

'I think so. But I don't know for sure. I don't even know how Edmund learned of it. I had no idea myself of its existence until Grandfather told me about it, shortly before he died. But I'm quite certain that Edmund cannot know precisely where we are going, only that it's somewhere in the north of England.'

'Then there isn't any immediate danger. There's more than one road out of London to the north, and though I've had my men keeping watch, there hasn't been any sign of pursuit.'

Caroline was still not altogether reassured. 'I can't fail now! I mustn't!' she said agitatedly. 'Colonel Ancroft, how far is it to Marrick and High Hutton?'

'About thirty miles or more to Marrick. And another eight or so to High Hutton.'

'Then we're close enough to outrun Edmund. We must leave Boroughbridge at first light tomorrow,' she urged.

'I agree. I'll warn the men to be ready.' He smiled at her. 'Try not to be so anxious. We can't do anything before tomorrow, but we'll start in good time, I promise. Now! The inn has some excellent brandy. Allow me to order a glass for you. I've noticed you enjoy one occasionally, and it will help you sleep.'

Caroline made an effort. She gave him a challenging

look. 'I suppose you disapprove of my drinking brandy? Maggie does.'

'Why should I? Though surely rum is a more usual tipple in Jamaica?'

'Neither rum nor brandy is considered suitable for a lady, not even in Jamaica.'

'But as you told me—you make your own rules, do you not? Drink the brandy, Caroline. It will help to calm you. It's very unlikely that your cousin will find us, especially once we've left the main road north. And if he does, we can deal with him, I fancy.'

They left the inn as planned early the next morning and were soon driving over a handsome stone bridge over the River Ure. They would leave the Great North Road just beyond Catterick, which was a mere twenty odd miles away. Caroline was restless. It would have helped if she could have ridden with the Colonel, but they had both agreed that that was out of the question. She must stay out of sight in the carriage.

'Do what you can to keep Bellerby happy,' John said. 'I think he's fretting at his inability to help. That arm is not healing as fast as it ought.' He regarded her critically. 'And you'd better sit well back,' he said with a frown. 'Your appearance is too distinctive. It's a pity you chose to throw away your widow's weeds.'

'Do not say so!' she begged. 'I was never so glad to be rid of any garments before! I'll sit well back in the carriage, I promise.'

It was as well she did so. After making good time along a straight road from Boroughbridge, they arrived at Catterick Bridge. From here the Great North Road went on to Carlisle and then into Scotland and Gretna Green. But, much to Caroline's relief, Colonel Ancroft and his party would at last leave the main road and turn west towards Richmond. Marrick Castle and High Hutton lay among the hills beyond.

They had stopped to change the horses before turning off, and found they had to wait. Another carriage, one travelling south, was already at the inn, the ostlers busy harnessing up a new team. The landlord came hurrying out to apologise for the delay, and offer the inn's hospitality while they waited. His face changed comically when he saw the Colonel.

'Eh, Master John! Well, I never!' He turned to the house and shouted, 'Annie! Annie! Come 'ere, lass, quick! It's Master John come back after all these years.' He took the hand John was offering, and shook it enthusiastically, grinning from ear to ear. 'Ee, it's good to see thee, lad! Where's tha been, all this time?'

His wife came out and gave him a shove in the ribs with her elbow. 'I'm ashamed of thee, Barnaby, I am that! Where's your respect?' She turned and curtsied. 'My lord, you'll 'ave to forgive my husband. He means no 'arm, but he forgets what's due to you now. May I say we're reet glad to see your lordship. We'd be honoured if you'd step inside a moment. And the rest of your party.'

'Thank you, Annie, but another time. My passengers are impatient to be at Marrick. And don't blame Barnaby. It's a wonderful welcome he's given me. Besides, it must be difficult to show too much respect to the scrubby boy he taught to ride. I've had many a cuff on the ear from him.' Annie laughed, and John turned to put his head inside the carriage. 'I ought to explain,' he said to Caroline, 'that Barnaby and his wife were once in service at the castle. Barnaby was head groom there, and taught us to ride.'

'Aye, you and Lord Philip both.' Barnaby's red face clouded over. 'That was a poor business,' he began, 'but there! His lordship was always too hasty for his own good... But we're glad you've decided to come back to us at last, Master John.'

'I say! Ho, there! Landlord!' The peremptory call attracted everyone's attention. Both John and Barnaby turned to look. An exquisitely dressed gentleman was stepping down from the other coach. His blue velvet coat and pale fawn breeches looked so out of place in these parts and at this hour that they all stared. Then John's eyes narrowed. He turned again and gave a quick glance at Caroline. Like everyone else she had looked out to see who had called the landlord, but she was now shrinking back against the squabs. Her face was white. 'Edmund!' she mouthed at him. John nodded and stepped forward, covering the window with his broad shoulders.

'Well, did you hear me? Landlord, I say!' snapped the exquisite.

'In a minute, sir!' said Barnaby amiably.

'No, dammit! Now! Come here, I want to ask you something.'

Barnaby looked at the Colonel, who said quietly, 'Be careful what you tell that gentleman, Barnaby.'

Barnaby ambled over to Edmund Willoughby. 'What can I do for you, sir?' he asked pleasantly. 'Are my men not doing their job to your satisfaction?'

'It's not that,' said Mr Willoughby impatiently. 'I want to ask about some travellers you might have seen. A Colonel Ancroft. I need to talk to him. Do you know anything about him? Have you seen him? I understand he belongs somewhere in these parts.'

'In these parts, you say? I don't think so, sir,' said Barnaby, the very picture of a slow-thinking landlord of a wayside inn. 'Give me a moment to think... And I'll ask the lad, too.' He looked round. 'Where is he, the young varmint? He should be dealing with the other gentleman's carriage. Unless you watch them every minute of the day they're back in the taproom! Excuse me, I'll be back in a moment.' He went to the door of the inn and roared, 'Jem! Where are you? Come out here and start your work before I use my belt on you!' He went over to John, apparently to apologise, but lowering his voice he said, 'What is it, my lord?'

Colonel Ancroft said quietly, 'I heard. I don't want him to find me, Barnaby. Put him off. He doesn't know the new title, so you can impress him with that if you have to. But no mention of Ancroft.'

Barnaby bowed and cuffed the ear of a puzzled stable lad, who was just coming round the corner. Then he went back to Mr Willoughby.

'Now, sir, I'm all yours. What was the name of the party?'

'Ancroft.'

'And why would you be wanting him, sir?'

'The er...the villain has abducted a cousin of mine. I suspect he's taking her to Gretna. They must be stopped before he succeeds! Have you seen them?'

'What makes you think they're anywhere round here?'

'They had rooms reserved in Catterick last night. I waited for them but they didn't arrive. I must find them. There'll be a substantial reward, landlord. Have you seen them at all?'

'I can't say I have, sir. We've had very little traffic through here these last days. Perhaps they're at Boroughbridge? We've had some weather recently, and that might have delayed them. Try Boroughbridge, sir.' He turned away.

'Just one moment! What about the fellow over there? Who is he? Don't just stare like that, you fool! Check them. There's someone who appears to be travelling north, *and* he has a female in the carriage with him, too!'

John Ancroft stiffened and strolled towards him. He stood looking coldly down at Edmund Willoughby. 'May I have your name, sir?' he asked.

'Certainly! And I hope to have yours. I am Edmund Willoughby of Kingston in Jamaica.'

'Ah! Jamaica, eh?' drawled John. 'I suppose that explains it.'

'Explains what, sir?'

'The uncouth manner you use in talking of myself and my wife. Colonial manners. I suppose I must forgive you.' And John turned away with insulting indifference.

Mr Willoughby coloured angrily and said, 'One moment! You have not yet told me who *you* are, sir! May I have your name?'

John raised an eyebrow and looked Edmund up and down. 'Certainly!' he said finally in a bored tone. 'Tell him, Barnaby.'

Barnaby said in tones of hushed respect, 'You're talking to the biggest landowner for miles around, sir. This is his lordship, the Marquess of Coverdale. It's more than my inn's worth to annoy him. So, if you don't mind, sir, I'd like you to be on your way. It doesn't do my business any good at all to have strangers coming here and insulting their betters.'

'Why, you impertinent—'

'On your way, sir!'

With bad grace Mr Willoughby got into the carriage and told his man to give the order. In minutes he was on his way south again.

John Ancroft watched him go, and then turned to the

landlord. 'Barnaby, you rogue!' he said grinning. 'You should be on the stage!'

'Oh, I can crawl with the best o' 'em, my lord—when it suits me.'

'I'm obliged to you. Now, we must make haste to reach the shelter of Marrick before Mr Willoughby discovers his mistake.'

Barnaby eyed him curiously, hesitated, then said somewhat awkwardly, 'May it please your lordship… Annie and I would like to give you our best wishes, my lord. You and your good lady. We didn't know your lordship was married, you see.'

'I'm not, Barnaby. The lady is merely a friend. I said it in order to put that villain off the scent. And before that dramatic imagination of yours gets to work, I'm not off to Gretna with her, either. Thank you. If the gentleman comes back again, don't provide him with any horses!'

'Don't you worry, my lord! And if I do, they'll be broken-down nags not worthy of the name! Give my regards to Marrick! They'll all be reet glad to see your lordship there.'

'Oh, will they?' muttered John to himself as they set off again. 'I doubt it, Barnaby. I doubt it very much.'

Just three miles further on, they stopped again in Richmond. A team of John's own horses which had been sent down from Marrick were to be harnessed up for the last stage of their journey. Caroline was fascinated by the warmth of the welcome the Colonel received from nearly everyone who saw him. John Ancroft may not have been seen in Richmond for nine years, but he had not been forgotten.

As they entered the inn he said to her, 'I've sent a groom to warn my steward up at Marrick to have rooms prepared for us all. The roads were pretty bad when I was last in the district, and from what I hear they're now worse, not better. High Hutton is nearly inaccessible at the best of times, and the recent rains have made the road up the valley dangerous. We'll stay the night at Marrick and then consider what's to be done.' He nodded reassuringly. 'You'll be as safe at Marrick as anywhere in the kingdom. It was once a fortress.'

Caroline nodded. Once again he had taken the law into his own hands without consulting her first. But this time she was ready to trust his judgement. However anxious she was to see her mission over, his better knowledge of the country must prevail. However, she could not resist teasing him once more. Putting on a mournful face she said wistfully, 'And I had *so* hoped you were taking me to Gretna, as my cousin said! Especially as you've told the world that we are already married!'

'Mrs Duval—'

'There's another thing! Last night you called me Caroline. But now I'm back to being Mrs Duval again. What have I done to displease you? Apart from running away with you to Gretna.'

John gave her a reluctant grin. 'You forget, I know you better now. You won't disturb me with your teasing. I know your views on marriage, and they agree with my own. But I think we're friends enough for me to call you Caroline, if it's your wish. My name is—'

'Oh, I know your name! It is the Marquess of Coverdale! And to think I thought you Captain Ancroft, a simple soldier in the service of the King…'

'You always knew I was a Colonel. And the Coverdale title is very new. My…my uncle died in April.' His face changed. 'I should perhaps warn you that I'm highly uncertain of our reception at Marrick. I only hope it won't affect you.'

'But everyone I've seen is delighted that you're back! How can you be uncertain?'

He hesitated and seemed to be debating within himself what to say. Then he walked to the window and peered out, examining the weather. He then turned back to her. Caroline was puzzled—John Ancroft was not usually so indecisive. She waited.

He said suddenly, 'Caroline, do you feel able to ride with me a part of the way to Marrick? All of it, even. It's no further than our ride to Aberford, and the weather seems promising. I think I need to talk to you.'

'Of course, I should be delighted! It won't take me long to change. I'll call Maggie at once.'

Once they were out of the town and on the road he kept up a good pace, and they had soon left the carriage far behind. The scenery became increasingly wild as they went on through a narrow valley. A river flowed alongside, its banks lined with thick woods, all in full leaf, and above the road, the upper slopes were covered in grass, interspersed with grey limestone rocks. Everywhere, small streams and rivulets rushed down to join the river at the bottom, filling the air with a constant sound of running water. And in the distance hills of grey and green were bathed in the afternoon sunshine. John seemed to be feasting his eyes on it, like a man starved of the sight for too long.

Some way along the valley they left the road and turned on to a narrow track which led to a grassy knoll above. To Caroline's relief, a halt was called, and they dismounted. John gave the grooms a signal to fall back, and they were left effectively alone. He led her to the edge of the knoll.

'I hope you don't object to this seclusion?'

'I'm no nervous maiden, John! And I imagine you have a good reason to want privacy. No, I don't object.'

'Good. Over there. Can you see?'

Caroline looked in the direction he was pointing. On a rocky outcrop some distance away she saw a large castle bathed in the afternoon sun. Even on a sunny afternoon it looked formidably uncompromising, grey and stark among the rocks. 'That is Marrick Castle,' he said.

'It's an impressive sight. How it dominates the countryside!'

'Yes. Marrick and High Hutton between them. For centuries, the Ancrofts and the Ainderbys have held most of the lands round here. They've been in turn enemies, friends, rivals, and allies.' He paused. 'And some have loved.'

Caroline caught her breath. Was she to learn something about the Ainderbys at last?

John Ancroft glanced at her and said, 'I should like to tell you something of our family history. This isn't idle gossip. I've invited you to stay at Marrick, and want to prepare you for whatever is waiting for us there.' He took a breath and began again, 'You said people were pleased to see me. Yes, I think you're right. The ordinary folk round here are pleased to welcome me back because they believe there'll be better times ahead. My uncle was a recluse for many years before he died, and the estate has been badly neglected. There's no shortage of money to make the reforms necessary. It was rather a complete abdication of interest on his part. They all hope that I'll do better by them.'

'But they seem to *like* you, too!'

'I suppose they remember me from happier times, when I was a lad among them. The folk round here are rather like your Joseph Bellerby—their respect has little to do with rank or position. You have to earn it. And if they once decide you're worthy, then they're yours for life.'

'I think you said once that you'd quarrelled with your uncle?'

'Yes. And this is why. He had a son, my cousin Philip, his only child. He and I were brought up as brothers. But there was an accident and Philip was killed, together with Gabriella. My uncle blamed me for it, and I must say he had some justification.'

The bare words, uttered without expression or feeling, hovered in the air between them. If Caroline had not heard the devastation in John Ancroft's voice in that bedchamber in Buckden when he talked of Gabriella's death, she might have thought that the tragedy now meant little or nothing to him. But the contrast between these matter-of-fact sentences and the anguish she had witnessed at Buckden could not have been greater. What she was seeing now was John's public figure. The private agony which she had accidentally provoked that night was not for the world to see. Never for the world. *'I saw her die,'* he had said. *'She and Philip together.'*

But was John Ancroft now saying that he believed himself responsible? Responsible for Gabriella's death! The depth of the agony she had witnessed that night suddenly became more comprehensible. She waited.

He took a deep breath and went on, 'In my fever at Buckden I mistook you for Gabriella. You...you strongly resemble her, you see.'

Caroline was silent. There was nothing she could say.

John went on, 'There are still some older people at Marrick who were there at the time of the accident.

They're sure to see this resemblance, even if they don't comment.' He turned and looked at her. 'In fact, Caroline, I suspect your grandfather may have had a closer relationship with the Ainderbys than you know. The physical likeness is striking.'

'I...I remember your saying so.' Caroline said awkwardly.

He gave her a swift tortured look. 'Yes,' he replied. 'Yes. Indeed. May I go on? Or are you tired? I've at least explained why you may be subjected to some strange looks. Perhaps that's enough.'

'No, please! Tell me a little more. Tell me about Gabriella's daughter. Your daughter.'

'Gabriella's! No, no! You're mistaken. Harriet is my *wife*'s daughter.'

Caroline looked at him in astonishment. 'Gabriella wasn't your wife?'

'No.' He paused. 'No. We were to have been married within the month when she was killed. My wife's name was Rose. Harriet is *her* daughter.'

'I see...'

He gave her a little smile. 'I'm quite sure you don't. But that's another long story and a sad one. I won't go into it more than I have to. My wife, you see...my wife...had been in love with Philip, and thought I had killed him deliberately. She persuaded Harriet to believe the same.'

'Your *own daughter*? But how did she manage that? Harriet wasn't even born when the accident happened!'

'No. Not till the following February. You mustn't blame my wife, however. She had help from my uncle... Oh God, Caroline, if you knew how difficult this is! But I must prepare you!' John turned away again and gazed out over the valley, as if to draw strength from it. He began again. 'After Philip died, my uncle's affection for me turned to a hatred which was so virulent that he would have harmed me in any way he could short of murder. He poisoned my wife's mind against me, and then set about turning Harriet away from me, too. With considerable success. Since she was old enough to understand, Harriet has disliked and feared me. As far as I know, she still does. That's what I wish you to know.'

Chapter Seven

'John! Oh, John!' There was no trace now either of mockery or of laughter in Caroline Duval's face. Nor was there the sentimental pity he had always feared from others. Her expression was a mixture of shock and pure compassion.

He was moved, but refused to show it. After seventeen years of steeling himself against the softer human emotions he was not about to melt at the sight of the first beautiful woman to show him compassion! On the whole he preferred her mockery. That could be dealt with far more easily!

'Pray don't be too sorry for me,' he said a little stiffly. 'There's no need. I hardly know the child. She was only seven when I last saw her, and even that was for a short two minutes. I have only told you this unhappy tale, to prepare you for her attitude towards me.'

'But what about the child?' Caroline cried. 'What about Harriet?'

'I believe she's a well-balanced, reasonably happy girl. Considering her beginnings, remarkably so. Mr Fennybright was good enough to find an excellent lady of education and breeding to be her companion, and I have regular reports from both the lady and Fennybright himself. No, Caroline, you need have no misgivings about the child. She's very bright. Shall we move on?'

As they made their way back on to the road, John Ancroft was wondering whether he had been wise to reveal so much. He could have satisfied many other women with a good deal less. But Caroline Duval was no fool. However short her time at Marrick, she could not fail to notice the situation. It was better to give her the facts rather than to see her speculating about his family affairs.

Besides, in a curious way, his dislike of revealing anything of his private concerns was balanced by a sense of relief at having unburdened himself, shared his trouble with someone he could trust not to offend him with excessive sympathy or pity. He was quite certain that his story was safe with Caroline Duval.

They arrived at the steep drive up to Marrick Castle not long after. Built on a rock, Marrick was accessible only by this drive, which ended in a bridge over a moat. The moat had long since been emptied and a wild garden planted in its hollows, but the wooden bridge and massive arch that had once been part of the defences were still in use. When they entered the main courtyard John's face clouded over at the sight of what looked like hundreds of servants gathered there. But his expression grew more amiable when an elderly man with a shock of white hair came towards him.

'Thomas!' he said, dismounting and shaking the man by the hand. 'Thomas Beckford! How d' ye do?'

'Very fair, my lord. But it's a grand day for Marrick!'

'Is it, indeed? It's an idle day for Marrick from the looks of things! What are all these people doing here?'

'Eeh, my lord! What do you think? We had to give the

new Marquess a welcome. There wasn't a soul for miles around but wanted to come when they 'eard you'd be back today, my lord.' Thomas's eyes passed to Caroline, who had been waiting in the background. The old man's eyes widened briefly in shock, but he quickly controlled it and became once again the well-trained servant.

'Mrs Duval, this is my steward, Thomas Beckford.' Turning back to the steward, John said, 'I hope you have some rooms ready for Mrs Duval and her people?'

'They're quite ready, my lord. If his lordship would come this way? Mistress Duval?'

The steps up to the great Hall were lined with servants, all bobbing and smiling at their new master. Some were even cheering. John spoke to some of the older ones and nodded to others. Walking behind him, Caroline had cause to be grateful for his warning. Not everyone was as discreet as Thomas Beckford. Numbers of people craned their necks and stared as she passed, and she heard a growing buzz of conversation behind her. But she lost none of her usual grace and composure as she followed John up the steps. Whether it was her likeness to Gabriella, or her possible relationship with the new master that was disturbing them, they would soon enough learn that she was but a temporary visitor to Marrick, with no part to play in their future.

Two people were waiting at the top of the steps, a girl and an older woman. But as they approached, the girl suddenly broke away and fled into the room behind. The woman who had been beside her looked vexed for a moment and turned, clearly debating whether to go after her. But then she changed her mind, came up to John and curtsied. 'Lord Coverdale, may I welcome you back to Marrick? I am Mrs Abbington.'

'Thank you.' John turned to Caroline. 'Mrs Duval, may

I present Mrs Abbington? Mrs Abbington has looked after Harriet for many years, and from all accounts very well, too.'

'Not so well as I should, apparently. You must excuse Lady Harriet, my lord. She must be over-excited. I'll fetch her presently.'

'No need for hurry, ma'am. I'll see her when she is ready. Now, will you perhaps show Mrs Duval to her room? I expect she needs a rest.'

'Certainly. Mrs Duval?' The companion led the way across a huge hall to a baronial staircase. 'I've arranged for you to be in the blue bedroom, ma'am,' she said as they traversed a long corridor decorated with stags' heads and pieces of old armour. 'I think you'll like the view.'

Eventually, after what seemed like miles, they came to a comfortable bedchamber with blue curtains and bed hangings. Caroline not only liked the view—she was struck dumb by it! Row after row of green and grey hills, purple now in the sun's lengthening shadows, stretched into the distance. To the right a foaming stream hurtled down over boulders and rocks to join the river in the valley far below. Over to the left, beyond a deep cleft, was an outcrop of rocks, overrun with tiny rivulets and infant waterfalls. 'It's breathtaking!' she cried. 'I don't think I've seen anything so impressive since I left Jamaica.'

'Jamaica? I didn't realise… You're a long way from home, ma'am!'

'Yes.' Caroline sobered, as she remembered that the task she had come from Jamaica to fulfil was still not complete. She took the strap of the bag that never left her, pulled it wearily over her head, and laid the bag down on the bed.

'Could you please find my maid, Mrs Abbington? And the valises.'

'I'll see to it with pleasure, ma'am. Er... Unless his lordship decides differently, we dine early at Marrick. Dinner is served at six.' Mrs Abbington gave a little bob and left her. Caroline was suddenly exhausted. So much had happened during the past twenty-four hours. And now, just over those purple hills lay High Hutton and the end of her quest. One more day and it would all be finished with.

And then what would she do?

After a refreshing nap she dressed carefully in another of her new gowns and came downstairs with fifteen minutes to spare. At the foot of the stairs she hesitated, but then a maidservant, whose shy smiles could not quite disguise her curiosity, led her through the Hall and into a line of rooms that had been laid out on the southern side of the castle. The sun had moved round, but there was still plenty of light, in spite of mullioned windows. She stepped forward into the room...and walked into what was clearly a family crisis.

John looked much as he had at their first meeting in Mr Turner's chambers—stiff, upright, cold, reserved. Her wooden soldier to perfection.

Mrs Abbington was nervous and distressed. She was holding Harriet Ancroft firmly by the arm, saying, 'Harriet, I will not allow you to behave so rudely! What do you suppose your father thinks of you—or me, either—when you show him such ill manners? Now, please prove that you do know how a lady should behave. For my sake, if not your own.'

The girl looked pale and tearful. 'Must I, Abby?'

'Yes,' replied the companion firmly. 'Now, if you please.'

Harriet Ancroft showed resistance in every line of her thin young body as she bobbed a curtsy to her father and then held out her hand, stretching her arm out to its full length. 'Welcome to Marrick, Father,' she said woodenly.

Caroline was briefly amused. Like father, like daughter, she thought. And as the pair stared stonily at one another, she saw that Harriet really was like her father, with the same dark hair and silver-grey eyes, as well as the same expression! But her amusement turned to dismay when she saw the girl snatch her hand back as soon as it was touched, her face suddenly a study in revulsion.

'Harriet!' said Mrs Abbington severely.

John turned away and said wearily, 'Leave it, Mrs Abbington, leave it. The girl hardly knows me, after all. Let her go back to her room, if she wishes.'

Caroline spoke up. 'But surely not before I have a chance to meet her?' She came forward and said to the girl, 'I'm disappointed. I was hoping to talk to you. Your father is so proud of you that I wanted to see you for myself.'

'Proud? Of me?'

'Why, yes!'

'How can he be? He hasn't been near me for nine years!'

'Hasn't he? But he gets frequent reports, I understand, from Mrs Abbington here, and also from Mr Fennybright. You know Mr Fennybright, do you not?'

The girl looked uncertainly at Caroline. She obviously liked what she saw, and indeed, Caroline was a very attractive sight in a gown of apricot silk and Honiton lace. Harriet decided to answer her. 'Yes. Yes, I do.'

'Shall we talk about what Mr Fennybright says over dinner? Or have you other things you'd like to discuss?'

'Abby says you come from Jamaica. I'd like to hear about that.'

'Why, there's nothing I like better than to talk about Jamaica. But what am I thinking of? Shouldn't your father introduce us first?'

John gave Caroline a straight look, as if to say that he knew what she was up to, but said simply, 'Mrs Duval, as I am sure you've guessed, this is my daughter, Harriet. Harriet, Mrs Duval is on her way to High Hutton, but I decided it was too dangerous to go over there tonight, so she is staying here.'

'It is! The Alne has flooded the road as much as three feet deep in places. You mustn't attempt it, ma'am! Besides, there's no one there.'

'What's that?' asked her father. 'What do you mean?'

The girl ignored him and addressed Caroline. 'The Ainderbys are in Kirkby Stephen. They'll be away for weeks.'

Caroline was stunned. All this way, nearly five thousand miles, weeks of travel, danger and discomfort...and after it all she was to be baulked at the last moment. Curiously, it had never once occurred to her that there might not be anyone at High Hutton to receive her.

'What are they doing in Kirkby Stephen?' John asked. 'Does anyone know when they plan to return?' Caroline listened apprehensively for the reply. When it came it was a shock.

'They are not expected back before the end of August, I believe,' said Mrs Abbington. 'They're visiting Mr and Mrs Paul Ainderby.'

'Paul is Martin's younger brother,' said John for Caroline's benefit. He said to Mrs Abbington, 'So Paul has moved to the other side of the Pennines? That's surprising. I thought the two brothers were fonder of each other than that.'

'Really?' Mrs Abbington sounded doubtful. 'From what I have heard, Lord Coverdale, they have been at odds for years. Mr Paul Ainderby went to the other side of the Pennines, they say, to get away from his family. This visit is an attempt at reconciliation. It will be the first time for many years that the two have met.'

Caroline was dismayed. 'But this means that I have to wait a month before I can see them!'

John turned to her. 'So it seems. It appears that we shall have the pleasure of your company for longer than we had thought!' He paused, then added lightly, but with a significance that was meant only for her, 'But you'll be safe enough here, Mrs Duval. Marrick has fended off many an attack in its time. Perhaps Harriet would tell you something of its history as a fortress? I know she has always been fascinated by the stories of the many who have found a safe haven here.'

'How would you know anything at all about me?' the girl demanded belligerently.

'Harriet!' exclaimed Mrs Abbington. 'What *has* come over you? Please use more respect when speaking to your father!'

'Because I listen to what Fenny tells me and I read the reports which Mrs Abbington sends,' said John patiently.

Harriet was diverted into a more natural manner. 'Fenny? You call him Fenny, too?'

'Ever since I was a boy,' said John, giving her a smile. But this was going too far. Harriet scowled, and turned to Caroline.

'I could show you round tomorrow, if you wish, Mrs Duval.'

Aware that John's real purpose had been to remind her that she herself would be safe here at Marrick, Caroline nevertheless pulled herself together, gave Harriet Ancroft one of her dazzling smiles and said, 'You're very kind, Lady Harriet. Thank you!'

Harriet blinked, then a wave of colour flooded her pale cheeks. 'May I lead you in to dinner, Mrs Duval?'

Caroline had plenty of opportunity to study Harriet Ancroft over the next week. The reports of her had not lied. She was a clever, accomplished girl, and when away from her father she had excellent manners. Her life had been more secluded than most, and she sometimes showed a certain awkwardness, a lack of grace, in company. But she was very bright, and really came to life as she took Caroline round the castle, recounting its history, dwelling with a child's relish on some of the more gruesome details, then switching to a young girl's delight in romance as she told stories of the love affairs that had unfolded within its walls. In return Caroline described life in Jamaica to her, and answered her many questions about the island. In the evenings the dinner table was lively with their talk. Once or twice Harriet actually forgot herself and addressed her father without prompting.

Caroline was even free of responsibility for the chalice for a while. John had persuaded her to leave her precious bag in the castle's strong room, a chamber without windows and heavily guarded from any possible intruder by thick doors and bars. The relief, though temporary, was enormous. It meant she could walk and ride with Harriet unencumbered by a constant reminder of the duty waiting to be performed. What was more, with the chalice in Marrick's strong room she was free for the first time in months of the fear of having it stolen from her by Edmund or one of his minions. Not that anything had been heard of her cousin since he had left the inn at Catterick Bridge, and she sincerely hoped he was still searching the inns further south.

She saw little of John. He was constantly in conference with his steward, his bailiffs, his farm managers, and, of course, the lawyers. Marrick was a huge undertaking and in urgent need of attention. So Caroline waited patiently for the Ainderbys' return, and meanwhile enjoyed the sunshine and cool breezes of the Yorkshire dales. And the company of Harriet.

She was without Joseph Bellerby. His arm was now almost as good as ever, but he had asked her to give him leave of absence.

'You're safe enough here, Miss Caro. For the moment you don't need me to look out for you. I've family living not far from here, and I've not seen them for nigh on forty year. I'd like to pay them a visit.'

Caroline eyed him in surprise. 'I didn't know you came from here, Joseph?'

'Aye, that I do. I came out to Jamaica to work for your grandfather when I was nobbut a lad.'

'How did you come by that?'

'An uncle o' mine had gone out with the master to Jamaica many years ago. When Uncle Ben got older, 'e sent for me to replace 'im. That's 'ow.'

'Why didn't you tell me this earlier?'

'It weren't my place to go chatterin' about your grandfather's business, Miss Caro! A very close man, the master. But now… Well, the master's dead, and I'm gettin' older myself. I'd like to see my brothers and sisters again before I die.'

'Well, you're not going to die for a good while yet,

Joseph dear, but I think you should see your family! Of course you can go! How long do you want?'

'I'm not sure. You can send me word when you want me. But I'll be back in time to go with you to High Hutton.'

If Joseph had been a local lad he might know more than he had told her. Caroline asked carefully, 'What do you know about High Hutton, Joseph?'

Joseph's face took on an obstinate look. 'Not much. But enough. It's best you wait and see, Miss Caro. That's what the master wanted.'

'But surely you could tell me!'

'It's best you wait, Miss Caro.'

Caroline sighed. 'Very well. I know I can't move you when you have that look on your face. Enjoy your holiday. And take care of that arm!'

He nodded and went. Afterwards Caroline asked Maggie if she had known that Joseph came from Yorkshire.

'He's never said, Miss Caro. He was already working for your grandfather when I came to look after you, and even when he was young he would never use two words when one would do. He and your grandfather were as tight-lipped as each other as far as their own business was concerned. But I thought once or twice he must be a Yorkshire man.'

'I shall be glad when this is all over, Maggie!' exclaimed Caroline crossly. 'I don't like so many mysteries.'

'I thought you were getting on rather well with his lordship?'

'Maggie,' warned Caroline. 'You needn't take that tone again. Lord Coverdale and I understand one another perfectly. We have no secrets now, and I even believe we are friends of a sort. He has certainly done more than anyone could have expected to help me. I can't imagine what we would have done if he hadn't invited us to stay here until the Ainderbys are back. But don't start looking for anything more than ordinary kindness in his actions. You know my views on marriage, and I think his are pretty similar.'

'He'll need an heir for this title of his…'

'Then he can look elsewhere for someone to marry! As far as I am concerned it is never again, Maggie. *Never* again!'

Maggie shrugged and started to take the pins out of her mistress's hair. 'It's a pity, that's all I can say. A great pity. What are you going to do when you're old?'

'I don't know!' Caroline looked at her defiantly for a moment, then she grinned and winked at her maid through the looking glass. 'I might find a handsome, poverty-stricken poet, forty years younger than I am, and pay him to keep my bed warm. What do you say?'

'Miss Caro! If I didn't know you better… You shouldn't say such things!'

'Then you shouldn't try to frighten me with questions like that, Maggie. How the devil should I know what I'll do?'

After a few days Mrs Abbington, who suffered from headaches in the heat, was content to leave Harriet and Caroline together on their afternoon walk. Caroline was sorry for the woman but glad of an opportunity to talk to Harriet alone. Some of the things the girl had said had made her wonder if the situation between her and her father was as hopeless or as simple as John believed.

They took one of the paths leading down from the castle towards the valley. When Caroline was doubtful about going so far, Harriet begged her not to spoil things.

'It's not really very far. I've often been down there by myself, and it's very pretty by the river. So cool and green.'

Since the day was still quite hot Caroline allowed herself to be persuaded and they set off down the path.

'It's a pity your father had to go to Richmond. It would do him good to relax with us occasionally,' said Caroline after a while. 'He works too hard. I noticed he was limping quite badly when he came back from Catterick last night.'

'Was he?' The girl's voice was noncommittal.

Caroline persisted. 'You know he was severely wounded, do you?'

'No, I didn't.' Harriet's reply came so quickly that her companion suspected it might not be true. The girl went on, 'Why should I care if he was wounded? Thousands of men were wounded at Waterloo. He wasn't the only one.'

So she knew where her father had been wounded! A poor liar, Harriet. But Caroline was careful not to say so. Instead she nodded. 'I suppose you're right. At least he wasn't killed. But doesn't it worry you to see him working so hard now?'

'Why shouldn't he work hard? Marrick is what he always wanted. And now he has it.'

'*Did* he always want it?'

'Of course he did! He killed his best friend, his own cousin, for it.'

Caroline seized the opportunity that Harriet had given her. She decided it was worth the risk of being thought a busybody in order to get the girl to tell her what she knew. 'Good heavens!' she said. 'Did he? Who told you that?'

'My mother. My Uncle Coverdale. Philip was my father's cousin, Uncle Coverdale's son. His only child. And my father killed him!'

'I can hardly believe it! What happened?'

'I'm not quite sure. All I know is that Philip was killed when his curricle crashed.'

'I see. It was an accident, then?'

'Oh, no! I am sure my father meant it to happen. Uncle Coverdale said so.'

'But how could he do that? Was your father in the curricle with Lord Philip?'

Harriet looked at her mutinously. 'I don't know. I don't suppose he was, or he would have been killed as well. Besides, Gabriella Ainderby was with Philip, so there wouldn't have been room. But Uncle Coverdale would never talk about it. He said it was enough for me to know that my father killed his son so that he could inherit the title, and that I must never, ever forgive him. My mother said the same. And I won't.' She paused, then said, 'I'm not sure why you are so curious about it, Mrs Duval.'

'Because I like and respect your father! And I'm curious to know why a bright, intelligent girl, such as yourself, has never tried to find out enough to form an opinion of her own! From what I've heard, you seem to have accepted what your uncle said without once giving it any real thought.' Caroline paused a moment, then went on carefully, 'That was perfectly understandable when you were a child. But you're not a child any more, my dear, and your father is now back in Marrick. It seems to me that he would like to get to know you better, but you put him off. Why? Because of this accident. Haven't you ever asked anyone else what happened?'

'The servants weren't allowed to talk about it. Besides, I don't need anyone else's version,' said Harriet mulishly.

'It's enough that my Uncle Coverdale said that he was to blame. My father, I mean. I hate him!'

Caroline looked shocked. 'But he *is* your father! And I've found him to be an honourable man, not a villain. Have you ever seen his army record?'

Harriet turned her head away, 'Yes,' she said. 'I... I have. Mrs Abbington showed me what the newspaper said of him. He's very brave.'

'Then why are you so convinced of his guilt? I don't know any more than you exactly what happened. But I do know that your father has been deeply unhappy about it ever since.'

'He doesn't look it.'

'Your father, my dear Harriet, is not a man who wears his heart on his sleeve.'

Harriet scowled at her. 'He has no heart! Why has he kept away so long? Why didn't he come when my mother died? Why is he leaving it to Fenny to organise my come-out? Because he is not interested. He has no heart! No, Mrs Duval! You are quite wrong to defend him. Please let's talk of something else!'

There was little point in pushing it any further, thought Caroline. She had done what she could. But what the girl had just said confirmed some of her suspicions. Part at least of John's crime in his daughter's eyes was to have ignored her existence for so long. 'I'm sorry,' she said swiftly. 'I was wrong to ask. Come, do I hear the sound of water at last? I'm so hot I could throw myself in!'

They wandered along the bank under the shade of the trees, and soon Harriet was more of a child again, laughing at the antics of the river creatures, and building up an impressive collection of stones, bracken leaves and other objects she could use in her painting lessons.

* * *

They went down to the river again the next day. And the next. The weather was still very hot, and the cool shade of the trees overhanging the water was more than welcome. It was on that day that Harriet herself brought up the subject of her father.

'I've been thinking about what you said,' she said abruptly.

'What was that?'

'About my father. About what happened in that accident. So I asked Thomas Beckford. Are you shocked, Mrs Duval? Abby always told me that I shouldn't gossip with the servants, but how else could I find anything out?'

'This was in a good cause. Did Thomas tell you anything?'

'He didn't want to at first. I told you, the servants had been ordered not to talk about it. But I could tell he wanted to, really. He likes my father, and I had the impression that he didn't like what my uncle had told everyone about him. So I asked him about the accident.'

'Was he there at the time?'

'Yes. He said that just before it happened my father was very angry with Philip. The curricle was standing in the courtyard, and the two of them came down the steps quarrelling about the girl he was engaged to. The girl my father was engaged to, I mean. The one who looked so like you. Gabriella Ainderby.'

'Did Thomas say that, too? That Miss Ainderby looked like me?'

'Oh, yes. But I knew that already. All the servants talk about *that*. They think my father is in love with you.'

Caroline smiled and shook her head. 'They're completely mistaken. He kindly agreed to escort me to High Hutton. And that's all. I promised my grandfather I would deliver something there, and when that is done, I'll thank your father for his help, and return to London. A little later I'll go back home to Jamaica.'

'I wish you and he would—'

It was not surprising that Harriet might hope for a match between John and herself, thought Caroline. The girl liked her, and the idea of a mother as well as a father would appeal to someone who had had neither for so long. But it was out of the question for more reasons than one. She must put the idea right out of Harriet's mind.

'Don't. I'm sorry, Harriet, but that's impossible.'

'Why? I thought your husband was dead?'

'He is. But I'll never marry again, not even if your father asked me. Which he won't. You must forget the idea. Now, tell me about your conversation with Thomas Beckford.'

'Thomas said my father was nowhere near the curricle when it crashed. Philip had got into the curricle, and shouted something at him. My father shouted back that he was welcome to go to damnation—I know I shouldn't say things like that, Mrs Duval, but that's what Thomas said he said—that Philip was welcome to go to damnation in his own way if he wanted to, but he was to leave Gabriella alone. He forbade Philip to take her in the curricle with him. Miss Ainderby was on the steps behind him.'

'And Lord Philip was too hot-headed to listen?'

'Yes. He shouted that he would soon show my father, and told Miss Ainderby she was to get in if she wanted to come. And as soon as she did, he took off. But he drove too fast down the drive and lost control on that first bend.'

'You see? It doesn't sound to me as if your father had anything to do with it at all!'

'But Uncle Coverdale said he did! Was he telling lies?'

Caroline paused and thought. It was important to get this right. She stopped and took the girl's hands in hers. 'Harriet, in my opinion Lord Coverdale didn't think he was. He had convinced himself that what he said was the truth.'

'How can that be?'

'I think it must be something like this. When people we love die, especially if they die when they're young, we have to find someone or something to blame. Your uncle was mad with grief for his son. He told himself, I believe wrongly, that your father had wanted Philip's death, and from there on it was a short step to believing that he had actually contrived it.'

'But my mother believed it, too!'

It wouldn't help Harriet to learn that her mother had been in love with another man, and equally distraught at his death. Caroline shook her head. 'I can't help you there. I don't know enough about your mother. But I *have* come to know John Ancroft. I can't believe him guilty. Remember, he too lost someone he loved in that accident.'

Harriet walked away and sat down on a log at the edge of the river. 'I don't know!' she cried. 'I don't know *what* to believe!'

'Why don't you ask your father?'

'I couldn't!'

'Yes, you could! My dear girl, you must! You must give him a chance!'

Harriet was silent. But she seemed to be thinking, and Caroline was content to leave it there. It was getting late, and Mrs Abbington would be looking for them. They retraced their steps along the river and up the path to the castle.

* * *

That evening before dinner she saw Harriet, rather pale but very determined, go up to her father and say something to him in a low voice. He looked surprised, but nodded immediately. And after dinner, instead of staying in the dining room with a glass of port as usual, he followed his daughter out of the room. They went into the library together and shut the door.

Caroline sat with Mrs Abbington for a short while, then decided that the tension was too much. She got up and said, 'Would you like a stroll in the garden, Mrs Abbington? It's a beautiful evening.'

To her relief Mrs Abbington shook her head. 'I have never trusted the night air, Mrs Duval. If you'll excuse me, I think I shall soon go upstairs. I still have that wretched headache. Can I ask your maid or one of the other servants to accompany you?'

'That's really not necessary. I'm sure I shall be quite safe, and I don't at all mind being alone. Goodnight. I hope your head is better tomorrow.'

Draping her stole more firmly round her shoulders Caroline went through the long doors that led out on to the terrace. She paused for a moment breathing in the scented air, and gazing at the dying light of the sun behind those purple hills. Then she descended the steps that led into the garden at the side of the castle. Harriet had told her how an earlier Ancroft had created this garden for his new bride, who had come from the south of England and missed the softer climate of her home. It was surrounded by a wall, and in its shelter grew numerous fruit trees, herbs and flowering shrubs, chosen to please her. Now, a hundred years later, their perfume still filled the evening air.

Caroline wandered along its paths till she came to an ornamental bench in a corner. Here she sat down and thought. It looked as if the long-standing animosity Harriet had felt for her father was about to end. She was a newcomer, a stranger, but she had become close to both father and daughter in these past days. She was happy for them. It was what she had hoped for, and father and daughter would both benefit from a new beginning. They each needed someone close to them.

So why this feeling of sadness? Self-pity? She hoped not! That was not something she allowed herself. During those far-off nightmare months in New Orleans she had sworn never to feel sorry for herself, never to weaken. Faced with Laurent Duval's duplicity and his unbelievable cruelty, she could easily have gone under if she had not held on to her inner determination to survive. It had been a close thing. She had the feeling that his death had released her just in time. Bruised in body and battered in spirit, but free at last of his viciousness, she had sought out her grandfather again, and he had taken her back with no questions and no reproaches. She had looked into the abyss in New Orleans, but had not succumbed. Her grandfather's love and confidence had restored her.

Since that time, whatever the scandalmongers may have hinted, whatever food she gave them for gossip, there had never been any substance in the rumours they had so gleefully spread. Since Laurent Duval's death no man had held her, touched her, as intimately as John Ancroft had held and touched her in the inn at Buckden. She had often aroused desire in the men around her, but before that night in Buckden she had never felt any desire herself. She had thought herself no longer capable of it.

In Jamaica she had led an independent life and, despite what the world thought, a decent one, deriving amusement from the antics of the people round her, and depending on no one but her grandfather for support. She had loved no one but him, and since his death Maggie and Joseph had had her affection, but no one had had her heart.

Was this her future? With only Maggie and Joseph to comfort her?

And if Joseph decided to stay in Yorkshire…

She sat contemplating this. She would have to encourage him to stay, if that was what he wanted. He was getting old, and she doubted now that that arm of his would ever truly heal. She would have to let him leave her… A tear slid down her cheek. And another. Confound it! This would not do! She jumped up impatiently.

'Don't go!'

She whirled round, startled. John was coming towards her. He must not catch her with tears on her face! Thankful that the fading light would hide any trace of them, she said as normally as she could, 'I thought you were with Harriet!'

'I was. We've had a…surprising conversation. And a very illuminating one. I actually believe that she no longer regards me as a monster.'

'That's very good news.' He was coming nearer and she turned slightly away.

'I think I might have you to thank for that, Caroline.' His voice was in her ear, he was very close. Too close…

'Nonsense!' she said huskily. 'It was only a question of time.'

He turned her round and looked at her narrowly. 'Good God! You've been crying!' he exclaimed. 'Why?'

'What nonsense! Of course I haven't,' she said angrily, pulling herself free. 'Something was in my eye. It's out now. Tell me about Harriet.'

'There's still some way to go, but she is at least questioning what my uncle told her.'

'May I ask something?'

'Go ahead.'

'I don't understand why your wife believed it too. Surely she knew it wasn't so. Didn't she owe you her loyalty?'

'Rose? She was never very strong. And in the end she was deeply unhappy, and seriously ill. She died when Harriet was eight.'

'But surely if she loved you—'

'She never loved me! Philip was her life. Oh, you needn't look like that, Caroline! I knew she was still in love with Philip when I married her. I was trying to make some sort of reparation, to give…to give Philip's child a name.'

'Harriet?'

He nodded. 'The child doesn't know, of course. As far as she and the world are concerned, she is my daughter.'

'What about you? How do you regard Harriet?'

'You know, it's strange. In spite of her antipathy I've always thought of her as mine, regretted the fact that she appeared not to love me. When I first married Rose I hoped that we would eventually be able to live together in amity, to create a home for the child. But I couldn't have been more wrong.'

'I see.' She stole a glance at him. He was staring into the distance, a frown on his face. Then he shrugged and turned back to her.

'Why did you do it?' he asked.

'Do what?'

'Persuade Harriet to talk to me.'

'Because she needs you!' At his look of doubt she said more firmly, 'She does, John! I've been talking to Mrs Abbington. Harriet was careful to keep it from Lord Coverdale, but in the past few years she's collected everything she can find about you and your career. She has a secret cache in her bedroom. At least some of her resentment arises from what she sees as your indifference to her. You must believe me. I feel for her. She needs you.'

'You *feel* for her? So the Widow Duval has a heart, after all?'

'Oh, no! Don't try to give me virtues I don't possess.'

John took her chin in his hand, 'I wasn't talking of virtues,' he said softly. 'Only of hearts.' He kissed her gently on the lips. Then smiled and kissed her again.

Caroline was surprised by the sudden rush of feeling that leapt into life as his lips touched hers. It had happened again, she thought hazily. The same witchery was at work, the magic that had brought her almost in a trance to his arms in Buckden. But there was a difference. John Ancroft had believed then that Gabriella Ainderby was in his arms. Tonight he was kissing Caroline Duval, and fully aware of it. For one moment the knowledge was like heady wine. Had she really thought she was no longer capable of desire? Then what was this, this heat in her blood, the feeling of weakness along her limbs? What would he do if she responded as ardently now as she had that night in Buckden? Would he kiss her as deeply, as intimately as he had that night? The temptation was almost too strong...

'Thank you,' he said gently, in a totally matter-of-fact tone, 'for your concern for Harriet. Now tell me why you were crying.'

It was like a shower of cold water. She came back to earth and removed herself carefully from his arms, telling her pounding heart to be still. 'I've told you,' she said defiantly. 'I wasn't crying!' He held her eyes, and after a moment she turned away and gazed at the garden. What the devil had she been crying about? She gathered her wits together and said, 'I think I'm going to lose Joseph Bellerby. He's gone to visit some members of his family near here, and I'm afraid he'll want to stay with them forever. He's getting old, and it's understandable that he might want to die in the place he was born, surrounded by his own family. But if he does...' She swallowed. 'I mustn't stand in his way, but I'll feel lost without him. I've known him all my life. He's the last link with my grandfather.' The tears were too close again. She shook her head angrily.

John took her hand and said firmly, 'My dear Caroline, don't meet trouble halfway. The Bellerbys are a quarrelsome lot. They're always falling out among themselves. After a week or so spent in the bosom of that family, your Joseph will almost certainly be glad to get away from them. But if he isn't... We must think of something else.'

What did he mean by that? What could he mean? Had there been something in his tone...? Confound it, thought Caroline, she was in danger of getting altogether too serious! It was time to pull herself together. With a brilliant smile she turned again and replied, 'Why, thank you, Lord Coverdale! Are you by any chance thinking of offering yourself in Joseph's place? Because if you are, I ought to warn you that I am a very hard...mistress...' She chuckled at his shocked expression and with a graceful wave of the hand went into the house, leaving John Ancroft staring.

Chapter Eight

John watched her go. She really was like no woman he had ever known! One minute weeping over the loss of a valued servant, the next making remarks meant to outrage him and laughing at him when she had succeeded! His lips twitched. She was very witty—a mistress of the double meaning. Yes, exactly! Mistress. There was that word again, raising all sorts of speculations in a simple soldier's mind! How many men had known Caroline Duval as their mistress? Ten? Twenty? Or none at all? It was impossible to guess. Her behaviour at Buckden had suggested that she was experienced—though not promiscuous. When it came to the final barrier she *had* drawn back. On the other hand, she had been remarkably self-possessed at the waterfall, had made no desperate attempt to hide herself, shown no maidenly panic. It was almost as if she was used to being looked at in a state of nudity. She had, of course, been married—apparently very unhappily. But who had been at fault in that?

He stood there for some minutes, his thoughts in a tangle. Harriet must be his chief concern. He would be very happy if he and Harriet could indeed make a life together. But what about a wife? A mother for the girl?

It might be better than a paid companion, especially if Harriet liked her—as she liked and trusted Caroline. That lady's behaviour in the past may not have been above reproach, but it was evident that she had the girl's interests at heart. And as a wife she would certainly be interesting!

John stopped short. What was he thinking of? Putting a woman like Caroline Duval in the place that was to have been Gabriella's? She might look like Gabriella, but how could he regard her as any kind of replacement for his lost love, the girl who, to him, was still the embodiment of everything a man could want in a wife—beauty, innocence, virtue, constancy… It was impossible! He could not do it!

But Caroline Duval, said the little voice inside him, has her own virtues. Not conventional ones, perhaps, but worth taking into account. Courage, humour, pride, compassion… All of these. And, whatever she might say to the contrary, she had a heart. If a man could capture her heart… He was lost in thought for some time. But then he shook his head. Time to sort out his thoughts and speculations when her business at High Hutton was resolved. Then would come the reckoning.

The next morning, Harriet pressed him to stay at home and accompany them on their walks.

With real regret John said, 'I'm sorry, my dear. I simply have to go to Richmond again this morning. If I could, I would very much like to spend the whole day with you, but I can't postpone my business there. What do you plan to do this afternoon?'

'If Mrs Duval agrees we shall go down to the river again. I need some different bracken for my watercolour.

The fronds I gathered yesterday are all exactly the same shade, and I want some variation.'

'How would it be if I joined you there this afternoon? I think I could get back early enough.'

The contrast between Harriet's enthusiastic response and her previous attitude towards him could not have been greater. Deeply pleased, he went off to Richmond, leaving her debating with Caroline what they should do that morning, while Mrs Abbington listened and looked on with approval. There was no doubt that Caroline had made friends there!

But others who were not at all friendly were also interested in Caroline's activities. Though neither Caroline nor Harriet had been aware of it, they had been under observation for the past two days by two ruffianly men, unscrupulous cutthroats. Dan and Billy Parker were always available for hire to any man who paid them well enough—and Edmund had promised them a great deal if they found and captured Caroline Duval. After a wide-ranging search they had tracked her down to Marrick, and were now ready to strike. For the past three days she had come along the river path every afternoon in the company of a young girl, and with no other protection. The two would almost certainly come today, too. From a suitable vantage point from which they could see without being seen, they noted John's departure along the road to Richmond. Then they sat down to wait patiently for their quarry… A large sum of money was practically in the Parkers' pockets!

Harriet and Caroline came down from the castle as planned, their pale muslin dresses easily seen as they walked through the trees, conversing animatedly all the way. The girl was a different person altogether, the scowls and sulks a thing of the past. She talked excitedly of her father, of what he had said the night before and the plans they might make for the future. A London season figured largely in her conversation.

The two were so absorbed that they did not at first register the unkempt, villainous-looking men blocking the path in front of them, one with a cudgel, the other with a wicked-looking knife. But it was soon clear that the men were looking specifically for them.

'That's the one,' said the man with the cudgel. 'The tall one with red hair. That's the Duval woman.'

'Harriet!' shouted Caroline. '*Run!* Quickly! Run back to the castle!'

'No, you don't!' said the first man before Harriet could even turn. 'We need you, too, sweetheart! You get her, Billy! I'll take this one.'

He made a lunge at Caroline and grabbed her round the waist. Billy caught Harriet with no trouble at all. The poor girl was too scared to put up any kind of resistance. Nothing like this had ever happened to her before, and she was paralysed with fright. Unfortunately, Billy enjoyed such a situation and liked inflicting pain. Though it would have been simple for him to drag the girl along the path, he took a handful of her hair and used that to pull her along, cruelly tugging and twisting it as he went. Harriet screamed with pain, tears running down her cheeks. Caroline was distraught. She yelled curses at them both and struggled frantically to get free, desperate to help Harriet. But Dan was too strong for her, though, unlike poor Harriet, she did not give in without a fight. Kicking, biting, screaming, she fought every inch of the way, and Dan had bruises on his shins and more than one scratch on his face before he was finished.

The riverbank was deserted, and the men were obviously well prepared. They knew exactly where they were going, and in a short while, too short for any hope of rescue, they arrived at a ramshackle stone building, in a small clearing just off the river bank. It looked empty. Here Caroline and Harriet were bundled unceremoniously down into a dark cellar and the door was shut and barred behind them.

Dan uttered a sigh of relief and wiped his face with his sleeve. 'You'd better make yourselves comfortable!' he shouted through the cellar door. 'You'll stay there till we've found our client. You've got a fine turn of language there, missus. Try it on the rats!'

'Bye, bye, *sweetheart*!' yelled Billy. 'I'll do yer hair for you again, when I see you next!'

Their raucous laughter at his joke died gradually away as they left and there was silence outside. They were left to the smells and airless darkness of the cellar.

'Harriet?' said Caroline apprehensively into the darkness. 'Harriet, are you all right?'

'I...I think so. It was very painful for a while, but I'm not really hurt,' the girl replied.

A hand touched Caroline's arm. With enormous relief she took firm hold of it and drew the girl to her. 'Splendid,' she said. 'That's one thing we don't have to worry about, at least.'

A giggle broke out near her. 'It's not much.'

'It's a beginning,' said Caroline firmly.

The giggle changed into something dangerously like a sob. 'What do those men want? Why were they so cruel? Are we going to die, Mrs Duval?'

'Of course not! They just want to keep us here until they can fetch my cousin Edmund.'

'But why? And who is your cousin Edmund?'

'It's a long story. I'll tell you when we're back in the castle. Don't waste your energy asking about it at the moment, Harriet, we have to find a way out.' Sensing the girl was near hysteria, Caroline kept her voice as calm and businesslike as possible. 'Now, is it my imagination or is there a glimmer of light over there? I think it might be a window or some kind of outlet. Let's go to see. Keep tight hold of me and try to follow where I tread. Right? Thank goodness we have our walking boots on! Silk slippers would be no use at all!'

They made their way slowly, gingerly to the source of light. Harriet went rigid and clutched Caroline's hand even more desperately, as various scratches and scutterings told them they were disturbing the cellar's usual occupants. But they pressed on and at last reached a small, very dirty, window. It was covered with cobwebs inside and weeds outside, but it was a window all the same.

'There! What did I say? Perhaps it's a way out for us, Harriet! There are some bars, but one of us might get through them… Let me see…' She took off her fichu and wiped one of the panes of glass.

Disappointingly, the bars were set too close together to allow either of them to pass through. Harriet gave another little sob.

'Oh, no, Harriet. This isn't the moment to lose heart! We're not finished yet! We can't travel but our voices can. Now I'm letting go of your hand, but don't you let go of me! Hold on to my skirt.' Caroline bent over and fumbled in the dark, swearing colourfully as she tried to unlace her sturdy boot. Then she stood up, wrapped the fichu round her hand and said, 'Turn your face away, Harriet, and keep as far back as you can!' Then swinging her boot, she dealt the window a hefty blow with its heel.

One pane broke and a welcome stream of air came into the musty gloom.

'So far, so good! At least we now have some air. Now for another!'

'How many panes are there?'

'Four, but I don't have to break them all, Harriet. We only need one each.'

'What for? Oh! To shout, you mean?'

'The sound should carry quite a way in this valley. With luck it may even echo. How good are you at shouting?'

'I can try.'

'Brave girl! Don't bother with "Help!"—"Yahoo!" or "Holla!" will carry further. Which would you prefer?'

'I like "Holla!" better.'

'Then come nearer the window and stand by me. That's right. Now, are you ready? When I say "three". One, two, three!'

They yelled with all their might through those two small windowpanes, then waited. All they could hear was a mocking echo sent back by the opposite side of the valley. *'Holla...a...a...a...a.'* When that died away there was silence.

She could feel the girl beside her shivering and said encouragingly, 'We'll try again in a moment. Swallow, to ease your throat first. It's so dusty here, and you need all the volume you can muster.'

'Oh, Mrs Duval...' Harriet's voice wavered.

'Swallow, Harriet! Don't give up! I expect your father will soon be on his way. He said he would try to meet us, you remember. He'll come to our rescue, don't you worry! He'll be so proud when he hears how well you held up. Ready again?'

They yelled again. But again there was no response.

'We'll have a little rest, then we'll have another shout. Are you cold?'

'A b…b…it. It's so d…d…amp in this cellar.'

'Then come here and let me put my arms right round you to keep you warm.'

A small voice said, 'Mrs Duval, you're so brave! How do you know what to do? Did you learn it in Jamaica?'

Caroline's rich chuckle sounded in the gloom. 'Not exactly. It's not regarded as part of a conventional upbringing even out there in the colonies!' She thought, then decided to distract Harriet by telling her about herself. The girl must be wondering what Dan and Billy had in store for them. She said softly, 'I don't tell everyone this, Harriet dear, so once we get out you'll keep it to yourself, I know. When I was only about a year older than you are now I ran away from home. I thought I loved someone enough to leave my grandfather, and all my friends. And I thought he loved me. I was wrong. It was the biggest mistake anyone could have made. Seventeen, with no money, and no one to protect me, I found myself in some very rough company. I had to fight to survive. On the way I learned some…unusual tricks. But I came through. And *we* shall too, I promise you.'

'I would never have guessed… Does my father know?'

'No. You're the only one in England I've told. So not a word. Now. Shall we try again?'

They yelled again. And this time they were rewarded. As well as the echo they heard the sound of a horse coming towards them.

Refusing to believe that it might be Edmund and his accomplices coming back to deal with them, Caroline called yet again.

A man's voice said urgently, 'Call once more, I can't see you! Where are you?'

It was John. For a moment Caroline was weak with relief, then she pulled herself together and shouted, 'Down below you. We're in the cellar!'

The grass was torn away from the window, and more light came in. 'Caroline! What the devil are you doing there?'

'Mind the broken glass! Don't ask questions, just come inside the house and unbolt the door to this place. Hurry! They'll be back soon.'

As John came round and they heard the sound of bars and bolts being drawn Caroline muttered furiously, 'What are we doing here, indeed! What does he think we are doing? Hunting rats?'

The door was opened and John came down the steps. He stopped in shock. 'Harriet is here too!' he exclaimed. 'What the devil is going on?'

Harriet stumbled and would have fallen, but John rushed to catch her. She burst into tears and he hugged her tight. 'Harriet, my dear girl…!'

'Don't waste time! We must go!' cried Caroline. 'Those men will be back with Edmund any minute now!'

'Too late, lady!' said a voice at the top of the cellar steps. Dan came down slowly, his cudgel in the air.

Caroline was amazed at the speed with which John responded. He thrust Harriet towards her, leapt up on to the steps and, ducking and twisting, dragged Dan down off them. The two men grappled with each other, and the cudgel dropped to the ground. Harriet screamed. Caroline, watching anxiously, drew her back into the shelter of the flight of steps and hissed, 'Be still! Your father knows what he's doing. He's a bonny fighter! But you mustn't distract him.'

A vicious fight ensued, but John slowly gained the upper hand. It was difficult in the half-dark to see exactly what was going on, but in the end the two men were on the ground, John's fingers round the other's throat, squeezing the breath out of him. Dan's struggles were growing weaker…

Another figure appeared in the door at the top. With a shout of surprised anger Billy rushed down, his knife ready. Harriet screamed again and John looked up. He was just in time to see Caroline, green eyes intent in the semi-darkness, waiting for Billy to reach the bottom step. Then she pounced on him from behind, throwing her fichu over his face and pulling his head back with it. Before he could turn, she had twisted his arm up his back. Billy gave a howl of agony and dropped the knife. Caroline laughed.

'Now who's hurting?' she growled. 'No! Don't try to move your arm, Billy, *sweetheart*! Nor anything else. I know what I'm doing, I've been taught by a master, and I'd *hate* you to break something. And that's what'll happen if you even *breathe* too hard.'

'Let go of me! Let go! Dan! Dan, you've got to help me! She's hurting me! She's going to break me arm!'

Caroline gave a laugh. 'I might, too. I have to do something, Billy *sweetheart*. And unlike my poor friend, *your* hair isn't long enough to get hold of. But confess now. Isn't this much more *fun*?' She gave a small tug and Billy howled again.

John had finished with Dan. The big man lay unconscious on the floor. He came over and picked up the knife. 'You can let him go,' he said.

Caroline stood back and John took over. He propelled Billy, who staggered whimpering over to his brother. 'You needn't worry,' he said drily. 'I haven't killed him. He'll come round in a minute or two.'

The stuffing had gone out of Billy. He sank down in a

heap beside his brother, holding his arm and rocking himself, still moaning, not taking the slightest notice as John helped his two ladies up the stairs.

John shut the cellar door behind them and made it secure. He carried Harriet outside and put her on to his horse. 'Hold on tight!' he said. 'It's quite a walk. We'll have to take the long way round up the drive.' He looked somewhat oddly at Caroline. 'My congratulations,' he said drily. 'But did you have to be so hard on the poor fellow?'

'You weren't there when he hurt your daughter!' she said briefly. 'I was. I ought to have been a lot harder!'

They made an interesting sight as they came painfully through the archway. Harriet was exerting herself to sit upright, but her hair was in wild disorder, and her white muslin dress black with dust. John, walking beside her and watching her carefully, had grazed knuckles, a streak of blood down his cheek and a tear in his jacket. Caroline was almost unrecognisable. Her hair was in as bad a state as Harriet's, and looked much worse. Its chestnut masses rioted down her back and over half her face, but failed to hide that she had an incipient black eye, and that her dress was torn and even dirtier than Harriet's. A filthy fichu was draped over her shoulders in an attempt to hide the worst of the damage. After a moment's shocked silence everyone in the courtyard rushed to the rescue. The three of them were taken to their bedrooms. Scullions were ordered to fill kettles and set them on the fire, and a train of footmen was soon hurrying upstairs carrying steaming cans of hot water, together with a variety of restorative drinks.

After an hour of Maggie's shocked ministrations, Caroline, clean, dry and once again her elegant self in a green muslin dress, received a message from John requesting her presence in the library as soon as she was ready. When she went down she found that John and Harriet were already sitting at the table, but there was no sign of Mrs Abbington.

'I sent some of my men out to release your attackers and take them to Richmond,' John began. 'But when they got there the cellar was empty. They're now searching the area.'

'Edmund must have arrived before them,' said Caroline.

'You're assuming that your cousin is involved and I think you're right, Caroline. But there's so far no evidence to connect him with it. Until we know more, I suggest that we say as little as possible. I've merely told anyone who asked that you were attacked on the river path. Harriet assures me she hasn't talked to any of the servants, nor mentioned your cousin to Mrs Abbington or given any reason for the attack. They are all under the impression that you were set upon by itinerant thieves. Have you said anything?'

'Only to Maggie. And she is discreet.'

'Good. Then we'll keep any speculation to ourselves.' His face altered and his voice was harsh as he continued, 'Harriet has told me what happened before I came on the scene.' He stopped, took a breath, then went on, 'I would very much like to get my hands on that pair again. Especially the smaller one. Billy. He deserved everything you did to him.'

'And more,' said Caroline. 'I can now confess to Harriet that I was not at all sure what would happen when they came back.'

'Quite. Thank God I came along when I did.' He

paused and said more calmly, 'But I was surprised you were so unprotected. I had assumed that you were always accompanied on these walks of yours.'

'Joseph Bellerby would normally have been with me. He's away at the moment, as you know. I can't tell you, John, how much I regret putting Harriet into danger. If I had known—'

'Harriet herself knows she was wrong not to have a groom or one of the other servants with her. She won't let it happen again.'

Caroline sighed. His tone was sternly uncompromising. Harriet and her father had evidently had words before she had arrived. She hoped this episode was not about to spoil the budding relationship between father and daughter.

But Harriet said, 'I won't, Papa. I promise. It was too frightening. But it was exciting, too! Mrs Duval was very clever.'

'Clever enough to get you both half-killed!' growled John Ancroft.

'But she saved you! When that second man came down the stairs I thought he was going to murder you, Papa!'

At first John regarded Caroline coolly. Then, reluctantly, he began to smile. 'I suppose I must thank you. There was certainly little I could have done to prevent him. Where on earth did you pick up a trick like that?'

'In a hard school, I assure you.'

John turned to his daughter. 'Er...Harriet, Mrs Duval possesses some remarkable skills—but they aren't the sort I would wish you to acquire, however strongly you admire her. They will hardly serve you in the kind of society I hope you'll encounter in London.'

'I've already told your daughter,' Caroline interrupted. 'I have a somewhat reprehensible past. I hope and pray she is never forced to rely on herself alone, as I was, to survive.'

John eyed her speculatively. 'I wonder if I shall *ever* know the real Mrs Duval,' he said. 'That widow's disguise was only the first layer, it appears.'

'Nonsense. I've told you. I'm now perfectly respectable.' Caroline turned to Harriet with a smile. 'For a beginner, you were remarkably good! But remember what I said in that cellar. I very soon bitterly regretted the day I left the protection of my home. You, Harriet, will never be so foolish. And now you must put it all behind you, and concentrate on other things. Your début, for instance. For that there are other, more pleasant, skills to learn. Can you waltz?'

Caroline's attempt to give Harriet something else to think about worked almost too well. The girl's face lit up and she said eagerly, 'Oh, could you teach me? Please do, *dear* Mrs Duval!'

Caroline laughed. 'I'd love to. But you'll have to be a quick learner! I shan't be here all that long. If your father wishes, I can show you the first steps before I go.'

'Then I could teach you the rest,' said John blandly.

When the two ladies looked at him in astonishment he burst into laughter. 'What made you both think I wouldn't know how to waltz? Do I appear to be so dull? My dear girls, no one would survive for long on Wellington's staff if they couldn't waltz! There's nothing his Grace loves better than a ball!'

'Then you must teach me, Papa! You and Mrs Duval together! And…and can't we have a party? We ought to celebrate that you've come back.'

'That's something to celebrate?'

Harriet flushed. 'I…I think so, Papa,' she said shyly. 'I think I've been wrong about you…'

'We've both made mistakes, child,' John said seriously, holding out his hand to her. 'Let's make a new beginning.'

Harriet came round and put her hands on his shoulders. She kissed his cheek. 'With a party? A ball?'

He laughed. 'Perhaps we shall. Why not? Marrick shall show what it can do! But first...' He grew serious again. 'We still have to sort out the question of Mrs Duval's delightful cousin.' He turned to Caroline. 'He must be stopped,' he said. 'But I think you'd rather avoid a scandal, wouldn't you?'

'Of course. Especially as it might involve you. But is it possible?'

'We'll have to see. If I can once get hold of him, I think I can frighten him into leaving you alone for good. Especially if he realises that his efforts have all been all in vain.'

'Can you convince him of that?'

'Believe me, I can, and will!' Harriet was still standing beside him. He put his arm round her waist and drew her closer. 'When Edmund Willoughby sent men to attack my daughter,' he said grimly, 'he started a fight I shall be only too glad to finish. You can forget about Edmund Willoughby, Caroline.'

'You sound quite bloodthirsty. Are you planning to dispose of him?'

'We'll see. Probably not. But I can see that he goes back to Jamaica too frightened to do anything more dangerous than look after his plantation, or whatever he does there. Would that do? Or would you like him sent to another island?'

'I think Jamaica will suit. Without the incentive of... of...'

'Of your grandfather's treasure?'

'Yes. Without that he'll leave me alone when I return.'

There was a short silence. Then John said slowly, 'To Jamaica? I hadn't realised… When do you plan to do that?'

'First I must go to High Hutton.'

'Yes, yes! But after that?'

'I shall probably travel a little. Perhaps do a season in London. But I'll go back to Jamaica eventually. My home is there.'

'Of course.' There was another pause. Then he said briskly, 'Of course! So, you're happy to leave everything to me?'

'Yes. This time I would! At the moment I have no desire whatsoever to see my cousin.'

Harriet had been looking on wide-eyed during this conversation. Her father turned to her and said, 'My dear, this must all seem gibberish to you. And I can't at the moment explain it.' He cast a glance at Caroline. 'I don't know the whole of it myself. But once it is over, with Mrs Duval's permission, I promise to tell you as much as I can. Will that do? Meanwhile what can I say to make sure you keep what you've heard so far to yourself?'

Caroline's heart lifted as she saw Harriet gave him a mischievous grin. 'That you'll promise to teach me the waltz, Papa?' she suggested.

John laughed. 'That's easy enough!'

'And that you'll give a party at Marrick.'

'That takes more effort…but, yes! Done!' he said.

The men sent to search found no sign of Dan and Billy. Nor was there at first any sign of Edmund. It was the next day before they found him. He was lying half in, half out of the river, ugly bruises on his cheek and covering his body, stripped of most of his clothing. He was carried up to the castle and put to bed.

The surgeon was sent for and after examining him carefully, he said, 'He's been subjected to a severe beating, as you can see.' He directed a look of enquiry at John.

'I suspect he was waylaid and robbed on the river path,' said John gravely. 'My daughter and a friend staying with us at the moment were attacked yesterday on the same stretch of river. We are at this very moment searching the surrounding countryside for the villains who did it. Will he live?'

'Oh, he'll live. I've given him a sedative. He's asleep, not unconscious. A couple of days of bed rest, and apart from some aches and pains he'll be fit enough. Unless there are complications, it won't even be necessary for me to come again. But it was lucky for him that your men found him in time. Another few hours and he might well have died. Who is he, do you know?'

'There was nothing on him to identify him,' said John carefully. 'But you needn't concern yourself with that. I'll see he's looked after and sent on his way when he's ready.'

The surgeon left and John was left gazing down at Edmund Willoughby. A weak face, he thought. And a mean-looking one. Eyes too close together and a small, petulant mouth... What should he do about him?

John put Betts in the bedchamber and told him to watch over his visitor, to look after his needs and to keep his own mouth shut. He was to be informed the moment the 'guest' seemed fit enough to talk. Except for a few moments when he took some water and a little soup, the invalid slept through the whole of the next day, but John was sent for the day after.

* * *

Edmund Willoughby was sitting up and looking a great deal better. 'It's about time! That damned servant wouldn't say a word! Who are you and where am I?'

'I'm Coverdale and you are in Marrick Castle.'

Willoughby regarded him sourly. 'Oh, yes, I remember now. Colonel Ancroft at Catterick Bridge. So you *are* one and the same. Clever that. You fooled me. How did I get here?'

'My servants were looking for the men you hired to attack Mrs Duval. They found you lying near the river bank and brought you in.'

A shifty look appeared in Willoughby's eyes. 'What men? I haven't hired any men to attack anyone. What do you mean?'

John said in a bored voice, 'Come, Willoughby! Some lies are possible to sustain, but not that one. You weren't set upon by gypsies! What happened? Did you refuse to pay your friends when you found out that Mrs Duval and my daughter had escaped? I'd say you were extremely unwise if you did.'

'They beat me!' said Willoughby sulkily. 'The damned scum beat me! How dared they! Of course I refused to pay them! They hadn't done anything!'

John sat down next to the bed. He spoke softly, but the menace in his voice caused Edmund to cringe back against the pillows.

'They had done a great deal, my dear fellow. They had frightened and distressed two vulnerable women, one of them still a child. They had treated them roughly, locked them in a cellar without air or light, and then left them to their fears. I suppose it's fortunate that I happened to come along to rescue them. If anything serious had happened to either of those ladies you, my friend, would have paid with your life! At least! As it is, someone will have to pay for what *did* take place, and I'm very much afraid you are the one.'

Willoughby grew even paler. 'You mustn't threaten me, I'm a sick man. It isn't fair!'

'I'm not *trying* to be fair, Willoughby. Those women were under my protection, one of them my own daughter. When you injured them you injured me, and I intend to have satisfaction.'

'You can't challenge a sick man!' Willoughby cried, sliding down in the bed. 'I'm a stranger in England, a foreigner. I refuse to fight you!'

John's lip curled. 'I don't intend to fight. Why should you think killing a worm like you would bring me any kind of satisfaction?'

'Well, what are you going to do?' Willoughby sat up and said eagerly, 'If you want money, I have some in London. A great deal. Let me go and I'll send it, I promise. I promise! I'm sorry for what I did. Really sorry. I didn't mean them to hurt Caroline, or your daughter. I didn't even know your daughter was with her! And you could say I've been punished already, couldn't you? Look at these bruises! If you let me go, I swear I'll go away and you'll never see me again.'

'Why should I believe a cur like you?'

'Because I'm telling you the truth! Nothing is worth what I've been through in the last year. I should never have chased her to England.'

'Why did you?'

'I wanted that chalice! I can't expect you to understand, Coverdale. No one who hasn't seen it could.' For a moment Edmund Willoughby seemed to have forgotten John's presence. There was a new note in his voice, a kind of awe. 'It was the chalice... I saw it once in Peter Leyburn's study. He always kept it locked in a special sort of cupboard, but one day he had it out when I came in. He was holding it in his hands and staring at it so intently that he didn't know I was there. The light… The colours… I have never seen anything like it before or since. It took hold of me. He was so furious that I had seen it that I think he might have killed me if he had dared. But I didn't care. I wanted it. I wanted it so badly that I offered him anything, begged him to give it to me, to leave it to me when he died. It became an obsession. But he always refused even to listen. Then when he died he left it to *her*!' He thumped the pillow angrily. 'I should have taken that chalice when she was still in Jamaica! It ought to have been easy, but somehow or other she always got away from me. That's why I followed her here.'

'It's now beyond your reach, Willoughby. Forget it. You'll never have it. Peter Leyburn didn't leave it to Caroline Duval, either. He sent it back to where it belongs.'

'Where is it now? Have you seen it?'

'That's something I'm not going to tell you. And, no, I haven't seen it. I didn't even know what it was until *you* told me. Caroline has always refused to talk of it.' He leaned forward and said earnestly, 'There is no chance that you will ever see it again, Willoughby. Put this madness out of your mind. You have more urgent concerns at the moment.'

Edmund seemed to grow smaller in the bed. 'What are you going to do with me?'

John looked at him for a moment. Then he said contemptuously, 'You're not worth a great deal of trouble. If I were to hand you over for the punishment you deserve, your cousin would suffer almost as much. I think I shall send you under suitable escort to be put on the next packet boat to leave Falmouth. But don't think you can take up where you left off in persecuting Mrs Duval. If I hear of any further harm to her, I shall make you pay. I assure you I can do it, Willoughby, even if you are as far away as Jamaica. Believe me.'

'Oh, I've learned my lesson. I'll be glad to go back. So Caroline is under your protection, is she? I didn't think you'd be fool enough to have married her, whatever you said at that inn. Well, make the most of it. She never stays long with the same man.'

John's lips tightened. 'Caroline Duval is under my protection as a guest! Nothing more! No! I don't wish to hear another word.' He got up. 'You'll leave tomorrow at first light, whether you feel fit or not. You've had my warning. I'd remember it if I were you, Willoughby.' He went to the door and called Betts in.

'Colonel?'

'Organise an escort to take this man to Falmouth as speedily as possible. He is to sail for Jamaica as soon as there is a packet, or any kind of boat, to take him. He is to be guarded until the ship sails. I'll provide you with the necessary funds tonight. Understood?'

Betts's training stood him in good stead. His 'Yes, sir! Right, sir!' gave no indication that the order was in any way extraordinary. Not even by a raised eyebrow. When the Colonel was in this kind of mood, a wise soldier did what he said without comment or delay.

Betts did well. Edmund Willoughby left Marrick the next morning in one of the castle's carriages. He was apparently being looked after by his valet, another manservant, a coachman and two grooms. On the journey down to Falmouth such an ostentatiously large entourage aroused frequent comment. What was the gentleman afraid of? He didn't appear to be particularly happy with his men.

But Edmund Willoughby still had a score to settle with Caroline. His last act before boarding the packet boat was to sit in the parlour in the King's Arms under the watchful eye of his escort, and write a letter. He sealed it, addressed it and gave it to Betts to take back to Yorkshire.

'I've written a letter to thank your master,' he said. 'See that he gets it.'

Chapter Nine

While Edmund was making his journey back to Falmouth and on to Jamaica, Marrick bustled with activity. After long years of silence and seclusion the castle hummed with excitement, as preparations got under way for the grand reception and ball at which John Ancroft, fourth Marquess of Coverdale, would renew his acquaintance with the neighbourhood. It would be an occasion, too, for Lady Harriet Ancroft, his daughter, to mix in society before her début in London the following year.

An army of servants was drafted in to prepare the castle for the ball, and Mrs Abbington was faced with a mountain of new, unforeseen duties.

'I am really not sure how I shall manage, Mrs Duval,' she confided to Caroline in a worried voice. 'Such a large number of guests wish to stay the night that I can't work out where to put them all. Many of the bedchambers have been shut up for years—they will all need to be aired, and cleaned and prepared. And as if that weren't enough, Lord Coverdale wishes to have a sit-down dinner for forty before the ball. He'll expect me to make sure refreshments are available throughout the evening, as well.'

'That really isn't difficult, Mrs Abbington,' said Caroline, in an attempt to encourage her. 'Thomas Beckford is a very good steward, and you have an excellent chef in the kitchens.'

Mrs Abbington was not to be comforted. 'But they aren't used to such large affairs! It's years since anything like this was done at Marrick, and they all need a lot of direction. There's a thousand things to do! How I am to plan it all I do not know. The main reception rooms have to be dusted and polished, chandeliers taken down and cleaned, curtains shaken, floors scrubbed, ornaments washed... Quantities of silver, china, linen to be looked out and checked...' Mrs Abbington came to a halt and held her hand to her forehead. 'And my head is aching so.'

Caroline looked at her with a great deal of sympathy. Mrs Abbington was a quiet woman, excellently suited to acting as companion to a young girl, and running a household that never had visitors or any kind of entertainment. The previous regime under Lord Coverdale had suited her very well. But she was now faced with a different world, and it was clearly too much. It was no surprise at all to hear the day after this conversation that Mrs Abbington had taken to her bed with a violent, and permanent, headache.

The situation was potentially desperate, and Caroline felt obliged to offer to step into the breach. Till now she had done her best to stay in the background while these preparations were going on. She was not a member of the family, merely an unexpected guest who would leave as soon as the Ainderbys came home. But things were different now and, in the circumstances, what could she do but agree to take over? This was something she loved and was well used to doing. Her grandfather may have despised Kingston society, but his business and political interests made it imperative that he entertained frequently, and often lavishly. A dinner for fifty, a musical evening for a hundred, a ball for two hundred—she had managed them all with ease. She was not at all daunted at the prospect of opening up a large castle in Yorkshire. To tell the truth, she was stimulated by the new challenge!

At first the servants looked askance at this guest who seemed to have taken over the household so firmly. But the new Lord Coverdale made it clear that he supported Mrs Duval in her efforts, and Mrs Duval herself soon impressed them with her command of the situation. The lady clearly knew what was needed, and, what was more, she saw to it that everyone else did, too!

John watched and marvelled as the castle slowly emerged from its years of sadness and neglect, and the servants learned to move swiftly and efficiently about their work. 'Mrs Duval says' was heard all over the castle, whether it was the gardener watering plants with anxious care—'Mrs Duval wants plenty of greenery for the ballroom, my lord'—or the chef trying out new recipes—'Mrs Duval is hoping for a worthy centrepiece, my lord.' Furniture was ruthlessly redeployed or moved away altogether, and when he questioned the men, they said with all respect, 'But Mrs Duval wants the hall cleared for dancing, my lord! As well as the ballroom.' John lost no time in putting a ban on any interference with the furniture in his library! Who knew what 'Mrs Duval' would want next?

And Caroline Duval seemed to achieve it all without the slightest loss of her calm, slightly lazy-looking grace. She appeared to find plenty of time to coach Harriet, too. John watched her patiently teaching the girl how to approach the different ranks of the *ton*, a curtsy with the correct degree of formality for some, a polite bob for others, a hand extended to yet others. He listened as she went through the proper forms of address, and laughed with his daughter as Caroline acted out a crotchety duchess, or a plum-voiced bishop to make the lesson fun. Harriet had been well educated by Mrs Abbington in the niceties of ordinary behaviour, but John was amazed to see that she was now being taught the manners of the cream of society. Taught by an expert, too. The most exclusive seminary for the young ladies of the *ton* could not have found fault with what Caroline Duval was teaching Harriet Ancroft! And in spite of her easy-going manner she was strict. Harriet was not permitted any lapses. Some of her own philosophy, it was true, sometimes surfaced, but nothing to take exception to. If Harriet stammered or apologised after she had been clumsy or forgetful, Caroline would say firmly, 'Never apologise, never make excuses. Hold that head of yours up, Harriet, and keep calm. The world will take you at your own valuation. Stay courteous, stay polite, but never, never cringe!' John looked and wondered. Once again, this woman had him puzzled. Loyal granddaughter, actress, impudent wanton, superb manager and chatelaine, and now a first-class mentor to his daughter… Where the devil was the *real* Caroline Duval?

Of course time was made, too, to teach Harriet all sorts of dances. A fiddler was brought up from the village, and John and Caroline between them demonstrated the steps needed for most of the country dances, and one or two others besides. The waltz was kept as a special treat, to reward Harriet when she did well with the others.

'It will do no harm for you to know the steps, Harriet. But from what I have heard, and I think your father will bear me out, you must not dance it in public until you have the approval of certain ladies of London society, the famous patronesses of Almack's. Is that not so, Lord Coverdale?'

'Quite right. There won't be any difficulty in obtaining their approval, however. Sally Jersey is an old friend of mine. But you must wait until you've got it.'

'I will, I will! But please show me how it goes! Dance with Mrs Duval, Papa! I can play the piano and watch at the same time. Go on!'

So John took Caroline by the hand, bowed and began to waltz with her. His touch was impersonal, the distance between them perfectly judged, close enough to guide, but a respectable distance apart. Nothing could have been more proper. Yet John was aware of every movement of her body, as they swayed gracefully round the room. For all her height she was as light as thistledown in his arms, matching his steps perfectly. He was sorry when they finally came back to the piano and a shining-eyed Harriet.

'That was wonderful!' she exclaimed, jumping up and clapping her hands. 'Now you must teach me!'

'You'll never have a better teacher,' said Caroline laughing. 'Your papa, Harriet, is the best partner I think I've ever danced with!' She turned to John. 'My congratulations! Wherever did you learn to waltz like that?'

'My dear lady, the two chief qualities necessary to be a success as an officer in Wellington's army were first to be able to march well, and second to be able to waltz even better!'

'There must have been one or two others,' she murmured. 'Ability to fight, perhaps? To command men? And…courage under fire?'

'Yes, but those were trivial matters compared with keeping the army on the move and the ladies happy, I assure you!'

'Shameful! You mustn't disillusion us, Colonel! We thought you all heroes.'

'He *was* a hero! I read about him. He was often a hero! They kept saying it. ''Bravery under fire.''' Harriet turned to her father. 'I was always afraid you would be killed, Papa. I know that's what Uncle Coverdale wanted, but I could never want that. I was always afraid for you.'

John stood looking down at her. He said finally, 'Strange. If I had known that, there might not have been so many commendations for bravery under fire.'

'What do you mean?'

'Never mind. Come, Harriet! If Mrs Duval will kindly oblige on the piano, we shall begin your lessons.'

After a while Harriet was sufficiently adept to start learning the turns. This needed another demonstration, and John and Caroline duly set off dipping and swaying down the room. To this point they had kept their steps simple for Harriet's benefit, coming back, not by changing direction with a turn, but by following round the curve of the room. But this time John pulled Caroline to him as he guided her into the turn. The contact was closer than he intended and gave them both a shock. He had to restrain a mad impulse to pull her closer yet, to hold her as he had held her in Buckden... For a moment the world was forgotten in a surge of desire. It gave him a certain amount of satisfaction to see that Caroline's eyes had widened and she was breathing rapidly. He wasn't alone, then, in this sudden and inconvenient onset of feeling... With an effort he pulled himself together, took up the correct distance once again and came down the room with her.

'That looked easy enough,' said Harriet.

'It was far from it,' muttered John. 'If you only knew, child!'

Caroline said hastily, 'It looks easy until you try, Harriet. Look, I'll show you where to put your feet.'

'Er…' said John. 'I must apologise. I've just remembered an appointment. I'll have to excuse myself for this afternoon.'

'Papa!' exclaimed Harriet in tones of deepest disappointment.

'It's all right, Harriet!' said Caroline swiftly. 'We can do the steps of the turn nearly as well without your papa. I can leave the piano—we don't really need music for it. We can count. Now, come over here.'

John looked back as he came to the door, and met Caroline's gaze. By Heaven, she was laughing at him again! The wicked look in her eyes told him that she knew perfectly well why he had no wish at the moment to demonstrate an intimately close turn—with his daughter!

They had taken to having a short stroll round the garden after dinner, using the tranquillity of evening to discuss the day's activities and plan for the next, and that evening John found himself waiting more impatiently than usual for the moment when Harriet would excuse herself and go up to visit Mrs Abbington and he and Caroline would be free to go outside. At last it came. They went out on to the terrace and started down the steps.

'The invitations have been sent out?' asked Caroline. This was one task which she had found impossible, and John had taken it over.

'The last of them went out today. I've had one delivered to the Ainderbys, though I'm not sure they'll be back in time to come. Still, they had to be invited. You may meet Martin Ainderby before you go to High Hutton. Will that disturb you?'

'I don't think so. I would still wait till we go over to High Hutton to talk to him. A ball wouldn't be the time or place to mention the...what I'm bringing.'

'You can call the thing by its right name, if you wish. Your cousin told me what it was.'

She grew pale and said fiercely, 'Did you ask him? He had no right to tell you if you did!'

'No, I did not ask him. It was obvious that you didn't wish the world to know, and I respected that wish. I'm surprised that you think I would!'

'I'm sorry. You're right. The world was not to know, not even someone like you. My grandfather was very insistent. He was furious when Edmund saw it. He made me promise to tell no one else. Only the Ainderbys were to know anything at all. I've kept my promise. Now I hear that Edmund has let it out the first time he meets you, and all my trouble has been wasted. What did he say? Have you...have you looked at it?'

This time John was really annoyed. 'Of course not!' he snapped.

'No, of course you wouldn't.' She gave him an apologetic smile. 'I just thought that if Edmund had talked much about it you might have been tempted. It's incredibly beautiful, you see. Mystically so. I can almost understand Edmund's obsession with it. Grandfather was the same.' She frowned as she said thoughtfully, 'You know, he was a strong man, my grandfather. I never saw him miserable or depressed. But when he talked of that... that...'

'Chalice?'

'Yes. The chalice. He was always disturbed. And every bit as fanatically determined as Edmund. It was to go to

High Hutton, those were almost his last words! Promising to bring it here was the only way I could make him easy in his mind. Oh John, I wish I knew what lies behind it all!'

'I can't help you,' he said taking her restless hands in his and holding them still. 'I was only twenty-one when I left Marrick, and before that time we'd had very little to do with the two Ainderby brothers, though they were much the same age as we were. My uncle had quarrelled with their father, and we never visited. I had a hard time persuading my uncle to allow my engagement to Gabriella.'

'How did you meet her, if you saw so little of her brothers?'

He shook his head. 'Gabriella wasn't their sister. She was their cousin.' He started to walk slowly down the path, still holding Caroline's hand.

'Tell me about her,' she said softly. 'Where *did* you meet her?'

The scents of the garden surrounded them in the warm air. The light was fading, and it seemed a time for confidences. For the first time in years John felt an urge to talk. 'I met her at a ball in Richmond when she was a couple of years older than Harriet is now. She was there with her mother. I thought her the loveliest thing I had ever seen, and fell in love there and then.' He smiled down at her. 'I had plenty of rivals for her favours. But in the end she took me.'

'How soon did you get engaged?'

'Two months later. We had to overcome considerable opposition. Gabriella's mother didn't like it any more than my uncle did.'

'Why not? You must have been a most eligible young man. Belonging to one of the most important families in this part of Yorkshire, handsome, well set up… What more could a mother want?'

'My fortune wasn't particularly handsome! My connections were good enough, I suppose, but at that time…' He paused. 'At that time I had no prospect of a title, and my own estates were not large. Mrs Ainderby was ambitious. She thought her daughter would be throwing herself away if she married me. But then she suddenly relented. Almost overnight. I never asked her why, I was only too happy that she had. We got engaged at the end of June and were to have been married in the last week of July. But by that time Gabriella was dead.'

They walked in silence for a while.

Then Caroline said hesitantly, 'What was she like, your Gabriella? She looked quite like me, I know. But what was she like as a person?'

He thought for a moment. 'She was still very young, of course. I've sometimes been reminded of her when I see Harriet now. All that openness, that shining innocence… She loved meeting people—company, dancing, concerts, going to balls. And wherever she went she was always surrounded by admirers.' He turned to Caroline. 'But I was always sure she was mine. And the night before we got engaged she told me she had always felt the same.'

He stopped and looked at her. 'I'm sorry! This can't be very interesting for you. I don't know what has come over me! I haven't talked of Gabriella for years. The last time was in Spain and I at least had the excuse of being wounded.'

'Who was your confidante that time? A lovely senora?'

'Far from it! An ordinary-looking Englishman, Adam Calthorpe. He was in the army with me. We were wounded together at Talavera, and we talked through the night to keep our minds off our aches and pains. Adam's a great fellow, I'd like you to meet him.'

Caroline laughed. 'That's most unlikely! Unless I come across him in London.'

'You might if you're still in England next year. He and his wife had a baby son last December, and missed this year's season. They'll almost certainly be in London next spring. In fact, I had considered asking Adam's wife, Kate, to help me with Harriet's début.' He paused. But he wanted to know. 'Will you be?'

She didn't understand him. 'Will I be what?'

'Be in London next spring?'

'I...I don't...I'm not quite sure,' she said, clearly disconcerted. 'I've no reason to hurry home. But I can't make any plans for the future until I've delivered the...the chalice.'

They had reached the farthest end of the garden. The sounds of the house hardly penetrated this far, and the countryside was still as the sun slowly sank, leaving the hills in shadow.

John took her hand again. 'Caroline, I want to thank you. For everything. For all the effort you're making to make this ball a success.'

'That's nothing! Really, John, I mean it. I enjoy the work.'

There was a brief silence, then he said awkwardly, 'You've done a lot for me personally, too. You've been generous about what happened in Buckden. You must have been curious, but until tonight you have never asked about...about Gabriella.'

'Was I wrong to do so now? Has it stirred up the unhappiness I saw that night?'

'No. I think it might even have done good. It's strange. I nearly didn't come back here at all, you know. If Fenny hadn't persuaded me that it was my duty I doubt I ever would have. I had decided I couldn't bear all the reminders. But somehow… That journey with you, meeting Harriet again, realising that I can be a father to her… And seeing Marrick and my people again… A lot of the unhappiness has disappeared. I can even talk of Gabriella with less difficulty. I suppose you think that after seventeen years it's time!'

'I can't answer that. We have to deal with what we can, when we can.' She hesitated, then went on, 'You, at least, didn't suffer the humiliation of learning that the person you had loved was completely worthless, as I did. But I got over it. And talking to my grandfather helped. It gave me confidence in myself, restored my pride again—along with a certain scorn for the way in which the rest of the world judges by appearance.'

'As I did with you?'

She looked at him for a moment. Then she said sombrely, 'I think you still do. But perhaps that's as well.'

It was most unlike her to sound unhappy. He drew her to him. For a short while they stayed like this, his only aim to give comfort. But then the intimacy of the dark, secluded garden, the heady scents of the flowers, the warmth of her body resting against his, slowly combined into an irresistible mixture. The urge to hold her yet more closely, to press her to him, kiss her was overpowering. He tightened his hold and she looked up, startled.

'John—' Any other words were lost as his mouth covered hers and an explosion of passion left them breathless. They clung to one another, locked together in a swaying embrace. The kiss went on and on, neither wanting to put an end to this swirling, intoxicating delight. This was what he had been waiting for! Caroline felt so right in his arms, he wanted to hold her like this forever. Her response excited him further, and he strained her to him. He was trembling when he finally raised his head. He held her face between his hands, searching in the dark to read the expression in her eyes. She looked desperate.

'I don't want this,' she whispered despairingly. 'It's too…it's too dangerous.'

He was surprised into a laugh. 'Don't be absurd. What do you mean? How can it possibly be dangerous?'

'You mustn't laugh. I mean it. I…I don't seem to be able to take you lightly, John. I can't treat you like the others. You get too close. Much too close.'

John was disarmed by her evident distress. He relaxed his hold, but still kept her in the circle of his arms. 'There's no need to be afraid. I don't want you to take me lightly.' There was a silence. Then he said slowly, 'Caroline, when your visit to Ainderby is over, would you consider staying on here for a while? Nothing would please Harriet more, I know, and I… I'd like time for us to get to know one another better. Harriet needs someone like you in her life…and I believe I do, too. You've said that you can't consider the future until you've taken the chalice to High Hutton, so I won't press you now. But afterwards when you're free…'

She pulled away. 'I…I don't know… I'd have to think. What you're talking of…it sounds as if it might become altogether too serious for me. Too close, too close.' She threw him a quick look. 'And yet…it's so tempting… I've so dreaded the thought of being alone.'

He wanted to take her in his arms again, but she held him off. 'No, don't! That doesn't help, it just obscures the issue. I mustn't let my senses rule my head! Once was enough.'

'Senses? Not heart?'

She shook her head ruefully. 'You keep looking for my heart. But I'm not sure I have one to lose. Not any more.'

He gave a slow nod. 'That's something that might be said about both of us, perhaps. But surely there are compensations? Interests in common, friendship, humour. And wouldn't you say that there's a certain...feeling between us?'

She pulled a face. 'I can't deny any of those—especially not the "certain feeling"! But I need more than that to convince me.'

'What?'

Caroline shook her head. 'Leave it, John! Give us both time to consider. Shall we go back to the house? It's getting cold.'

John had to acquiesce. Perhaps he was not altogether sorry. His invitation to Caroline to stay longer at Marrick had come almost as much of a surprise to him as it had to her. The magic of the night, of that kiss, might well have had a lot to do with it. But even when he thought about it in the cool light of day it kept its appeal. Caroline, it was true, would never be able to replace Gabriella, but she was a woman of beauty, intelligence and passion. His daughter was on the way to loving her and, from what he had seen, Caroline Duval would in her totally individual way be a good mother. Whatever her own standards of behaviour might have been in the past, she was strict enough with Harriet. Yes, he could do a lot worse than consider Caroline Duval as his future Marchioness...

He was annoyed therefore when Caroline announced on the day before the ball that she was proposing to remain in the background for the whole of the evening.

'What do you expect us to do?' he asked. 'Who will

give the servants the necessary orders, receive the guests, be in charge?'

'I've asked Mrs Abbington. She says she's well enough.'

'But, Caroline—'

'I don't think you've thought about this. Mrs Abbington has been Harriet's companion and managed the household for many years. She will be regarded as the proper person to act as your hostess tomorrow night. You needn't worry. She'll do it well. And I'll make sure that there are no crises.'

'But you've done all the work!'

'In the eyes of the county I'm merely an unexpected guest, waiting for the Ainderbys to return. Unless you want all kinds of unwelcome speculation about my position here, you'll pay me no particular attention, nor give me any undue importance. I mean it, John. I know what gossip can do, and the last thing I want is to spoil what ought to be a perfect evening for Harriet. Don't you agree?'

'You don't mind about spoiling my evening?'

'You'll be busy looking after Harriet, and making sure your guests are happy and well fed. You're a great man, now, John! And *noblesse oblige*, you know!' She laughed at his disgusted expression.

But her laughter was stilled when he said, 'I hear the Ainderbys will be back tomorrow, though I doubt they will be in time to come here for the ball. Shall I send a message asking if we may visit them the day after?'

'Yes,' she said, suddenly breathless. 'Yes, of course! So they're coming back at last... And my journey to Yorkshire will finally reach its end. It seems almost strange to think that it will soon all be over.'

'Your grandfather's part will be over. But not his

granddaughter's. I still hope to see her continue to play a part in Yorkshire, Caroline, though perhaps not at High Hutton.'

Caroline dressed early on the evening of the ball, then sent Maggie to see to Harriet. When Maggie had gone she sat down in an armchair by the window, put her head back against the cushion and gazed out on the hills. Tonight was a climax of a sort. She had done her best for a girl she had come to love, and now she could only be an onlooker. Harriet was bound to be a success, here and in London. Perhaps she should make sure she was in London for Harriet's début whatever happened up here in Yorkshire in the next few days. What *would* happen? She guessed that John Ancroft might well ask her to marry him, and wondered what she would say if he did.

There were, as he had said in the garden, sound reasons for considering it. Interests in common, friendship, humour...and a certain 'feeling' between them. He had meant a strong physical attraction, of course. And when he had asked what more she wanted to convince her she had been unable to tell him. Not out loud... How could she have said, 'I'm sure you won't hurt me physically as Laurent Duval did. But physical hurt was more bearable than what he did to the real me, Caroline. If I let myself trust you, let you near me, how can I be sure you won't hurt me as he did, betray my trust, my belief in you? To give anyone, but especially a man, such power over me fills me with horror... I would need very strong reasons to risk that a second time. I'm not sure the ones you gave me are enough.'

She had sworn never to marry again, and part of her still rejected the very idea. But John was not Laurent Duval. She believed she could trust him not to hurt her as

Laurent Duval had hurt her. He had a basic respect, a basic kindness, which had been totally absent in her late, unlamented husband. And most women would think her a lunatic to turn him down. Refuse the prospect of marriage to the Marquess of Coverdale! Quite mad! In the eyes of the world it would bring so much—a great position, wealth, security, Marrick and other houses all over England.

But she had never set a great store by position. She had all the wealth she could ever need. If security meant money to buy servants and houses, then those were hers already… But marriage to John would bring so much more. Harriet as a daughter, a family, perhaps children of her own, a home. And John.

She got up and walked about the room the train of her grey silk dress rustling behind her. John. Her wooden soldier. Someone she had seen in every possible state of mind—cold reserve, despair, black anger, and amusement, laughter. A man of authority, yet liked by those under him. Someone who was at ease with Barnaby and Thomas Beckford, but who had clearly mixed with the great and the good of Europe. A strict man, but very kind. How could she have ever thought him simple? And this man, against all the odds, seemed to respect her, value her. So much so that he might ask her to marry him. Dared she risk it?

It was time to go down, and she was still no nearer a decision!

Harriet looked enchantingly pretty in a white dress with pink silk roses round its sleeves and hem. She was carrying a small bouquet of pink roses in a silver filigree holder, which John had presented to her before the evening began, and her dark hair was held in a delicate silver clasp given to her by Caroline. The guests were disarmed by her shy charm, and her silver-grey eyes shone like stars as she joined in the country dancing with grace and enthusiasm. Her presence at the ball could be counted a great success and augured well for her London début.

Caroline herself had stuck to her decision and stayed severely in the background. She had dressed herself for the part, getting Maggie to skewer the rebellious waves of her hair into a discreet twist with a small diamond aigrette and a fall of Venetian lace covering the many pins that held it in place. Her dress of grey silk *gros de Naples* had half-sleeves and a train, its neckline trimmed with more lace. The stones in her diamond necklace, though not extravagantly large, were of the first water. She looked unostentatiously elegant. A woman of distinction. She was careful to allow John to put his name on her card for only two dances, and refused to go into supper with him.

'I am surprised at you, Lord Coverdale! Do I have to remind one of Wellington's stars that the host takes in the senior-ranking lady present? Lady Randolph, you may be sure, will be well aware of her status, and expect no less! Do your best to charm her for Harriet's sake, if not your own!'

Lady Randolph was a formidable dowager who terrorized her family and everyone else who came within her orbit. She loved gossip, and with the aid of her cronies was always *au fait* with the latest scandals. She would make an excellent ally in restoring Marrick's position in the neighbourhood, but it would be dangerous to offend her. Fortunately John saw the sense of this, remembered his manners and led Lady Randolph into supper with all the address and polish at his command. Caroline, watching, was once again impressed with a new facet of John's personality. When Lord Coverdale chose, he could be a real charmer! The old lady was delighted.

After supper the dowager captured Caroline, sailed with her into an alcove and subjected her to a polite, but ruthless examination. A lesser woman would have been afraid, but Caroline remained undaunted. She was a past mistress in fending off unwelcome questions, and expected to enjoy the promised verbal fencing match. In the conversation that followed Lady Randolph learned a great deal about Jamaica, but very little about Caroline Duval. After a while she decided that subtlety was getting her nowhere and tried a broadside attack. She suddenly said, 'Hmph! I suppose you realise that you're the image of Gabriella Ainderby? Is that why Coverdale is so taken with you? Are you and she related?'

'Not as far as I know. But I've heard the name, of course. Was Lord Coverdale engaged to her at one time?'

'Yes, more's the pity!'

Caroline was startled. 'I beg your pardon?'

'It was a sad end for her, but it would have been a sadder one for him if she had lived.'

'Lady Randolph, I'm not sure what you are trying to say.'

'I'm not *trying* to say anything, Mrs Duval! I'm *telling* you that he would have been a sight unhappier married to that girl than he was when she died.'

Caroline decided that she must change the subject. She badly wanted to know more, but this old harridan must not be allowed to see how very interested she was. She said sympathetically, if a little disingenuously, 'Miss Ainderby is dead? That must indeed have been a sad blow for Lord Coverdale. But his daughter must now bring him a great deal of pleasure. I think she looks charming, don't you? Do you have granddaughters, Lady Randolph?'

'Three,' snapped the dowager. 'All dull as ditchwater. But I'm happy to say that they have never given their mother a moment's worry. They've all made very good matches.' She gave Caroline a crocodile smile and leaned forward. 'Which is more than could be said for the Ainderby girl! What a time Mrs William Ainderby had with her! And all the other Ainderbys, too! Of course it's water under the bridge now—mother and daughter have both been dead these many years. But I happen to know that the family would have thrown them out of High Hutton within the month if Gabriella had not managed to get herself engaged to John Ancroft. And I tell you this, there were a good few of us who were very sorry for him when she did!'

Caroline's mind was reeling, but, not without difficulty, she held on to her air of polite interest. She would not betray herself to this woman! She said calmly, 'Lord Coverdale was saying tonight that he thought the Ainderbys were back at High Hutton. Have you heard?'

Lady Randolph looked at her sourly and decided to give up. She knew when she had met her match. Mrs Duval was either not interested in old scandals about her host, or she was too clever to let it be seen. Either way, even *she* felt she could not in decency drag in the subject of Gabriella Ainderby for a third time. She switched to other, more recent scandals.

Caroline was released soon after by one of the other guests, a Mr Dalton. He was some years older than John but still very handsome with bold, dark eyes and a dashing moustache. He asked her to dance. She was so relieved that she gave him a brilliant smile and got up immediately. She excused herself to the dowager, who smiled briefly in response and immediately looked round the room for another prey. As Caroline accompanied her rescuer into the ballroom he said with a grin, 'You seemed to survive the ordeal remarkably well, Mrs Duval. Lady Randolph's victims are usually more crushed when they leave her.'

'I've met quite a number of Lady Randolphs in my time, sir. I rather enjoy their company—for a while! But I admit I was very glad when you came over.'

'Really?' He seemed to be assessing her. For a moment there was an element of familiarity in his gaze which didn't altogether please her. They danced for a while, then he said, 'I expect others have already said how like Gabriella Ainderby you are. It gave me a shock, I can tell you, when I first saw you. It might have been Gabriella herself come back to haunt us all.'

'*Am* I so very like her?' she asked coolly.

He went on, 'Of course you are! The same red hair, the same wicked eyes, the same charmingly enticing smile! How much further does the resemblance go, I wonder?' With a shock Caroline felt her hand being squeezed.

'I think I must have misheard you, sir,' she said pleasantly, removing her hand from his grasp. 'At least, I hope I did. I'd hate to believe that these are Yorkshire manners. My name is Caroline Duval, not Gabriella Ainderby. I am from Jamaica, and at present Lord Coverdale's guest. Is that enough for you? Now, we'll talk of other things. Do you live far from here, sir? I find the roads very uneven in quality. How difficult is it to get about in winter?'

He gave her an odd look, but remembered his manners enough to follow her lead. Though he still eyed her speculatively from time to time, there were no more overfamiliar remarks.

Caroline was puzzled. She knew that her normally

rather striking appearance could lead to misconceptions about her behaviour. She had sometimes played on it out of sheer mischief. But this evening she had deliberately set out to make herself unexceptional. Nothing could be more sober, or more respectable, than her grey dress, and her restrained hairstyle with its lace cap and diamond aigrette. What was it about her likeness to Gabriella Ainderby that caused such a strange lack of good manners?

By the end of the evening Caroline was seriously worried. More than one gentleman had been sufficiently misled by her superficial resemblance to Gabriella to assume she was an easy target for their gallantries. She had soon disabused them. That was not the problem. But it was possible that her presence in Marrick might stir up more potential grief for John than he had yet experienced. For seventeen years Gabriella had lain quietly in her grave, forgotten, as far as she could see, by all but John. But her own resemblance to the girl was stirring up old memories, old scandals. John Ancroft had put Gabriella on a pedestal, and worshipped at its foot for seventeen years. What if his image of her had been false?

She avoided talking to John by the simple expedient of going upstairs to bed while he was still dealing with his guests. In her present state of mind it would have been difficult to know what to say to him. But though she was very tired, sleep eluded her. She tossed and turned, her mind swinging like a pendulum between her two enigmas. The impression she had gained tonight of Gabriella Ainderby was very different from everything John had told her about the girl. Where was the truth? And as she got nearer to High Hutton and the delivery of the chalice, she began to wonder about its history. So many mysteries surrounded it. Would she learn the truth about *that* tomorrow?

The chalice and Gabriella Ainderby. She was not sure that the truth about either would turn out to be very welcome.

Chapter Ten

Caroline got up early the next morning, pale and heavy-eyed, still wondering how she could talk about the ball the previous night without letting John see how concerned she was. He was already downstairs and dressed for riding.

'I wondered about you when you disappeared last night,' he said, looking at her with a frown. 'Have you been doing too much?'

'No, no! Of course not. But you were busy when I wished to go to bed, and I thought it best to leave you and Mrs Abbington to deal with the guests. When are the people who stayed overnight leaving, do you know?'

'Oh, we're a hardy lot in Yorkshire! We don't keep London hours. Some have gone already, and the rest will depart soon after breakfast. Caroline, Harriet has been invited to a party the Lawsons are giving tonight at Brough. I'd like her to go. The Lawsons have a large family, some of them around her age, and it would be good for her. And it fits in quite well with our plans. We shall be out for most of the day, and I don't think this visit to High Hutton is a suitable occasion for her. Do you mind?'

'I think it's a wonderful idea!'

'Good. Good!' He looked pleased. 'I'll tell her. Er... shall we set off for High Hutton about eleven o'clock? I think everyone will have left by then.'

'Certainly.'

He looked at her closely. 'You *are* tired! Shall we postpone the visit?'

'By no means!' exclaimed Caroline in a panic.

'If you're sure?'

'Absolutely certain!'

'I had thought we would ride cross-country. It's a long way round by road. But it looks as if it might be better to take the carriage after all...?'

'No, I should prefer to ride. I haven't had enough fresh air recently. It might do me good.'

'In that case, why don't you have a rest before then?'

A rest in her room would keep her out of John's way for a little longer. Caroline said thankfully, 'I think I will.'

He accompanied her upstairs, and escorted her to her room. 'Maggie, see that your mistress lies down for a while. I think she's been overdoing it, whatever she may say!' He turned to Caroline. 'Stay up here till it's time to go. I'll say goodbye to Harriet for you. And try not to worry so much about today.'

'He's right, Miss Caro. You look washed out. Let me take that dress off and fetch your wrapper. I'll draw the curtains in a minute, too. By the way, Joseph is back, and says he'll go with you.'

'Did he enjoy the visit to his family?'

Maggie smiled broadly. 'Perhaps for the first day or two. But after that he was glad to get away. The rest of the Bellerbys are a noisy, quarrelsome lot from what he said.'

'So he doesn't wish to stay in Yorkshire after all?'

'I don't think so.' Maggie paused. 'That is, not with

his family. But I don't know what he'd do if you decided to stay?' She looked at Caroline inquiringly.

'Don't you start,' said Caroline wearily. 'It's all so confused. And I still have to deal with the Ainderbys.'

'I expect his lordship will see to any problems. A very capable man, his lordship. And a gentleman with it. Anyone who had him to look after her could count herself lucky!'

'You think so?'

'I'm certain of it!'

'If only I could be sure… The prospect is tempting, but how could I ever marry again? To hand over such power…'

'You could trust his lordship, I'd stake my life on it!'

'Wouldn't we all miss Jamaica?'

'Not if you were happy. And married to the Colonel.'

'Not so fast! There are a few problems to solve first!'

'Such as what they say about Miss Gabriella Ainderby?'

Caroline sat up. '*What* was that?'

'Miss Ainderby. You should hear what the servants here have to say about her. The older ones, that is. They remember her quite well, and she was a proper little madam, from all accounts. Wasn't happy until she'd got a man where she wanted him—wrapped round her little finger. Then once she had him so as he didn't know whether he was on his head or his heels, she lost interest. But up to that point she'd try anything. She was up to all sorts of tricks. It didn't stop with kissing, either!'

'Be quiet, Maggie! I won't listen to this!'

But Maggie was not to be stopped. 'Our poor Colonel! The servants here say *she* was the one who really caused the accident, not him! The two cousins were both in a rage, but that was because they'd quarrelled over her! The

Colonel was angry with Lord Philip because he thought he was flirting with Miss Ainderby, but it was the other way round. Miss Ainderby wouldn't leave Lord Philip alone! You may take it from me, Miss Caro, Gabriella Ainderby was far from being the saint the Colonel makes her out to be!'

'Oh, Lord!' Caroline put her face in her hands. Maggie could be right. The people last night had given her the same impression. She looked up. 'How can we stop him from finding out?'

'If you ask me, it's time he did find out.'

'No! I can't bear to think what it would do to him.'

Maggie was silent. Then she said slowly, 'I think you're much fonder of the Colonel than you admit, Miss Caro.'

Caroline stared at her. 'Am I? I don't know! I never thought I'd ever fall in love again with anyone. Not after that first time. But what if you're right? Oh, Maggie, what a coil I'm in!'

'And I think the Colonel is pretty sweet on you, Miss Caro. He's a changed man since we were in Barnet. If he knew you loved him, he might not mind about Miss Ainderby as much.'

'You think so? If I could only be sure of that.' She leaned back against the pillows. 'Since you already know so much, you are probably aware that Lord Coverdale has asked me to stay on here for a little. Just as a guest, for the moment. Do you think I should?'

'Yes, I do, though it's not my place to say so.'

'Whenever has that stopped you from saying what you wanted?' asked Caroline.

Maggie ignored this. 'You said yourself you'll be lonely in Jamaica without your grandfather. And the Colonel is a good man. You'd be safe in his hands.'

A yawn caught Caroline unawares. 'He has a friend in you, at least.' Then she added sleepily, 'I'm not so sure that I want to be in any man's hands, Maggie. Not metaphorically, at least. I wouldn't at all mind being in a good man's hands literally...'

'Miss Caro! You watch what you're saying! If you're going to be a Marchioness, you'll have to learn how to behave!'

Caroline didn't reply. Her short night had caught up with her. She was asleep.

However, she was ready when one of the servants came to say that Lord Coverdale was waiting for her. She came downstairs in her green riding habit and met him at the bottom of the stairs.

'You look much better,' he said. 'Do you feel it?'

'Thank you, yes. You have my bag there, I see.'

'I took it out of the strong room five minutes ago. I suppose you will carry it, won't you?'

'Yes. For this last stage.'

'Don't be nervous. I'll be there whenever you want me. The Ainderbys are not monsters.'

'I'm sure they aren't! And I'm not nervous! It's just... Oh, confound it, John, I'm *horribly* nervous! I hate not knowing what's ahead!'

'Is there any kind of message or letter for them?'

'Two letters. One to give them, and one for me to open at the same time.'

'Then let's be on our way! The sooner we're there, the sooner you'll know. And remember! Whatever happens, I'll be nearby.'

'I...I'd like you to be present. All the time.'

He turned and gave her a long look. 'Thank you,' he said at last.

* * *

It was another warm, sunny day, but there was a cool breeze on the hills. It made for very pleasant riding. The climb was quite steep, and at the top they dismounted and gave the horses a rest. Below them the river ran like a silver ribbon threading its way through the surrounding trees. Above them the sky was a deep, clear blue. Caroline stood with Joseph just behind, looking down over the hills and dales which spread in every direction, a patchwork of green and grey, brown and purple, with here and there a single square of pale green or gold, where the farmer had planted wheat or some other crop.

'So, Bellerby. What do you think of Yorkshire after all these years?'

'It's a grand place in summer, your lordship. But the winters are none so great. Jamaica is warmer then, I'm thinking.'

'Did you find out from your family when it was that your uncle left these parts for the West Indies?'

Joseph shot a glance from under his brows. 'It were a long time ago. Too long for most folk to remember,' he replied evasively.

'Joseph! That's not an answer!'

'Better to wait, Miss Caro. After *that's* handed over.' He nodded to the bag round her middle.

'The sooner the better! Shall we go?' John waited while Joseph helped Caroline into the saddle, then set off once again.

The Ainderbys were waiting for them in the main doorway at High Hutton, and as she and John rode up with Joseph close behind, Caroline inspected them with interest. Martin Ainderby was tall, as tall as John or her grandfather. He would have been a handsome man but for a general sourness in his expression. Beside him was his wife. She was a plain woman, with a short, rounded figure, wispy hair, and an air of defeat about her. Not a prepossessing couple, thought Caroline. By now she was used to expressions of surprise when people up here saw her for the first time, but the Ainderbys' reaction was stronger than any she had seen before. Shock and amazement, yes, but mixed with something approaching antagonism. She was even more apprehensive about the coming meeting, but waited calmly to be introduced. This John did, and they were invited in. They were in a large hall with rooms opening off at either end. The door at one end was open with an inviting glimpse of an airy, sun-filled room. But Mrs Ainderby walked over and shut it before turning to her visitors again. She said,

'You've had a long ride. I expect you'd like something cool to drink. Martin, would you take Lord Coverdale and Mrs…Mrs Duval into the library, while I find one of the servants? Will your groom have his in the kitchen, Lord Coverdale?'

'Thank you kindly, ma'am. I'll wait here in the hall, if you don't mind,' said Joseph stiffly.

Mrs Ainderby looked surprised, but said nothing. Instead she pointed to a chair by the door, and went off, presumably in the direction of the kitchens. The others followed Martin Ainderby into the room at the other end. There was a slight pause while they sat down, then Mrs Ainderby came in again, accompanied by a servant carrying a tray of drinks. There was another pause, during which Caroline felt herself being eyed uneasily by their hosts.

Mrs Ainderby gave her husband a glance. He cleared his throat and said, 'I was a little surprised at your note, Coverdale. You said Mrs Duval wished to speak to us, but as far as I knew…' he threw Caroline a glance '…as far as I *know*, we have never met the lady before.' He turned to her. 'Am I wrong?'

'No,' said Caroline. 'Unless you have been to Jamaica, sir? I have never been in England before this spring.'

'Really?' He seemed about to say more, but changed his mind. After a short pause he went on, 'Then, how can we serve you, Mrs Duval?'

Caroline carefully opened her bag and took out two letters. 'Forgive me if I appear to be acting mysteriously. But I must ask this. May I confirm that you are Martin Ainderby, the eldest son of Thomas Ainderby, of High Hutton?'

Martin Ainderby coloured angrily. 'Of course I am, ma'am! Who else could I be? What *is* all this about?'

'I'm sorry if I've offended you, but I had to make certain. The truth is, I am not sure myself what it is about. My grandfather died last year in Kingston, Jamaica, Mr Ainderby. Almost the last thing he did was ask me to deliver this letter to you. And, if the others will excuse me, he also gave me a letter addressed to me, which I was to read at the same time. Here they are.' She handed one letter to Martin Ainderby, and held the other in her hand, waiting till both could be opened at the same moment.

Martin Ainderby took his letter over to the light and stood by the window reading it. Caroline stayed where she was. The two other people in the room waited in silence and suspense.

John watched Caroline anxiously. She had grown very pale, and was obviously agitated. She had first scanned her grandfather's letter rapidly, then with a smothered exclamation had gone back to the beginning again, devouring the page with her eyes.

Martin was no less affected. He read more slowly, and when he had finished he came back to the table in the centre of the room and put the letter down on it.

'Where is it?' he asked heavily.

John had never seen Caroline in such distress. She could hardly speak. 'I'll show you,' she said, and started to open the bag again.

'No!' said Martin. 'Not here! You'd better come with me. You too, Ellen!' When John got up, he said fiercely, 'Not you, Coverdale!'

'I'm coming,' said John evenly. 'I don't know what this is about, Ainderby, but I can see that Mrs Duval has had a shock. I insist on coming with her.'

'And I wish him to come,' said Caroline. 'Lord Coverdale is to know...everything.'

Martin looked from one to the other, and saw their determination. Without another word he went over to a large bureau that stood in a corner, unlocked it and took out a heavy bunch of keys. 'Follow me,' he said briefly. 'Bring the bag with you.'

He led the way across the hall. Joseph, sitting stiffly on his chair, followed them with his eyes. He looked troubled. Martin took up a lamp from the table, lit it and went through a leather-covered door. John made sure he was close to Caroline as they followed him through the door and went a good way along a narrow passage, till they came to another door, which Martin opened with one of the keys. On the other side, they were in a part of the house that was obviously much older than the rest. Another door, another lock, then steps downwards. The air was cold but dry. There was some ventilation, though no window was visible.

Martin put the lamp down in a niche in the wall and turned up the wick. John saw that they were in a small stone chamber with an altar-like table at one end. A large oak cupboard stood on the table. Its wood was black with age, but its handles and locks shone bright in the lamp-light. Another lamp stood to the side, evidently kept permanently lit. Martin turned this up, too. Then he turned round and faced Caroline.

'If this is a trick, you will be cursed forever. If it is not a trick, then your grandfather is cursed.'

'My grandfather has returned the chalice. He is not cursed,' she said steadily. 'I have it here, ready to give you.'

'Do you swear secrecy, Coverdale? Otherwise you will have to leave this chamber now.'

'I'll swear whatever you suggest. But I'm not leaving this chamber while Mrs Duval remains. Get on with it, Ainderby. It's damned cold down here. I give you my word that I'll keep your secret, whatever that is.'

Martin selected a small key and opened the black wooden doors. John drew in his breath. It was an amazing sight. The inside of the cupboard was a blaze of reflected light. Brilliant streaks of red, green, blue, the bright sheen of gold streamed out, dazzling in their intensity. When his eyes were more accustomed to the display he saw that the cupboard had three shelves. In the centre of one of the shelves was a large gold dish, a paten, tilted on to one edge. On another was a krater-like bowl, also of gold and also tilted. Both objects were encrusted with jewels. The centre shelf was empty, a pool of darkness amid all the splendour.

Caroline went over to a side table and took a leather pouch out of her bag. She undid the pouch, took what was inside out of its linen wrappings and held it up. Her hands were quite steady. In them was one of the most beautiful objects John had ever seen—a graceful chalice of gold, chased and, like the objects in the cupboard, embellished with jewels that caught the light of the lamps and threw it back at them in a blaze of colour. It was obviously very ancient.

'The Ainderby Chalice!' Martin breathed the words with reverence and awe.

Caroline stepped slowly towards the cupboard and placed the chalice on the middle shelf, where it shone even more brilliantly than its fellows. Then she stepped back and made a curious little bow. 'It is done, Grandfather,' she said in a low voice. Then she came back and stood by John.

For a moment he was speechless with astonishment. Caroline Duval had carried this priceless artefact, centuries old and, as she had said, worth a king's ransom, all the way from Jamaica, worn it next to her body, carried it in a pouch over her shoulder... How could she have taken such enormous risks! It might so easily have been lost forever or damaged beyond repair during her long journey. She saw him looking at her.

'It was well protected in its own case for most of the time,' she said almost apologetically. 'But the case was stolen during the attack on Hounslow Heath. Since then I have protected it as best I could. I couldn't confide in anyone, not even you. Don't condemn me, John.'

'I don't condemn you. But I should like to know how your grandfather came to have it in the first place.'

She said expressionlessly, 'He stole it.'

'*Stole* it? But how? This place is like a fortress. And how could he have known about it? I was brought up only eight miles away, and have never heard a breath of anything like this.'

Martin regarded him coldly, obviously regarding his presence as an unwelcome intrusion. 'The presence of these relics has been kept secret ever since they were entrusted to the Ainderby family by the Abbot of Belvaux Abbey. They were part of a treasure brought back from the Holy Land many hundreds of years ago, and were ancient even then. The Abbot wished to protect them from King Henry's men, when the Abbey was dissolved. He himself was later hanged for his part in the Pilgrimage of Grace.'

'What was the Pilgrimage of Grace?' asked Caroline.

'A rebellion in the north against the King. For nearly three hundred years we have kept them faithfully here in this chamber, and only members of the Ainderby family have had access to it,' said Martin. 'But their access has been free and untrammelled.'

Caroline turned to John. Her distress was real, but she had control of herself. Her deep voice was calm and clear. 'My grandfather's real name was Peter Ainderby. He was the youngest son of William Ainderby, this Mr Ainderby's great-grandfather. He…he ran away to Jamaica when he was twenty, taking the chalice with him. He says in my letter that he was very wild as a youth, and at the time was full of resentment about an inheritance, which his father had denied him because of his behaviour. He was ordered to leave High Hutton and on a mad impulse took the chalice with him. He realised almost straight away that he had done something very wrong, but once it was in his possession he found he couldn't give it up. I told you. It had the same effect on him as it had on my cousin Edmund.'

'He was a thief!' said Martin harshly. 'He betrayed the family's trust.'

Caroline spread her hands in a gesture of appeal. 'But he sent it back! Doesn't that count for something?'

Ellen Ainderby had been silent till now. But she suddenly spoke. 'You'd better go,' she said. 'We don't want you here! Your grandfather was a thief, and you bring back too many unhappy memories.'

'*I* do?'

'Yes! You're too like your cousin Gabriella.'

'Of course,' said John. 'Caroline, you're an Ainderby! That's why there's such a likeness. You and Gabriella had the same great-grandfather.'

'And the sooner she is out of this house the better.' Ellen turned to her husband. 'Get her out of here!'

'You can't blame Caroline for her grandfather's crime!' John exclaimed. 'She's brought this chalice back to you at great personal risk. You can't be so unjust!'

'No,' Caroline said nervously. 'Leave it, John. I agree with Mrs Ainderby. I bring too many unhappy reminders. Please let's go. Now!'

Martin took a last look at the chalice, then closed and locked the cupboard. The little party retraced its steps back to the hall. Joseph was standing by the door, and he gave Caroline a look of inquiry.

'It's back,' she said briefly. Then she added, 'You knew. You knew, didn't you, Joseph?'

'My uncle told me afore he died. He went to Jamaica with the master when he were a lad, and knew most of what had happened. He told me, but I kept it quiet for the master's sake. Lately I've done my best to help you put it right, Miss Caro. It were what he wanted.'

Caroline stood by the door, not quite knowing what to say. The day's revelations had left her feeling drained. Joseph, her grandfather, and Gabriella… She wanted to leave High Hutton as soon as possible, suspecting that the Ainderbys had something to say about Gabriella that she would not want John to hear. The sooner they could go the better. She turned to Martin. 'I've done what I came to do,' she said. 'You must be happy to have your treasure restored, and I am happy that my grandfather's wish has been granted. So we'll take our leave. Mr Ainderby? Mrs Ainderby?' With relief she started for the door, not caring how abrupt her farewell had sounded.

'What is that girl doing in the house again?'

The voice rang across the hall. They all turned round, startled. An old woman dressed in black and walking with the aid of a stick came out of the door that Mrs Ainderby had closed so carefully an hour before.

'Mama! Why aren't you still asleep?'

'Never mind that, Martin Ainderby! I told you to throw that girl out of my house, and, as soon as I turn my back, you've got her here again!'

The two Ainderbys both started to speak at once. Ellen Ainderby won. 'My mother-in-law is confused,' she said. 'It's better you should go.'

'As for you, ma'am,' said the old lady, scornfully raking her daughter-in-law with a glittering eye. 'I'd have thought you had more pride! Hasn't that girl brought you enough pain? Ready to see your husband making love to that…that hussy all over again, are you? Under your very nose again? Well, I shan't get rid of her a second time! You'll have to put up with it!'

'Wait!' said John sharply. 'This must stop. I can't stand by and listen to such insults to the lady I brought here, a friend of mine.'

Old Mrs Ainderby gave a raucous laugh. 'Friend, is she now? I thought she was to marry you, John Ancroft.'

Martin went over and took his mother's arm. 'Mama, you're mistaken! This is Mrs Caroline Duval from Jamaica. Let me take you back to your sofa—'

She shook him off angrily. 'Don't you try any tricks on me! I'm not blind, boy! I can see who she is! She's

Gabriella Ainderby, and if you don't send her packing she'll cause you as much trouble as she did before. What about your wife? She's looking sour enough. Is she to watch once again while you make a fool of yourself over that girl? Shame on you!'

John had gone pale. He was staring at the old lady as if he couldn't believe what he was hearing. 'Mrs Ainderby, are you talking of your *niece*, Gabriella? Is what you are saying about *Gabriella*?'

'Of course I am! Look at her! White as a sheet. She don't want you to know, but it's time someone told you, John Ancroft. She wrecked my family and she'll wreck yours! That girl can't leave anything in breeches alone till she's made him her slave. My poor Martin went out of his mind over her, and my other son Paul, too! Why do you think they don't speak any more? I sent her packing. I told her mother. I'll give you a week to find somewhere else to live, I said. I don't care where, but your daughter is to leave High Hutton and not come back.' She gave another cackle. 'She didn't waste any time, either! She'd got her daughter engaged to you before two days were up. What happened? Why isn't she your wife? Did you see through her before you married her? Your cousin Philip did, but you were as innocent as a newborn babe!'

'Mama!' Martin was trying in vain to take his mother away, but John stepped forward and held his arm.

'Gabriella is dead, Mrs Ainderby. She won't do you or yours any further harm. But...' He turned to Martin. 'Tell me what she's talking about! It doesn't make sense. What does she mean about Gabriella?'

Martin looked uncomfortable. 'She shouldn't have said anything. You must forgive her, Coverdale. She's old, and a little out of her mind.'

Ellen Ainderby had been growing increasingly agitated.

Now she suddenly spoke up. 'She's *not* out of her mind! Except that she is confusing Caroline Duval with Gabriella Ainderby, and that's natural enough. For one moment I thought myself that it was Gabriella at the door! No, Martin, I *will* speak! Most of what your mother's been saying is perfectly true! I'm glad that that chalice is back at High Hutton, but I wish to heaven that that woman had not been the one to bring it! She reminds everyone of that accursed cousin of yours! She reminds *me* of how Gabriella ruined my marriage, how you and I have never been happy since. And she reminds *you* of how you and Paul fought over her, and how the two of you haven't been friends since. Aren't I right? Aren't I?'

Her husband looked away in pain. It was more explicit than any acknowledgment. Ellen Ainderby drew a shuddering breath, and turned back to John.

'Your precious Gabriella demanded *every* man's homage, and didn't care how she got it, or who was hurt until she did. It sickened me to my soul to see the air of innocence she put on. Innocence! She was a *serpent*!'

'No! I don't believe you! Not Gabriella! It can't be!' But John's desperate cry lacked conviction.

Ellen went on remorselessly, 'You'd have found out sooner or later, Lord Coverdale. She was after your cousin even while she was engaged to you, but he at least knew her for what she was. I was *glad* she died! You deserved better.'

John turned away and walked to the door. He swung round. 'I...I can't—' He broke off and shook his head.

Martin said dully, 'I'm sorry, Coverdale. My wife shouldn't have spoken as she did, but what she says is the truth. I'm sorry you had to hear it from us. I...I don't think there's any more to say. Excuse me. Come, Mama. You must rest again.' He left them in the hall.

Ellen Ainderby was back in her shell, once again a quietly unhappy woman. She said, 'I'm not sorry. Except that you've seen what our life here has been for the past seventeen years. Goodbye, Mrs Duval. Lord Coverdale.' She followed her husband.

John looked at Caroline and saw her expression. He said incredulously, 'You're not surprised! You knew! You knew all this and you didn't say a word! I trusted you with my deepest feelings, you knew how I felt, but you didn't say a word!'

'How could I?' asked Caroline helplessly. 'You loved her.'

He gazed at her in silence for a moment, then he turned away. 'Bellerby will see you back to Marrick,' he said curtly. I…I need to think. Bellerby!' He strode off in the direction of the stables. The last Caroline saw of him was of a figure galloping off as if all the hounds of hell were after him.

Caroline and Joseph rode back to Marrick in near silence. As they came in through the archway she saw that the carriage that had taken her cousin Edmund to Falmouth was there. Betts, John's man, was beside it.

'Good evening, ma'am,' he called. Caroline roused herself.

'Betts! You're back again. Come and see me when you are ready. I'd like to hear how my cousin fared.'

'I will that, ma'am. As soon as I've reported to the Colonel.'

'I'm not sure you'll find him in the castle, Betts. He went for a ride, and I doubt he's back yet.'

'I'll have a look, ma'am. If he isn't, shall I come to see you?'

'Please. But not if you're too long about it. I'm rather tired.'

'Very good, ma'am. You may rest easy, though. Mr Willoughby is safely at sea somewhere on the Atlantic Ocean.'

'Thank you. Till later, then.' Caroline dismounted and went slowly up the now familiar steps. The castle seemed deserted. During the day the servants had dismantled all the arrangements for the ball, put nearly all the furniture back in its usual place, and swept and cleaned the rooms. Now most of them had gone. Mrs Abbington was with Harriet at Brough. Unless John came back soon she would be alone for dinner.

Maggie was waiting for her when she got to her room, but when she saw her mistress's face she forbore to ask questions.

Only later, when Caroline had rested and was getting ready for the evening, did she risk it.

'You saw the Ainderbys, Miss Caro?'

'Oh, yes, Maggie,' said Caroline wryly. 'I saw the Ainderbys. I've done what my grandfather wanted me to do. Did you know that he was really an Ainderby? That Peter Leyburn of Kingston, Jamaica, was really Peter Ainderby of High Hutton in the county of Yorkshire?'

'No, I didn't know, but I thought there must be something like that about it. He was always something of a mystery, your grandfather, and you couldn't be so like Miss Gabriella Ainderby just by coincidence. So, it's all done?'

'Yes, it's all done...' And Caroline astonished her maid by bursting into tears.

'There, there, now!' Maggie soothed her mistress as a

nurse would soothe a child. 'There, there, Miss Caro! It's over! You can put it behind you now.'

'It's not that, Maggie,' sobbed Caroline. 'It's the Colonel!'

'You told him about your grandfather? He was annoyed? Surely not! Not just about a little thing like a name!'

'There was more to it than a name, but no, that wasn't it. He was very sympathetic about my grandfather. But… oh, Maggie, the Ainderbys told him about Gabriella! He knows now what she was really like. They said everything that you told me this morning.'

'What happened?'

'He sent me back with Joseph and rode off by himself. I don't know when he'll return.'

Maggie was silent, then she said, 'It's not altogether a bad thing, Miss Caro. He would have heard about her sooner or later. Better now. Then he can put it all behind him before he settles down properly.'

'He took it badly. He was even angry with me. He thought I should have warned him.'

'Oh, he won't hold that against you, once he's himself again. He'll see for himself that you couldn't. Don't worry, Miss Caro.'

There was a knock on the door. Caroline started up. Maggie said, 'There! That's probably the Colonel now, come to see that you got back safely.' But when she opened the door Betts was there.

'Mrs Duval asked me to see her, miss,' he said.

'Betts!' called Caroline 'Come in! Is your master back yet?'

'Not yet, ma'am. But he'll probably be here any minute. It's getting a bit late for dinner. A very punctual man, the Colonel. I came to tell you about Mr Willoughby.'

'Yes! He's now on the high seas?'

'He is that. From what he said, he wasn't looking forward to it, neither.'

'No, he isn't a good sailor. How did he seem otherwise?'

'Resigned, you might say. I don't think he'll forget what the Colonel said to him. Powerful impressive the Colonel can be. You'll be all right now.'

'Thank you! Could you ask your master to let me know when he is back?'

'I will. Thank you, ma'am.' Betts gave her something like a military salute and left, winking at Maggie as she stood by the door ready to close it.

'Maggie, see if the kitchens can put dinner back by an hour. Lord Coverdale arranged it for seven, but he can't possibly be ready by then.'

Maggie went and Caroline was left to her own thoughts. This should have been a day of relief, the dinner tonight a celebration of a burden lifted. But she could not rid herself of a sense of impending disaster.

Betts went back to his master's quarters. The Colonel was still not back. He busied himself about the bedchamber, sorting out clean linen and a change of clothing for the evening. He looked round. Everything was laid out ready. With a shake of the head for his forgetfulness, he fetched Mr Willoughby's letter from his own bag, and laid it on the dressing table next to the Colonel's brushes. No doubt Mr Willoughby had little of importance to report, he was probably just grateful for the standard of comfort the Colonel had provided for him. More than he deserved. All the same, the letter should be handed over as soon as the Colonel came in.

Chapter Eleven

John Ancroft rode furiously along highways and bridle paths, over fences and hedges, heedless of danger. He was desperate to get away from High Hutton, to leave the Ainderbys and their tales of Gabriella far behind him, to escape from what he had heard. Once or twice he very nearly ended it all as he took a fence too recklessly or rode without caring under low-branched trees in the woods. He paid as little attention to his safety as he had in those early battles in the Peninsula, when all he had wanted was to satisfy his uncle's desire to see him dead. But fate protected him now as it had protected him seventeen years before. In the end the thought of Harriet and her need of him slowed him down, forced him to take more care.

Then, once he started to think, he realised that, run as he might, he could not escape from the truth. He believed what the Ainderbys had said. For seventeen years, he had lived with a fairy tale, a mirage. He had cherished an image of a girl who had given herself to him in love and innocence, who had died forever young, forever unsullied. He had seen himself as the most fortunate, and at the same time, the most unhappy of men, a man who had gained a peerless bride, only to lose her a few short weeks before their marriage. And it had all been an illusion.

He came to a halt and found himself high up on the hills gazing down on Marrick, the pain almost more than he could bear. What a damned, blind, insanely stupid dolt he had been! Why hadn't he seen Gabriella for what she was? It was clear to him now that Philip had known, had tried to show him how faithless Gabriella could be, but he had refused to look. Before the accident, on that last fateful day, Philip had quite deliberately flirted with Gabriella, and he, John, had been so blind that he had accused his cousin of envy, of wanting Gabriella for himself, of being unfaithful to Rose. In the face of these accusations Philip had lost his temper. He had always been quick to take offence, and John usually used his influence to calm him down. But that day John had shouted back, and soon they had both been in a black rage with each other, the worst they had ever known. Gabriella had brought devastation to the Ancrofts as well as to the Ainderbys. Almost her last act had been to trip lightly into that curricle, quite indifferent to the havoc she had caused between the hitherto devoted Ancroft cousins, perhaps even enjoying her power. In the accident that followed he had lost a man he had regarded as a brother, for the sake of a worthless, empty-hearted little whore. For a while he felt the pain of loss as acutely as he had seventeen years before. But this time it was for Philip alone.

After a time his thoughts turned to Caroline Duval. He was certain she had known about Gabriella before the Ainderbys' revelations, but how? Was it such common knowledge at Marrick? Or had she been talking to guests at the ball, the old Randolph harridan, for example? *Why* hadn't she said something to him? She could have saved some of this pain! It would have been hard to hear the truth about Gabriella from anyone, but to hear it like that, from the Ainderbys, to witness what she had done to them... Why hadn't Caroline warned him? He tried to remember what her excuse had been. 'How could I?' she had said. 'You loved her.'

Damn the woman! Why couldn't she have seen that living in a fool's paradise was far worse than any reality, however painful? He had thought that his relationship with Caroline Duval was based on truth. After those two dramatic encounters on their journey north, when so much had been revealed, he had believed that the only secret between them was exactly what it was that she carried to High Hutton.

So much had been revealed... Or had it? Was it only her body that had been revealed at Buckden, and at the waterfall, and nothing of her *real* self? He had been so wrong about Gabriella Ainderby. Could he not be equally wrong about Caroline Duval? After all, she had begun their association with an attempt to deceive him. Perhaps the resemblance between those two was more than one of appearance... Perhaps Caroline Duval's real reason for attempting to hide the truth about her wanton cousin Gabriella was because she feared it might damage her own hopes for a future at Marrick—as Marchioness of Coverdale.

John's heart twisted as he gazed down at Marrick. Recently he had actually begun to hope that his return to Yorkshire, to Marrick, would mean an end to seventeen years of living in the wilderness, a return to life itself. He had begun to laugh again, to feel the warmth of affection, to look forward to a future with a woman he felt he could love. Had it all been deceit on her part, self-deception on his? Did Caroline Duval have a heart? He had begun to hope so, though she herself had always denied it. Or did the beauty she shared with Gabriella hide the same corrupt mockery of one?

The shadows were lengthening, the sun well to the west. It was time to go back, time to find out.

Betts hurried up to him when he entered his room, prepared to scold. 'I've been a touch worried, Colonel! It's getting late, and Bellerby told me you had sent him back with Mrs Duval, so I knew you didn't have a groom with you. If you'd met with an accident...'

'Well, I didn't and if I'm late for dinner it's not the end of the world.'

'Mrs Duval has set it back an hour, Colonel.'

'Good! So get on with it, man, instead of scolding me as if you were a nursemaid, not a valet! Fetch some brandy, while you're about it. I'm damned tired.'

Betts hastened to do as he was bid. The Colonel did indeed look tired. And not at all his usual neat self. Dishevelled, he was. Very dishevelled. Judging his priority, he brought the brandy first, then produced as if by magic quantities of hot water and towels. Within a short time John was sitting down at his dressing table looking altogether more himself.

'What's this?' John held up the letter which Betts had carried back from Falmouth.

'Mr Willoughby asked me to deliver it to you, Colonel.'

'Willoughby, eh? You saw him off, did you?'

'Yes, sir! Mr Willoughby won't trouble you or Mrs Duval no more. He's on the high seas.'

'Good,' said John. 'Shall I read it now, or leave it till later?'

'There's still some time before you need to go down, sir,' said Betts helpfully.

'Bring me another brandy, Betts, and I'll read it now.'

'Mrs Duval wanted to be told when you got back, sir. Shall I go to tell her?'

'Do! This won't take long.'

Betts left, and John sat sipping his brandy, reading Edmund Willoughby's letter.

Coverdale,

I could see you were taken with Caroline Duval. That doesn't surprise me. She's a handsome creature, and you're by no means the first to fall. But perhaps I should tell you one or two things you ought to know before you get too involved with her. Take it as an attempt to show my gratitude for your leniency towards me in the matter of my unfortunate treatment of your daughter.

She and that old reprobate, Peter Leyburn, kept Kingston society pretty well under their thumbs. As a result, half the tricks Caroline Duval got up to, especially in New Orleans, never reached the ears of society. If Duval was her name. There was some question as to whether she had ever actually been married to Laurent Duval, but we'll let that pass.

For instance, has she told you that she posed without a stitch on for some of the most disreputable so-called artists in Louisiana? When she came back to Kingston old Peter spent a fortune on buying up as many of their portraits of her as he could lay his hands on. There was a time when you had to pay half a year's income in a certain house in Kingston just to see the one that he had overlooked. But believe me, it was worth the money… Even the most jaded palates were stimulated.

Has she told you about the duel fought over her, and how one of the participants died? He had a wife and children, too… But that was in New Orleans, so in the lady's mind it probably doesn't count.

She was more circumspect in Kingston, though there are a good few unhappy wives who could tell you something about her. But perhaps you really should ask her about Senator Coburn's son, though I doubt she will admit to anything. When he committed suicide they blamed it on his gambling debts. Her part in the affair never came to light. However, if his mother is to be believed, she had a great deal to do with it.

I could go on. There's quite a lot more. But perhaps I have written enough to show you the sort of woman you have in your house, keeping company with your daughter.

Believe me, it is not easy for me to reveal these family embarrassments to you. I hope you take it in the spirit it is meant. I return to Jamaica, knowing, as one connected to the family, that the names of Leyburn and Duval will always call forth the sideways looks and raised eyebrows so painful to a gentleman of my standing. I must bear it as I can.

I have not forgotten your kindly warnings. You may be assured that when my cousin eventually comes back to Jamaica I will not hurt her. In fact, I will do all I can to protect her as my uncle Leyburn protected her—though without his resources I fear it will prove extremely difficult.

Betts has been insisting for some minutes that I end this letter and join him on the quayside ready to embark. I cannot say I have liked his attitude towards me. Anyone would think I was a prisoner!

With best wishes for your future happiness

Yrs etc.

Edmund Willoughby

John's first impulse was to tear the letter up and throw it away. It had obviously been written by a man eaten up with resentment and anger, a man who had failed in his attempt to capture the chalice, and was now wreaking what revenge he could on his cousin and on the man who had helped her.

But then he took up the letter and read it through again. He had asked himself a while ago if Caroline Duval had a heart. Was this the answer to his question? Edmund Willoughby's malice was evident, but he seemed to have some evidence. John's doubts of Caroline redoubled as he considered Edmund's accusations…

She had posed for portraits without a stitch on. That was possible. Had he not seen for himself that she remained perfectly composed when caught under the waterfall? If what Edmund claimed was true, she was well used to being seen, stared at—studied even—when she was naked.

A duel had been fought over her. He had not had a real opportunity to study Caroline Duval's behaviour when other men were present. At the ball the other night she had certainly behaved with circumspection. But was that her normal behaviour or had she been anxious to impress? If she had teased hotheaded gentlemen of Louisiana as Gabriella had teased hardheaded Yorkshire men, there might well have been a quarrel that led to a duel. But would she allow a married man, a father, to lose his life over her? Before today he would have sworn it was impossible. But not now. Not now, by God! He had been deceived by Gabriella. Perhaps Caroline Duval had deceived him as much.

Her behaviour in Kingston. That was more serious. In Kingston she was not an impetuous seventeen-year-old, but a woman who had been married, a widow, the pampered granddaughter of a very rich man. Surely by then she would know what effect her actions might have on others? She was far from stupid or unthinking. Yet to drive a young man to suicide…?

But he must not get carried away by Edmund Willoughby's letter. He must be fair. If asked whether the man could be trusted, he would reply that he couldn't. Not at all! It was perfectly possible that a disappointed, frustrated man would exaggerate small incidents, enlarge gossip to huge proportions, and calumnify a woman he had every reason to hate.

John drank his brandy and poured himself another. He felt battered in spirit. After the day's revelations about Peter Ainderby, about Gabriella, and now about Caroline—how was a man to trust anyone? Until he had fallen in love with Gabriella the Ancrofts had in general steered clear of the Ainderbys. The two families had never really felt at ease with each other. In the recent past his own uncle had quarrelled with Martin Ainderby's father and frowned on John's engagement to an Ainderby. Now, it seemed, history had been right all along. Old Peter Ainderby had been a thief, and Gabriella Ainderby had been a faithless hussy, to put it at its best. And what about Caroline? An Ainderby by blood, if not by name. Yes, what about Caroline?

He sat drinking brandy and brooding about the Ainderbys until Betts came to remind him that it was time to go down to dinner.

* * *

Caroline had taken some trouble with her appearance. The occasion was not likely to be one of celebration. On the other hand she wanted to forget her grandfather's misdeeds and remember only his love and care for her—and that he had tried in the end to make reparation. What was far more important for her tonight was to make an effort to raise John's spirits. She could remember the devastating humiliation she had felt at the betrayal of her love for Laurent Duval, at the discovery of his true nature. John had today gone through the same agonising process, not gradually over a period of weeks as she had, but brutally, in as many minutes. Like Maggie, she did not believe he would continue to blame her, once he had calmed down a little, for not passing on to him what she had heard of Gabriella. He had probably already seen for himself that it would have been impossible. Her new task, her new aim, would be to do what her grandfather had done for her—to restore his pride and self-esteem, to show him how highly she regarded him. And, if the occasion arose, how much she loved him.

So she dressed with care in her white silk dress, and Maggie arranged some yellow roses from the garden at its neckline. She wore no other ornament. Maggie had brushed her hair until it shone like silk, several strands of it bleached by the sun to copper. Her eyes were huge, shadowed by the emotions of the day and the lack of sleep of the night before. Looking at her before she went down, Maggie thought that she looked unusually fragile, but more beautiful than she had ever seen her.

John was waiting when Caroline came into the saloon. He had a glass of wine in his hand and fetched another for her as soon as he saw her. They drank.

'Shall we go in to dinner?'

The question was uttered in a cool, formal voice, almost like the one she had first heard in Mr Turner's chambers. Her heart sank. So he was still angry, after all. But Caroline was not a fighter for nothing. She lifted her chin and gave him a smile. 'Of course. It will be strange, will it not, to be quite alone? Not even Harriet and Mrs Abbington for company. The house seems very quiet without them.'

Caroline had secretly been pleased that Harriet and Mrs Abbington were away, thinking that their absence would make it easier to talk more freely to John. But by the end of an hour she was wishing desperately that they had stayed. For the sake of the servants she made conversation, about the ball, about the weather, about Harriet's appearance, all so trivial that she could have screamed with frustration. John responded suitably, but with such an indifferent manner that she began to wonder if he was quite himself. He seemed to be carrying on some inner debate, occasionally staring at her fixedly, then looking away when he caught her eye. She noticed that he was eating little, but drinking fairly heavily, filling his glass from the decanter beside him with disturbing frequency.

The servants cleared the table and brought in the last course. 'That's all,' John said abruptly. 'Leave the rest. We'll call you if we need you.'

Caroline's heart ached for him—he looked so unhappy, as if the black burden of Gabriella's fall from grace was almost too much to bear. She had kept silent about Gabriella out of a wish to spare him, not for any other reason, but if he wished to vent some of his bitter anger on her she would try to be patient. But his first words astonished her, they were so far removed from what she had expected from him.

'Tell me about your time in New Orleans,' he began.

'It must have been hard. I believe you were on your own?'

His tone was hard, judgmental. She replied carefully, 'No, I was married.'

'Ah, yes! To Laurent Duval. So you said.'

Had there been a very slight question in his tone? Surely not! She was imagining things. 'I said I was unprotected. Duval wasn't an ideal husband.'

'I remember. You told me once that your marriage had been unhappy.'

'That's perhaps one way of putting it.'

'Why? What other way is there?'

'It was a nightmare.'

'Oh, come! If it was as bad as that, why didn't you leave him?'

The scepticism in his voice was a shock, but she said calmly enough, 'John, why do you sound so critical? Have you ever been to New Orleans?'

'No, I haven't.'

'Then I must tell you that it is not the sort of place where a penniless seventeen-year-old girl should run away from the only man who might keep away others even worse than he was. It would have been suicidal folly. Curiously enough, I felt some obligation to my marriage vows, too. Whatever Laurent Duval did, however he behaved, I had promised to love, honour and obey him, to stay with him for life. For that I had given up my home in Kingston and deeply hurt my grandfather and everyone who loved me. I couldn't simply abandon my marriage when things got difficult. I had made my bed, as they say, and had to lie on it. I did run away after he was dead, of course. But by then I was a little more experienced.'

'Experienced. Yes. I suppose you were as beautiful then as you are now—and tonight you are quite extraordinarily beautiful! It can't have been difficult for you to find protectors.'

How odd, thought Caroline painfully, that when he eventually pays me a compliment it should have such a sting in the tail! She said, still calm, 'I wanted none of the sort I think you mean. What's going on, John? What are you trying to say?'

'Nothing. We're alone after dinner. Relaxing after a somewhat difficult day. I just want to learn more about you. What's wrong with that?'

'I don't know...'

'Tell me, Caroline. In New Orleans, were you forced to do things you wouldn't normally have wanted to do? Have your portrait painted, for example?'

Her first impulse was to tell him to go to the devil. What had this to do with what had happened today? But then she decided to humour him. His questions were not idle. John was working to an end, but what it was she was not yet sure. She answered with care. 'Yes. We lived in an artistic community. Laurent had friends who wanted to paint me, and he...he made me pose for them.'

'Naked?'

'Why do you ask?' When he didn't reply she went on, 'I see. I suppose that worm, Edmund, told you while he was here of the pictures my grandfather suppressed. I'm surprised that you listened to him.'

'I learned it from Edmund, yes. So, you had a colourful time in New Orleans?'

'Is that what you would call it? Then, yes, I did. A reprehensible past. I told you that myself.' Caroline's anger was growing. These questions arose from something more than John's resentment at her omission to tell him about Gabriella. He was quite deliberately probing old hurts that she thought she had managed to forget. Why was he doing it? Surely he wouldn't be so cruel as to soothe his own sense of humiliation by reminding her of hers! He seemed to be reviving what Edmund had told him weeks ago with the express aim of wounding her. Of one thing she was quite, quite sure. Whatever his motive, John Ancroft was not about to see her crumple. She might have become foolishly soft about him, but she would not let *any* man see how much he was hurting her. It was time to gather her defences together.

'Well,' she said, sitting back and making herself smile, refusing to give way to the growing apprehension which was sending icy shivers down her spine. 'This *is* fun! What other misdeeds can I confess? There's no shortage, I assure you.'

'The duel?'

'Now that's one I can't remember. I don't think I ever actually fought a duel—'

'A duel fought *about* you. In New Orleans.'

Cousin Edmund *has* been busy with his lies, she thought. And, fool that I was, I thought John Ancroft would never believe them! She pretended to consider. 'No,' she said finally. 'It would have been amusing, but I'm sorry to say that I've never had a duel fought in my honour. Isn't it a shame? I can't have been misbehaving badly enough!'

She threw him a glance to see how he took this, but his expression gave nothing away. With a mental shrug she went on, 'I do remember a duel in New Orleans, you're right there. But that was over some cheating at cards. Poor man. He left a wife and family behind, too. But there! If you're going to be caught cheating at cards, you at least need to be a good shot, and he wasn't very good at that, either. As my grandfather always said, if you can't cheat well, you shouldn't cheat at all!' This wouldn't do, the icy shivers were gaining ground. 'Are you having some more wine? May I have a little?'

He got up and brought his own glass and the decanter over. He filled her glass and, instead of going back to his own place, sat down beside her.

'Let's drink to your misdeeds, then,' he said softly, touching her glass with his. He was too close.

'John, I—'

'Drink!'

She drank and felt the wine warming, giving her courage. The questioning continued.

'What about Kingston? You were older then. And protected.'

'Protected?'

'I mean by your grandfather, of course. What else did you think I meant?'

'I don't know. In this present mood of yours you might mean anything.'

'My present mood has little to do with the facts, Caroline. What happened in Kingston?'

She drank some more wine, then said lightly, 'Those good people of Kingston! How they talked! But the cream of it was that there never were any *facts*.' She gave a little laugh. 'No one could actually prove I had done anything at all!'

'Perhaps not. But surely young Mr Coburn's death was a fact? Didn't you feel anything about that?'

Caroline felt as if she had had a blow to the heart. It took her a moment to conquer the feeling of nausea that nearly overcame her. But she held on to her nerve. John Ancroft was not the man she had thought him. She was *damned* if she would let him see how violently affected she was! She got up, went round to the other side of the table and faced him across it.

'What are you trying to do, John?' she demanded, her deep voice harsh, but holding little trace of the tumult inside. 'Are you punishing me for what Gabriella did to you? Is that it? I hadn't realised how much filth Edmund must have poured into your ears, while he lay on his sick bed. But why bring it up now? You've never so much as hinted at any of it before!'

He made no reply, but drew Edmund Willoughby's letter out of his pocket and threw it across to her. 'I hadn't heard it before. Willoughby wrote to me before he left Falmouth. Betts gave me the letter tonight. Read it.'

She picked the letter up and scanned it. Then she threw it back and said contemptuously, 'It doesn't surprise me. He spread such insinuations about me in Kingston, too. Some were even believed. What I can't understand is why *you* appear to believe them.'

'Defend yourself, then! Be serious for once!'

Caroline shook her head. 'I won't. I can't. But I'm disappointed in you, Lord Coverdale. You aren't the man I thought you. Trying to make your own hurt easier by making mine worse is unworthy. Completely unworthy! But yes! If it makes you feel happier—yes, I made a mistake with Robbie Coburn.' She paused. 'I let my feelings get the better of me, and I'm sorry for it. You can't possibly know how sorry!' She knew she sounded hard. The effort she was making to control her voice allowed no softer tone. And from the look of contempt on his face he thought she sounded hard, too. She said angrily, 'But I refuse to excuse myself to you or to anyone else! Damn you all!'

John finished his wine and strode over to her. 'Look!' he said grasping her arm and pulling her to the large mirror over the side table. He stared at their reflection in the mirror, his eyes glittering with anger, his face flushed with the wine. 'Look at you! In that white dress, roses disguising that superbly enticing bosom, the picture of innocence itself! Do you know how like Gabriella you are? Did you hope that I would think of marrying you, as well? And, fool that I was, blind, wilful idiot that I was, I *did* think of it! What supreme irony that would have been! That I should escape from Gabriella, only to fall into Widow Duval's trap! Look at you! How can anything so beautiful be such an agent of destruction? You and Gabriella—cheats, both of you!'

Caroline wrenched herself free. 'How *dare* you call me a cheat! How *dare* you confuse me with Gabriella! I don't cheat! I never even pretended to be an innocent!'

'You could hardly do that,' he said with a contemptuous laugh. 'It was obvious at Buckden that you were well used to flaunting your body to anyone who cared to look. What stopped you that night? Was I too much of a fool for you? Too far gone? Why didn't you close the trap on me? I'd have thought a sick man would be an easy target for your kind of game!'

Caroline slapped his face hard. 'I was not playing games,' she shouted. 'I thought to comfort you!'

He swore, then snatched her to him and tore the roses from her bosom. 'You don't need these,' he said, his voice thick with desire. 'No games, no pretence, you said. *Now* is the time I need comfort. Damn your past! Damn your empty heart! I want to see you again as I saw you at Buckden! To know you fully this time. To bury this torment in the comfort of your body. Tomorrow you can go your own heartless way, but tonight I need you, I want you, Caroline Duval!' He kissed her cruelly, then, forcing her back over his arm, wrenched her dress off her shoulder and buried his face in her breast.

Caroline's deep sense of hurt was overcome by a wave

of pure fury. She broke free and ran to the table. Snatching up the decanter she smashed it against the fireplace and held its jagged edges in front of her like a weapon.

'Marrick has seen a good deal of drama in its time,' she said fiercely. 'But I don't think you'd like your daughter to see you held on a charge of rape. That's what it would be. What I give, I give freely or not at all. And I don't choose to make love with you, not just to drown your *pathetic* illusions about Gabriella Ainderby! If you come any nearer I will use this decanter, don't think I won't. I've had plenty of practice in *this* sort of *game*, though I never thought I'd have to use it against an English *gentleman*!'

Her swift and deadly reaction seemed to have sobered him. The wildness in his eyes slowly died, and he shook his head in self-disgust. He turned away. 'You can put that thing down,' he said, his voice full of shocked loathing. 'I must have been mad. You shouldn't have struck me.' There was silence in the room, as he sought to regain his calm. Then he faced her again, and said deliberately, 'Don't worry! I don't want anything you can offer. I prefer to buy my pleasures. It's at least an honest transaction. No hidden costs—or none that I'm not prepared to pay.'

Caroline hesitated, suspicious of this change of mood.

'Go!' he said. 'I won't stop you. I've had enough.'

She pulled her dress up and stepped warily round to the other side of the table. He didn't stir. Moving with more confidence, she laid the remains of the decanter down at the other end and went to the door. When she looked back he was still standing motionless, watching her as she left. She went out.

One or two of the servants were gathered in the hall, looking apprehensive.

'Has there been an accident, ma'am?' asked one of the footmen.

'Yes,' she replied calmly. 'Fortunately no one was hurt. A broken decanter, that's all. You'll have to watch out for the pieces. Goodnight!'

She went up the stairs and along to her room, where Maggie was waiting. Caroline shut the door and leaned against it. She was suddenly exhausted. Maggie took her arm and led her to the chair. 'The sooner you're in bed, Miss Caro, the better! Let me just get this dress off you. There! What happened to the roses? It's a pity if you've lost them. They were so pretty.'

'I must have dropped them,' said Caroline wearily. 'Don't bother too much with the dress, Maggie. I shall never wear it again.'

'Was...was the Colonel still angry?'

'You could say that. But not because I hadn't told him about Miss Ainderby. He had a letter from Edmund Willoughby. My cousin had excelled himself in raking up the old scandals. He had even improved on them.'

'The Colonel wouldn't believe them, surely?'

'He seemed to believe every word. I even tested him. He asked me about...about Robbie Coburn.'

'There was nothing wrong in that!'

'There was after Edmund had rewritten the story.'

'And you lost your temper. You let the Colonel carry on thinking the worst! Oh, Miss Caro, why did you?'

Caroline made a gesture of despair. 'It wasn't worth the effort to disabuse him. I said I had let my feelings get the better of me. He didn't ask what I meant, he came, without a single moment's hesitation, to the same conclusion as all the gentlemen of Kingston. Together with their wives. Caroline Duval had shared her bed with Robbie Coburn, and then abandoned him. It was just like Kingston. Instant, unthinking, condemnation. That hurt!' She caught her breath. 'Oh, *how* it hurt! I thought he was different. I trusted him, thought he liked me. I'm such a *fool*, Maggie! Why did I let him get so close to me? Why can't I *learn*?'

'But you should have told him! You didn't do anything of the sort with Mr Coburn! You never did do anything of the sort. Not with any of them!'

Caroline laughed harshly. 'Try telling that to the gossips of Kingston! Or even to the gentlemen of England! No, Maggie, I'd rather let them stew in their own prejudice.' She drew in a long shuddering breath. 'And now we shall forget it.'

Maggie knew when to stop. She went about her work in silence, fetching water and towels, brushing Caroline's hair, dressing her in her nightgown and wrapper. When she had finished she asked, 'Is there anything more, Miss Caro? Can I fetch a warm drink? Or a sleeping draught?'

'No, thank you, Maggie. You go to bed. I'll just sit here for a while. Tomorrow we must think about our journey back to London.'

Maggie went into the small dressing room next door and made herself ready for bed. But she lay for a long time listening to the stifled sobs coming from Miss Caro's room. Miss Caro never cried. Not even when her parents had drowned. Not even for her grandfather. She had gone about the world pale and withdrawn, but she had not cried. Colonel Ancroft, for all his gentlemanly ways, had dealt her mistress a mortal blow.

But there was no sign of this the next morning. It was as if the night before had never been. Caroline was a touch pale, but as she said, the visit to the Ainderbys had been a harrowing experience. She was full of plans for their return to London.

'What about Lady Harriet?' asked Maggie.

'Lady Harriet will be back at midday. We can leave an hour later. I'm sure we can rely on Lord Coverdale's stables to take us as far as the inn at Richmond, and we'll hire a post chaise to take us onward. Joseph can ride ahead to arrange it. We should be able to reach London in four or five days, but it doesn't really matter. We might even try a different route, spend some time on the way, perhaps go through York.'

'I'll see to the packing, then. At least we don't have to worry about that blessed chalice!'

Before Caroline went downstairs she spent some time in the little solar room composing a letter to Mr Turner, intending it to catch the mail in time to reach him well in advance of her own arrival. In it she reported the success of her mission and asked him to look for a suitable lodging for a few weeks until she could make up her mind what she wanted to do. John found her here. He was looking pale and stern, and said stiffly, 'I've been looking for you. I wanted to apologise. My behaviour last night was unworthy. I can only say in extenuation that the experiences of the day, and my efforts to drown them in brandy, had done more damage than I realised. I hope you will forgive me.'

Caroline replied with equally cool formality, 'It was a difficult day for everyone, Lord Coverdale. The events after dinner are best forgotten.'

'You are generous. Thank you. However, I cannot believe that I shall forget, or recover my self-respect, for some time.' He paused. 'I hear that Bellerby has gone to Richmond to reserve a chaise from the King's Head for your journey south. My carriage will convey you there at whatever hour you wish.' He paused a second time. 'Harriet will be glad that you stayed to see her.'

'I don't break promises lightly.'

'Are you planning to be in London next spring?' When Caroline raised an eyebrow in mock surprise, John added even more stiffly, 'Harriet will be eager to know.'

'Ah, yes! Harriet. I'm afraid that's a promise I cannot make to Harriet at the moment. My plans are not yet fixed. Perhaps. But since you're here, Lord Coverdale, I must thank you for your help in delivering the chalice to my grandfather's family. I don't think I could have done it as easily, or even at all, without your support. I am only sorry that the visit was such a personal disaster for you. For us both.'

He nodded and said with no perceptible warmth, 'I owe you thanks, too. I think the barrier that existed between Harriet and me would not so soon have been breached without your encouragement.'

Caroline gave a small, ironic smile. 'How civilized! Obligation acknowledged on both sides. We must both take satisfaction at the small good we have achieved out of our acquaintance.'

The bags and valises were packed and put into Lord Coverdale's carriage. Caroline went off to make the rounds of the servants to thank them and show her appreciation of their efforts on her behalf. Maggie was upstairs collecting the last of Caroline's things from the room. John saw her there and came in.

'I'm sorry, my lord. My mistress isn't here. She's seeing your lordship's servants,' she said, very formally.

'What's this extreme politeness, Maggie? I'm not used

to it from you. You used to call me Colonel, and I rather liked it.'

'His lordship is very kind,' said Maggie woodenly.

He gave a sigh. 'I wanted to give you this…' He held out a small purse. 'And to ask you to take care of your mistress on the road to London. I've already spoken to Bellerby.'

'And I'm sure Mr Bellerby's reply was the same as mine, my lord,' said Maggie, curtsying, but refusing to take the purse. 'Thank you, but we need no rewards for looking after Miss Caroline. She's always been the sweetest-natured creature you could ever want to serve, and except for the time when she was married to that black-hearted villain in New Orleans, who beat her black and blue and starved her till she did what he wanted, we've done it all her life. I don't think Mr Duval made her as unhappy as she is now, though.'

'I'm sure she will recover,' said John coldly, offended at Maggie's forthright manner.

'That she will. She's a lady with courage, my lady. And a heart.' Maggie paused, then made up her mind. 'It isn't my place to say so, my lord, but we shall probably not see you again and I'd like to put something right. I love Miss Caroline, you see.'

'I really don't think—'

'Excuse me, my lord, but that's just it! You *haven't* thought!' she said. 'You *know* Miss Caroline! Do you really believe, with all that pride in her, she would throw herself away on a scrubby young fellow hardly more than a schoolboy? When no one else in Kingston could come *near* her, however hard they tried, and that included her own cousin!'

'Edmund!'

'Yes, Edmund, for all he was married!' Maggie shook

her head. 'Why did you have to believe that good-for-nothing? Did you really think that young Mr Coburn died because of her? She gave him *money*, not anything else! He was too frightened to go to his father for it. He owed *thousands*. He begged Miss Caro to lend him money, and in spite of herself, Miss Caro felt sorry for him and gave him something to pay off the worst of his debts. But he betrayed her…' here Maggie threw him a quick glance '…just like all the other men she's let herself trust. He spent her money on more gambling, more drugs, and killed himself in the process. She still blames herself, says she should have taken more trouble to find out the real problem, persuaded him to talk to his father. But that's what really happened, my lord, and I'll swear to it in a court of law.'

John said nothing. He should have silenced Maggie earlier, she had overstepped the line in talking to him as she had. But her indignation had been genuine, and an innate sense of justice told him that he had deserved it.

'It's a pity your mistress didn't bother to explain,' he said after a while, 'Though it would have made little difference in the end.'

'The pity of it is that you're the one who could have made her happy,' said Maggie bitterly. 'I know you could. But I doubt she'll ever let you or anyone else as near again.'

Caroline entered, but came to a halt when she saw John. She looked from one to the other and gave them a glittering smile. 'Oh, Maggie,' she said. 'Have you been trying to rehabilitate me? What a waste of time! Lord Coverdale knows me for what I am, you see. I think we'd better leave before he hangs me from the battlements, or buries me in the dungeons. Would you take these shawls down to the carriage for me, please?' Maggie went and

Caroline gave John a curtsy. 'Harriet has arrived, and I've been saying my farewells. You would have been touched. I didn't say a word about reprehensible pasts and the like. No, I gave her some excellent advice. I told her again: Never cringe, never apologise. Hold on to the code you carry inside you. And hold your head high—whatever the rest of the world believes.' She looked at him with her familiar air of mockery. 'So, I'll take my leave, Lord Coverdale. Allow me to wish you all happiness and success with Harriet. She's a lovely girl. Make sure you look after her. If we meet in London, don't be afraid that I'll embarrass you by claiming any…intimate acquaintance. In fact, I can *promise* you I won't!'

With that she turned and went out of the solar and down the stairs. John followed her, and waited at the top of the steps outside until she was in the carriage, and it had swept round and started down the drive. Harriet was crying, and Mrs Abbington took her in. John followed them inside and went to his own room. He looked for a while at some crumpled yellow roses lying on the dressing table. He must have brought them up to his room after that dinner, though he couldn't remember doing so. He picked them up and threw them away angrily. He wanted no reminders.

Chapter Twelve

Caroline's only wish when she left was to put Marrick, High Hutton and the whole unhappy story of the past few weeks as far behind her as she could. Except for a determination to avoid the places she had travelled through on her road north, she had no other plans. The weather was still warm, and her original intention of going back to London was an uninviting prospect. When Joseph suggested they should leave the Great North Road soon after York Gate and stay the first night at Ripon, she agreed without argument.

At Ripon she met some travellers who had been touring Derbyshire, and their enthusiastic account of the accommodation and entertainment to be found at the spa resort of Buxton persuaded her to try it. Here she spent some time in the hotel at one end of Buxton's impressive crescent, trying the waters, and making use of the many excursions to be made in the surrounding countryside. Though the season was well advanced, balls and assemblies were still being held in the Assembly rooms, and she made herself attend one or two. It helped to put aside for a time some of the anger and hurt which were still burning beneath the graceful self-possession she showed the world.

From Buxton she travelled on through the Derbyshire Dales, among some of the most beautiful landscapes in England, stopping for two or three nights wherever she found an inn which she liked, and spending a great deal of time walking in the hills. She wanted no companion other than Joseph on these walks. He was exactly the sort of escort she preferred—there to protect her, but otherwise silent and self-effacing. Her sore heart found solace in the sunshine and shade of these hills and dales, so unlike the brightly coloured luxuriance of the scenery in Jamaica, and so different from the spare hillsides of Yorkshire. She sometimes walked for hours, returning exhausted to the inn, with energy only to eat her evening meal, wait till Maggie had undressed her, and then drop into bed. But she still could not sleep.

It was not as if she had not suffered before in her life. But the struggle she was now engaged in was different. In the years since New Orleans she had grown into a mature woman, a woman who had sworn never to be caught again in the trap of love, never to be reduced again to the state she had been in on her return from New Orleans. She had taught herself to despise the weaknesses of men, and her weapons had been cynicism and mocking laughter, which she had used against herself as well as against the world.

But John Ancroft had caught her off guard. He had crept into her heart so insidiously that he was there before she noticed. The man she had first met, the wooden soldier, the rigid authoritarian, the humourless hero, was too easy a target for her laughter to represent any kind of danger. But during the night at Buckden he had been unexpectedly revealed as a vulnerable man, a man who had suffered and was still suffering, and she had been moved by the anguish he had involuntarily shown into an attempt to comfort him.

Pity alone, however, would still not have been enough to capture her. Her whole acquaintance with him had been a voyage of discovery. He had turned out to have a sense of humour as strong as her own, to be capable not only of taking her mockery in his stride, but of turning the tables on her. Unlike other men of her acquaintance, he had not been put off by her more outrageous statements, refusing to accept them at face value, and seeing through, she had thought, to the defensive woman beneath. More than all that, she had found in him someone who had an extraordinary power to re-awaken feelings she thought she had put behind her forever. In his arms she had re-discovered physical desire, but this time it was that of a mature woman, where desire was mixed with compassion, and physical excitement with tenderness.

As their curious friendship progressed she had begun to think that here was a man who could look beyond the mask of the sophisticated woman and see the untouched heart behind. She had begun to believe that here at last was someone she could trust not to hurt her. And she had fallen in love. Not that she had known that, or realised how deep it went, until she had been forced to leave Marrick.

And then had come that disastrous day at High Hutton and the scene in the dining room at Marrick that had followed it. After Gabriella's true character had been revealed, his idol shattered, she had *expected* John to be angry. As indeed he had been. Knowing from her own experience how bitterly humiliated he must feel, she had waited to offer him comfort, as she had offered it once before. No, it was not his anger that had surprised and distressed her. It was his readiness to accept Edmund's calumnies as truth, to believe the worst of *her*, to condemn *her* along with Gabriella. His harsh questions, the ruthless contempt he had shown that evening, had struck her to the heart. But John Ancroft had not cared. He had not cared. His apology the next day had been formal, without feeling. A sop to the god of hospitality.

During her long walks Caroline gradually came to acknowledge that she had made a mistake. Influenced perhaps by Maggie's dire warnings about future loneliness, she had persuaded herself that John Ancroft was someone he was not. She had thought him someone special, whereas in fact he was just another man—no better and no worse than all the rest. She had been a fool, and now she was paying for it in deep unhappiness. But not for long! She would get over him as she had got over Laurent Duval. And sooner! If only she could recover from this sense of loss!

As the days passed the beauty and solitude around her began to make her feel better, and she started to think of what she would do. Marrick was behind her, she must look to the future. That night she announced to her two faithful servants that she had decided to leave Derbyshire the next morning and make for London.

'Mr Turner will be wondering what has happened to us—he hasn't heard from me since Buxton. Maggie, Joseph, what would you say if I decided to spend the winter in England? I should like to see something of London life—we saw very little of it when we were last there. Joseph, what about you? Is the winter over here likely to prove too cold for you? Do you want to return to Jamaica? I shan't stand in your way, if you do.'

'I told the master I would look after you, Miss Caro. I

won't leave you. Not till you pension me off! London would suit me pretty well.'

'Maggie?'

'Well, someone has to keep an eye on you, especially if you'll be mixing with all the nobs, Miss Caro! What would you do without me to dress you up and remind you how to behave? No, I'm not letting you stay in London on your own!'

Caroline smiled in relief. 'Then let's hope Mr Turner has found a house to suit us! I'm quite looking forward to it—we'll have a lot to do to make ourselves comfortable during our stay. I shall find out what other servants we need, and engage them, and if the house is not as well furnished as we like I shall visit the showrooms and buy extras. It will be an adventure!'

Maggie was much relieved at the excited note in Caroline's voice. She had begun to think that John Ancroft's defection had changed her mistress forever.

They arrived in London on a glorious day at the end of October. Mr Turner had reserved rooms at the Pulteney Hotel in Piccadilly for them and asked if he might call on Caroline the day after her arrival. He came armed with details of houses for rent in the fashionable quarter of London.

'However, if I may, I should like to draw something to your attention.'

'What is that, Mr Turner?' she asked, leafing through the papers he had brought. 'This house in Bruton Street might do, perhaps?'

'It may not have occurred to you that it won't be easy to live in London on your own.'

Caroline looked up. 'What do you mean? I have Maggie and Joseph, and will engage a whole houseful of other servants. That could hardly be called living on my own!'

'But it's not what I meant. You are still, if I may say so, a young woman. Now "Mrs Hopkins" could have lived alone in London as long as she liked, with no word of criticism. But you are still of an age where society will look askance at it. I assume you wish to enjoy a social life, to move in the first circles?'

'I have every intention of doing so.'

'Then you will need someone to keep you company. I could, if you wish, look for a respectable lady, someone in need of employment, to live with you.'

'You mean a paid companion?'

'Yes.'

'Must I have someone? For a while my grandfather employed a companion of that sort for me, and I found her a dead bore. She agreed with everything I said! I am sorry for such ladies, of course, but they are always so nervous, so afraid of offending! And that really doesn't suit me. Can't you think of something else, Mr Turner?'

'I'm afraid not. It won't be easy…' He frowned and thought. 'Unless… I wonder… It could be the very thing. Mrs Duval, I need to consult someone else before I say another word. You are happy to stay here at the Pulteney for a little? Could you leave it with me for a day or two?'

Caroline said, 'My dear sir, if it is true that the Tsar of Russia chose to put up at the Pulteney in preference to staying at St James's Palace, it would hardly be becoming in me to complain! But, in fact, I find the hotel extremely comfortable and very well appointed. Of course I can wait!' They went on to talk of other matters.

At the end of a short, but satisfactory discussion about the arrangements for financing Caroline's London stay, Mr Turner exclaimed, 'But I am remiss! We have been so occupied with business, that I have not asked about your journey north! Was it a success?'

'A great success,' said Caroline trying to inject some enthusiasm into her voice. 'My grandfather's...bequest is once again in place—with the Ainderbys in High Hutton.'

'Ah!' said Mr Turner in a satisfied tone. 'Mr Fennybright rather thought it would be there. Am I to understand that your late grandfather was an Ainderby?'

'Yes,' said Caroline abruptly.

'Quite!' Mr Turner's tone gave her the impression that he knew more about past events in Yorkshire than he was prepared to admit, and understood her reluctance to talk about it. 'And Lord Coverdale?' he went on. 'Is he well? Mr Fennybright tells me that his lordship has reached a measure of reconciliation with his daughter.'

'Yes, he has. They are both very happy.'

'And now it will be Lord Coverdale himself who will see to Miss Ancroft's début. A highly satisfactory conclusion. Tell me, what did you think of Yorkshire, ma'am?'

'It is very beautiful. But then so is Derbyshire. Did I tell you I came south through Buxton and Matlock?' To Caroline's relief Mr Turner rhapsodised about the beauties of the Derbyshire countryside for most of the time left, and did not refer again to Yorkshire, or to the families who lived there. He took his leave, promising to let her know more about her possible future home as soon as he had consulted another of his clients. Caroline admired his discretion, but was very doubtful if he would propose anything that would appeal to her. On the whole she would prefer to defy convention and live by herself in spite of society's possible frowns. It would not be the first time she had braved criticism. But she would wait and listen to Mr Turner's suggestion.

* * *

Mr Turner wasted no time. He made an appointment to see a certain Lady Danby who had recently come back to London and taken up residence in her house in Charles Street.

'What can I do for you, Turner?' she said briskly once they were settled. Lady Danby was a favourite of Mr Turner's. She belonged to one of the best families in Somerset, and though she wouldn't stand for any nonsense she was usually ready to listen to any reasonable suggestion or argument. She knew how to treat her visitors, too. On a small table at his side was a glass of first-class Madeira.

'Last week, when I expressed surprise at seeing you so soon in London again, Lady Danby, you said, I think, that you had found life in Somerset somewhat dull.'

'I certainly did! I don't mind telling you, Turner, I couldn't bear it a moment longer. I miss my goddaughter, d'y'see! When she married my nephew this summer I lost the company of both of 'em. Not that I'm complaining about the marriage! I was delighted at that. Perfect match! Jossie will keep Ivo in line, mark my words. There'll be no more scandals about my nephew! He's well and truly caught.'

'The new Lady Trenchard is a delightful young lady. It will surprise no one that Lord Trenchard is in love with her.'

'Absolutely besotted! They both are! And now he's taking her round the battlefields of Europe for a bridal trip!'

'Good heavens! What a very strange sort of thing to do! Lord Trenchard fought under Wellington, of course. I suppose it is natural for him to revisit the scene of the great victory at Waterloo. But what does his new wife think of it?'

'It was she who begged him to take her! I wouldn't be surprised if she knew more about that battle than anyone else, except perhaps the Great Duke himself!'

'Astonishing!'

'Not if you know my goddaughter. But I don't suppose you're here to gossip about my nephew and his wife, Turner. So, what *are* you here to say?'

'During that conversation, Lady Danby, you voiced a doubt that you would feel any better in London.'

'It was the lack of company! It's a strange thing. For years I lived quite happily on my own in Lyne St Michael, then my goddaughter came to live with me for just twelve months and now I find I dislike living alone! I suppose I miss all the bustle and activity of her début, too. What a time we had! Lyne St Michael was deadly dull without her, and I fear London might prove the same, but I have to give it a try. Why don't you tell me what you've come for? I can see you're working your way round to a suggestion that you don't think I'll like.'

'Have you ever thought of engaging a companion?'

'Never! Poor creatures, most of 'em. If that's your suggestion you can take it away again!'

'That isn't it exactly...' Mr Turner took the plunge. 'Among my other clients I have a highly respectable widow, who is alone in London...'

'And you want me to give her a home. No, Turner. Even if you aren't suggesting that I pay her, she would still be too dependent on me to hold her own in an argument. I'd be bored in a month!'

'Mrs Duval is a very wealthy woman.' He gave a dry cough. 'And I think she is not at all averse to expressing her views. I may say, she rejects the idea of a paid companion every bit as energetically as you yourself.'

'So what are you suggesting?'

'Mrs Duval needs somewhere to live. She wishes to experience something of London society.'

'Respectable, you said?'

'She belongs to one of the first families in the Caribbean. Her grandmother was a Willoughby. Her late grandfather was a prominent citizen of Kingston, Jamaica.'

'Jamaica, eh? That sounds interesting… What does she want?'

'Mrs Duval is not familiar with the views of our London *ton*. I have told her that society would not look favourably on a young and attractive woman living alone. If she will not engage a companion, then she ought to look for some congenial person who would be prepared to invite her to stay for a while.'

'Are you suggesting that I start letting out the rooms of this house?' Lady Danby demanded.

Mr Turner permitted himself a small smile. 'I would not dare to suggest anything of the sort, Lady Danby. There would be no question of money between you. Mrs Duval has a groom and a maidservant, and I dare say she would expect to pay for their keep. But for the rest she would be a charming and interesting guest. I really think you would enjoy her company.'

'Where is she staying at the moment?'

'At the Pulteney.'

'Well, that's a good enough address. If she can afford to keep herself, a groom and a maid at the Pulteney she cannot have any shortage of funds! I'll come to see her. Can you arrange a meeting? I'm not promising anything, mind!'

'I'll see to it straight away. Will tomorrow be too soon?'

'No, if I am to consider your mad scheme at all, then the sooner I meet your widow the better!'

* * *

After a little skirmishing on both sides, the two ladies found they had enjoyed their meeting—so much so that Lady Danby invited Mrs Duval for an indefinite stay, with the proviso that either lady could terminate the arrangement at any time. But the outlook was favourable. Lady Danby was soon treating Caroline like a young relative, calling her by her first name, and talking freely to her about the rest of the family. Both ladies had lively, independent minds, but they soon discovered that they liked each other's company. They were not always together, of course. Caroline had a small suite of rooms upstairs, which she could retire to whenever she wished, and Lady Danby kept one of the reception rooms downstairs for her own use. But on the whole the arrangement suited them both more than Mr Turner could have dreamed.

Lady Danby had a wide circle of acquaintances, who never left the capital except in the height of summer, and she took Caroline with her to the various parties, musical evenings and soirées held in their houses. Autumn in London was really quite pleasant. The streets and parks were not as crowded as they were in the season, but there were plenty of theatres, exhibitions, concerts and other amusements to go to, and riding or driving in the Park was very agreeable. Caroline joined in all this whirl of activity with enthusiasm, and managed to forget her strange sense of loss, sometimes for as much as a whole day. She made an impression, of course. Before very long the house in Charles Street had a good few callers looking for this ravishing newcomer to the London scene.

'It's almost like last season, when I had Jossie here!' said Lady Danby, sitting back in relief when the last of the four gentlemen to call that afternoon had just left. 'So many callers! I really cannot claim that life is dull since you've been here, dear Caroline.'

'I'm sorry, ma'am! Do these constant visitors tire you?'

'Not in the slightest! In fact, I think I enjoy them rather more than you. Did you have to be quite so offhand with Mr Powerstock?'

'Unfortunately, yes! I know the type. Young and impressionable. One word of encouragement from me and he will convince himself he is in love.'

'Is that such a bad thing?'

'Since I have no intention of marrying again, yes, I think it is. Mr Powerstock could be hurt. I prefer to flirt with gentlemen who know the rules of the game, Lady Danby. Of the four who were here this afternoon, Sir Anthony is much more to my taste.'

Lady Danby frowned. 'You should be careful, my dear. Sir Anthony Grainger may know the rules of the game, but I'm not at all sure he abides by them. He is not a desirable acquaintance. Ivo never approved of him.'

'From what I have heard, Lady Danby,' said Caroline with a grin at her hostess, 'your nephew was in no position to approve or disapprove of flirts! According to your own friends, he was the worst flirt in London!'

'My dear, you do him an injustice. Before his marriage, he was the worst flirt in *Europe*!' She started to laugh. 'I wish you could have been here when he suddenly discovered that he was in love for the first time in his life! The greatest flirt in Europe trapped by a nineteen-year-old innocent! London was stunned. It upset quite a few ladies, I can tell you! But then, Jossie is someone special.' She smiled reminiscently. Then she went on, 'Ivo may have been something of a rogue, Caroline, but he was always fair. You might say that the ladies he charmed were all well able to take care of themselves. I didn't approve of his antics, mind, but he never flirted with débutantes or indeed anyone else who was vulnerable. Sir

Anthony is quite different. He has no such scruples. Besides which, he's a gazetted fortune hunter.'

Caroline smiled and raised a sceptical eyebrow. 'You think me vulnerable?'

'Neither vulnerable nor even susceptible. What *have* you done with your heart, girl?'

'Oh, I threw that away a long time ago. It was too inconvenient. But since you say I am neither vulnerable nor susceptible, why are you concerned about Sir Anthony?'

'He's not someone you should trifle with. I notice, even if he does not, that under that charming air of attention you adopt towards him you are laughing at him in the same way as you laugh at all of them. He has the pride of the devil, Caroline. Be careful.'

'Well, since your brother has been kind enough to invite me to join you both in Somerset over Christmas, I shan't see very much of any of my beaux for a while. Perhaps Sir Anthony will have forgotten me by the time we return. Now, are you going to take me to this famous dressmaker of yours?'

'Caroline! Never let her hear you calling her a dressmaker! A mantua maker, perhaps, or a modiste… But never a dressmaker! There's no dressmaker born who could afford premises in Bruton Street. But you're right, we should think of going. We dare not be late. I would rather keep the Prince Regent waiting than I would Madame Rosa!'

Meanwhile, up in Yorkshire John had become deeply involved in Marrick's affairs. Mr Fennybright had been right when he had stressed how badly the estate needed a new hand to guide it, and it would take months, if not years, to restore it to its former splendour. But John had no desire to see it a museum piece, its old ways carefully preserved. A new age was beginning, and all the Ancroft possessions would have to respond to the demands of the times. That took study and consultation, visits of inspection and commissioning of designs… John was kept more than busy in the months that followed Caroline's departure.

He took time to cultivate his daughter, too, and was rewarded with an increasingly loving relationship with her. He devoted a great deal of time to her, riding with her, talking of his adventures abroad, about the Great Duke and others he had known, discussing books they had both read, listening to her… He gradually pieced together a picture of a lonely childhood spent in the limited company of his uncle, various nurses and, later, Mrs Abbington. Her mother did not seem to feature greatly in her accounts. Rose had apparently been an invalid for much of Harriet's childhood.

One day at the beginning of winter they had been for a long ride and had ended up looking down at Marrick from the hill above. John suddenly asked her, 'Why did you regard me with such horror the last time I came here?'

Harriet's reply was indirect. 'When I was a child I was terrified of my Uncle Coverdale. He spent all his time in his study, and it was always so gloomy in there. The curtains were never completely opened, even in summer. There was a portrait of his son on the wall beside him with a lamp in front of it, and he used to sit staring at the picture for hours. One day he stood me in front of it, and asked me if I knew who it was. I did, of course, but I wasn't sure what he wanted me to say. So I told him all of it—his son, Lord Philip Ancroft, my papa's cousin.'

'What did he say?'

'He got so angry! He shook me till my head rattled, and told me never to mention you again. That you had killed his son, and I was never to forget it. He threatened to put me in the deepest dungeons Marrick had, and leave me there for the rats to eat me, if I ever spoke to you or let you near me.'

'My poor child!'

'Papa, I used to have nightmares about those rats. I would dream that you came and I couldn't stop you from coming up to me, I couldn't even speak to you to tell you why you mustn't. Then Uncle Coverdale would suddenly appear and drag me away from you... I used to wake up screaming.'

John swore under his breath. 'I knew the loss of Philip had turned his mind. But not that it was as bad as that. I thought you were safe and happy at Marrick. Poor, poor Harriet!' He took Harriet and held her. She spoke from the shelter of his arms. 'Papa, Uncle Coverdale said something else. He said that I was the only bit of Philip he had left. What...what did he mean?'

There was a silence. John let Harriet go, then took her hands in his. 'I'll tell you. But first I want to say something else. Since coming back to Marrick, I've found that I really have a daughter after all, someone I can love and be proud of. It's been a wonderfully powerful consolation in a difficult time. Do you believe me?'

'But I'm Philip's child, aren't I? Not your daughter at all,' she said in a small voice.

'Your mother loved Philip very much, and if he hadn't been killed she would have married him. You were born of that love. But you're *my* daughter, Harriet. In far more than name.'

Harriet gave a contented sigh. 'I'm glad, Papa.' She hesitated, then said shyly, 'I thought at one time you liked

Mrs Duval, Papa. I should have liked it more than anything if you had married her.'

'No! That was impossible!'

'But why? She was always so kind and amusing. And I think she loved us both quite a lot. Think of all the things she did for us!'

'You're young, Harriet. You don't understand. Mrs Duval might have been everything you say, but her past life hardly made her a suitable person to be in charge of you.'

'How can you say that, Papa! She taught me so much about how I should behave.'

'Dancing and curtsies and the like?'

'Not just that! She explained about morals, too.'

'Morals? Caroline Duval?'

'Yes, Papa,' said Harriet gravely. 'Mrs Abbington and the Reverend Smythe have taught me the usual rules, but Mrs Duval explained them better.'

John stared at her. 'You'd better tell me what that woman has said to you!' he said grimly. If Caroline Duval had taught his daughter her own cynical scorn for the conventions…

But when Harriet told him he was amazed. The only part of what he might have called Caroline's own philosophy came in the form she had already told him—he remembered her saying it in the solar on the morning she left. *'Never cringe, never apologise. Hold on to the code you carry inside you…'* The curious thing was that, according to Harriet, the code emphasized honesty, pride in one's own integrity, loyalty, straight dealing—all qualities that he valued himself.

'There doesn't seem to be anything wrong with that,' he said gruffly. 'But I still think we are better off without Mrs Duval. So let me hear no more of her.'

* * *

But through all the work, all the discussions, he was conscious of a gap, a constant feeling that something precious had gone from his life. At first he thought it was his youthful dream of Gabriella, until one day he realised that she no longer meant anything at all to him, good or bad. Though he had clung to her memory for so many years, it was now on the way to being forgotten, simply a part of the dead past. But the gap, the sense of loss, remained. And now, though Harriet obeyed him, and never mentioned her name, Caroline Duval came back to haunt him. The curious thing was that his memory of her, of their whole acquaintance, was still as clear and as vivid in his mind as if it had happened the day before. He lay awake at night going over their time together, always ending with the evening of the day at High Hutton. That evening, the memory of all those years spent mourning Gabriella had eaten into him like a canker. And he realised that he had made Caroline Duval a scapegoat.

Maggie's reproaches the day she left now burned into his memory. Had her defence of Caroline been rooted in the *facts*, not a faithful servant's blind loyalty? In his futile anger at Gabriella's fallen image, had he rejected something much more real? Not a faultless idol, the object of veneration by an infatuated young man, but a woman of warmth and passion, a woman who was not afraid of the truth, who placed a high value on loyalty, keeping faith… Someone who would be a companion for a lifetime, a friend to laugh with… John punched his pillow and tossed restlessly in his bed. Damn Caroline Duval! She remained a tormenting enigma still!

Christmas came and went, and after Harriet's birthday in February they started to make plans for her entry into London society. Kate Calthorpe had already agreed to sponsor Harriet, and now wrote to offer her help in choosing a suitable wardrobe.

Though, from what I hear, Jossie Trenchard would be a better person for you to consult on that. Her come-out dresses are said to have been exquisite. I hope she will be in London when we are there. She and Ivo can't stay in Europe forever—they must run out of battlefields soon! But what do you think? They met Countess Leiken in Brussels, and she and Jossie got on enormously well. Ivo says he felt quite left out! Adam was wishing he could have been there to see it.

He was saying the other day what a splendid thing it would be if we were all to meet in London next year during the Season—you and Harriet, Ivo and Jossie, and Adam and I. Ivo and Jossie might have come down from their honeymoon cloud by then. I shall get Adam to write to Ivo to suggest it.

Baby Tom is robustly healthy and looking forward to showing you how well he can walk, my loving lord and master sends his salutes, and I send my best regards and love to your daughter. Tell her I cannot wait to meet her!

Yes, thought John, folding the letter with a smile. Kate Calthorpe was just as her brother had been, warm-hearted, impulsive and amusing, though with a good deal more sense. What would she have made of Caroline Duval? Or, indeed, what would she *make* of Caroline Duval! They were bound to meet. The world of London society was too small for it not to happen. Fennybright, who was under the impression that Mrs Duval's movements would be of interest to Lord Coverdale, had said in his last letter that Mrs Duval was intending to take part in the Season before returning to Jamaica. So she would be there. He would see Caroline Duval again. Would he find the answer to his enigma then?

Chapter Thirteen

The winter passed and spring came early. The daffodils in London's parks and gardens blew merrily in the winds of early March, inviting the world to come out and enjoy them. Society slowly returned to the capital to prepare for the great excitement of its year—the London Season. Hordes of servants arrived to open up the great houses round Berkeley Square, Grosvenor Square, Brook Street, Mount Street and the rest, and London suddenly grew busy. Caroline was enchanted. Jamaica and all its problems had never seemed less attractive. This England, so different from her Caribbean island, delighted her in all its moods and situations.

The new arrivals to the London scene were equally pleased with Mrs Duval. Charming, was the general verdict. As well as rich, of course. She was invited everywhere, and was frequently seen driving or riding in the park, sometimes with Lady Danby, or more often with an attentive gentleman at her side. The number of callers at Charles Street increased. Even mothers with daughters to marry off liked Mrs Duval—she was seldom seen with any of the young men they considered to be ideal husband material, but seemed to prefer the company of older, more experienced admirers. Soon Mrs Duval was an acknowledged success, and no function was considered complete without her.

Caroline came in from a drive one day to find Lady Danby reading her *Gazette*. She did this faithfully every day, eager to learn the names of the latest arrivals in town.

'Caroline! Come and sit down, my dear! Did you enjoy your drive? Who was it this time?'

'Sir Anthony, ma'am.'

Lady Danby frowned. 'He is still attentive? I hoped he would have forgotten you.'

'He might forget me, but I doubt he'd forget my fortune. You needn't be concerned. I think I have his measure.'

'Then why encourage him?'

'He's amusing. And not at all dangerous, I assure you. Unlike some others, he is most unlikely to break his heart over me. I quite enjoy fencing with him.'

'I don't suppose it's any use warning you again, but I think you may be mistaken. Sir Anthony Grainger is not as harmless as you believe.'

Caroline shrugged her shoulders. 'I can manage him. Who are the latest arrivals, ma'am?'

'A most interesting one!' She read out, 'Lord Coverdale has taken up residence in his house in Mount Street. His lordship is accompanied by his daughter, the Lady Harriet, who is to be presented to society this coming April.' She turned to Caroline. 'There! Do you know who that is? Before he succeeded to the title, Lord Coverdale was Colonel Ancroft, Ivo's commanding officer!' Fortunately Lady Danby was not paying attention to Caroline's reaction to her news. She was frowning down at the newspaper. 'It's strange, Ivo never said anything about a daughter. And there's no mention of a wife here...'

'Lord Coverdale's wife died some time ago. The family lived up north in Yorkshire while he was with the army,' Caroline said, keeping her voice cool. 'It's possible that your nephew wasn't aware of the daughter's existence.'

'You know them?'

'I spent some time in Yorkshire before I came to London,' said Caroline.

Lady Danby glanced at her curiously. Caroline's voice seemed rather constricted. 'I didn't know that. I thought you had come direct from Jamaica?'

'No, before he died my grandfather asked me to visit his family in High Hutton. That is quite near Marrick Castle, the Ancroft family seat. I went there first.'

'I see. So you knew the Ancrofts up in the north,' said Lady Danby, satisfied.

By this time Caroline had got her voice under control. 'Yes,' she said more naturally. 'I liked Harriet. She is a lovely girl, though rather shy.'

'I thought her father was a stiff sort of man. But Ivo liked him, and they became quite friendly after they had both left the army. I should imagine he'll be pleased his Colonel is in London again.' Lady Danby went on to talk once again about her nephew, and Caroline, who had heard some of these stories before, was left to her own thoughts.

She did not know how to feel about Lord Coverdale's arrival. She had known he would come eventually, and in the narrow world of London society their paths were bound to cross. How would he behave towards her? How was she to behave towards him—especially under the critical eye of the *ton*? She had discovered that the polite world in London was much like the polite world anywhere else. Scandal and gossip occupied a great deal of its time. What would the polite world here say if they even suspected what had passed between Lord Coverdale and herself? Even in the middle of her horror at the thought, Caroline could not suppress a grin. That would give the tabbies something to talk about!

Then she sighed. Their parting in Yorkshire had been very final, and their likely meeting in London would not change the situation. The sadness that still waited to pounce and twist her heart at unwary moments was not for this Lord Coverdale. However much she missed John Ancroft, whatever pangs she might suffer when she was reminded of him, the man she had begun to love had not really ever existed. When the Lord Coverdale mentioned in the *Gazette* came to London, she would have no need of him. He would simply be one man among many others, and not by any means the most handsome, or the most charming of them. London was full of attractive men, all eager to please her. And he would mean as much as any of the rest to her—which was nothing at all.

They finally met at a soirée given by Lady Marchant, though John had been observing Caroline for some minutes before they actually spoke to one another. He had seen her as soon as he entered the room. She was over by one of the windows attended by a number of admirers, looking even more lovely and more self-possessed than he remembered her. The ball at Marrick had been the only event during their extraordinary relationship when he had seen her dressed for a formal evening, and on that occasion, in a grey silk dress and a modest amount of jewellery, she had deliberately set out to underplay her appearance. Tonight she looked magnificent. The rich chestnut locks of her hair were dressed on top of her head *à l'antique*, held with a crescent of diamonds and pearls. One or two curls had escaped to frame her face, to fall behind to the nape of her neck. Diamonds sparkled in her ears and at her throat, and the lines of her superb figure were discreetly hinted at under the dull sheen of her ivory silk dress. For the first time John saw her in her proper setting, a beautiful and wealthy woman holding her own in the most demanding society in the world. The sight took his breath away.

His hostess came up and led him away to meet someone on the other side of the room, and during the conversation that followed he needed all the discipline he had learned during interminable social evenings spent with the Duke in Europe to disguise his complete lack of interest in what his companions were saying. As soon as he decently could, he made his excuses and escaped. He needed to be alone, to think, to sort out the rush of feeling he had experienced on seeing Caroline Duval again. His recent depression, the sense of loss, the feeling that something precious had disappeared, were all accounted for in that one vision. He now realised that all his efforts to forget Caroline Duval had been a waste of time. There was no enigma, not about her, nor about his feelings for her. She was everything and more that he wanted. She was *part* of him in a way that Gabriella had never been. The lift of her head, the lazily mocking expression, the deep voice, all so instantly familiar, all newly exciting. Even from such a distance, he could tell with no trouble at all what she was thinking as she stood there, enchanting her companions with her slow smile and wicked green eyes. Caroline was bored. If it was any comfort to him, she was as remote, as securely hidden behind her defences, as ever. No rivals there!

Lady Marchant came up to him again. 'Lord Coverdale! You're alone. What can I do to please you?'

'I should like to talk to the lady by the window, if I may.'

'Ah! You are not alone in wishing to meet her, Lord Coverdale. But I shall do as you ask.' She led the way through the crowded room...

The rooms were crowded, the atmosphere very warm. Caroline had dismissed her entourage and was standing by the open window enjoying a breath of air and a moment of quiet. She heard Lady Marchant's voice behind her.

'And this is our new star from the West Indies, Lord Coverdale,' said Lady Marchant. 'Mrs Duval, may I present Lord Coverdale?' Caroline turned slowly, her heart suddenly pounding. John was looking at her, his expression difficult to read.

'Mrs Duval and I already know each other,' he said calmly.

'Really?' said Lady Marchant, obviously intrigued. 'In Jamaica or England?'

'England,' said John at his most wooden. When neither party seemed inclined to enlighten her further, Lady Marchant said with a significant smile, 'In that case I shall leave you to talk. I see that poor Lady Parker needs a helping hand. Excuse me.' Neither of her guests noticed her going.

'You're looking well,' John said.

Caroline had control of herself. 'Thank you,' she said, in her slow, deep voice. 'London agrees with me, I think. How is Harriet?'

'A little overpowered by the city. I left her at home tonight in the care of Mrs Abbington. You were frowning just then. Was it wrong of me to say that we had already met?'

'Of course not. I wouldn't want you to be less than honest, Lord Coverdale,' she said ironically. 'And even if I was prepared to dissimulate, I couldn't ask it of Harriet. As a matter of fact, I have already told Lady Danby that I know you.'

'What did you say?'

'That I knew the Ancrofts in Yorkshire where I had been to visit my grandfather's family.'

'I see. No more?'

'I don't think there's a need to say more. After all, we're strangers, aren't we?'

'I don't feel like a stranger, Caroline. How can you call me one?'

'Very easily. We discovered that we hardly knew each other, as far as I remember. We certainly parted as strangers, and now we meet again as such. I remember promising you we would.'

'Caroline, I—'

'I really think it better if we're more formal, Lord Coverdale. I should prefer you to call me Mrs Duval. We meet, as I said, as comparative strangers, and I've no desire to cause gossip.'

'This is a different Caroline Duval from the one I knew. She was ready to shock the world.'

'That was a different world. At present I'm happy to be a respectable part of this one. Why the frown? Aren't you relieved to know that I'm now a reformed character?'

'I see,' he said grimly, unamused by the mockery in her voice. 'Well then, *Mrs Duval*, since it's obviously impossible to have a lengthy conversation here, may I call on you tomorrow?'

'I don't think—'

'I should like to bring Harriet to see you. She's feeling a little lost. Lady Calthorpe will take her under her wing when she arrives, but the Calthorpes have been delayed.'

'I see. Well, in that case…'

'Good! May I have your direction?'

'I'm staying with Lady Danby in Charles Street.'

Lord Coverdale looked surprised. 'Ivo's aunt? I know her quite well. There should be no difficulty about my visiting you.'

'Not from Lady Danby, no,' agreed Caroline pleasantly.

He ignored this. 'Is Ivo back yet?'

'Not yet, though he and his wife are expected any time now. Lady Danby talks a great deal about them. I have to say that I can't wait to meet the famous Lord Trenchard.'

He frowned and said disapprovingly, 'Ivo's wife is a lovely girl and he's deeply in love with her. You'll be disappointed if you're expecting to amuse yourself with a rake. He's reformed.'

So his opinion of her had not changed! She gave him a slow look through her lashes, her green eyes full of amusement. 'So am I,' she said solemnly. 'Had you forgotten? Lord Trenchard and I can compare notes.'

'He's a married man! Wouldn't that stop you?'

'Not at all! Married men are much more fun!'

'I refuse to believe you mean what you say, Caro—Mrs Duval!' he said angrily.

In a voice full of mock reproach she replied, 'Really, Lord Coverdale, I can't understand you! The last time we met you were angry because you believed I had seduced Robbie Coburn who, as far as I know, had never married. Now you're angry because I say I want to meet Lord Trenchard, who is! There's no pleasing you!'

'If, as I suspect, you are amusing yourself at my expense, then I warn you—'

'Yes, Lord Coverdale? What will you do?' She shook her head and said with a malicious smile, 'I don't think you had better punish me in your usual manner. That wouldn't do at all, not in Lady Marchant's drawing room. What *would* the *ton* say? Indeed, may I suggest you keep your voice a *tiny* bit lower? I'd hate anyone to overhear this conversation.'

'Dammit, that was not my usual manner!' he said in a low voice. 'I've already apologised for my behaviour that night, or have you forgotten?'

'No, I haven't forgotten exactly. But your apology wasn't exactly handsome. I wasn't sure afterwards whether you had meant it or not. You might try again, perhaps, if we are ever in a more private situation…'

'Caroline—'

'Though that's most unlikely. It wouldn't be proper, you see.' She sighed. 'Being a reformed character is sometimes *most* inconvenient.'

'I can see you don't mean to be serious,' he said, irritation in his voice. 'Let's hope Harriet finds you in a more amenable frame of mind tomorrow.'

'I assure you she will. She at least has a special place in my affection. And now I see Mr Powerstock coming towards us. I think we have talked for long enough. Till tomorrow, Lord Coverdale. At three.'

After he had gone Caroline felt exhausted, and as soon as she had managed to escape from Mr Powerstock she sought out Lady Danby and excused herself.

'I think I'll go back to Charles Street. I have the headache. It's the weather, I expect.'

'My dear child! I'm sorry to hear that. You'll take the

carriage? John Coachman can bring it back for me. Or would you like me to come with you?'

'No, no! I'd rather slip quietly away. But I'd be obliged if you would make my excuses to Lady Marchant. I can't find her at the moment.'

'Of course! Have a good night's rest, my dear.'

Caroline fetched her shawl. To leave Lady Marchant's house discreetly was impossible—no fewer than four footmen were waiting at the door. But once outside she congratulated herself on escaping without being observed by any of her admirers. She could not have borne a journey back to Charles Street in the company of any other person. She needed peace and tranquillity to persuade her unruly heart to settle down. All her brave thoughts had been quite useless. John Ancroft would never be just another one of the crowd to her. The mere sight of him had roused the sharp unhappiness she had tried so hard to forget. It had taken all her strength to keep a smiling mask in place, to treat his words with lighthearted irreverence when what she really wanted was to hurl reproaches at him for having betrayed the trust she had so stupidly placed in him, to berate him for throwing so much away. A useless exercise, if ever there was one!

But peace was to be denied her. The other door of the carriage opened and John Ancroft got in beside her.

'What are you doing here?' she demanded.

'Seeing you safely home,' he said briefly.

'But I don't need you!'

'I think you do. London streets are hardly safe at night. Don't bother trying to dissuade me, Caroline. I shall accompany you to Charles Street.'

She sat back against the squabs and said ungraciously, 'I suppose I can't throw you out, much as I should like to. But I don't have to talk to you.' She turned her head towards the window, and prayed that the darkness hid the sheen of tears in her eyes. Her time for recovery was not yet, it appeared.

His voice came out of the dark. 'Then I'll talk to *you*. You said I had not apologised handsomely enough. I'd like to remedy that. Caroline, I'm truly sorry for the way I behaved. I was driven mad that night with anger and humiliation. I had worshipped at a shrine for seventeen years, and suddenly the illusion had been ripped away and I was left with a very ugly reality. And…and in my madness I linked you and Gabriella together. Edmund's letter was the final straw. I didn't really believe the things I said to you, even while I was saying them, but it's true that I wanted to hurt you. And I did. Believe me, I bitterly regret what I did that night, how I behaved. Can't you forgive me?'

'You mustn't blame yourself too much, Lord Coverdale,' she managed to say coolly. 'Perhaps I was hurt, but that was entirely my own fault. I *let* you hurt me! It won't happen again. I believe I once said to you—I make many mistakes, but I do try not to make the same mistake twice.'

'What does that mean?'

'That for a while up in Yorkshire I was in danger of forgetting a resolve I made many years ago.'

'And that was?'

'That I would never again take *any* man seriously enough to be hurt by anything he did.'

'You haven't forgiven me, then?'

'I'm not sure what you want me to say. I understood at the time how you felt. I still understand. As I said afterwards, it shall be forgotten.'

'Then, can't we go back to the beginning? Start again?'

'You haven't been listening, Lord Coverdale. No!'

'Why not?'

Caroline took a deep breath and turned round. 'Circumstances threw us together on that damned road north. We both behaved uncharacteristically, and it was a mistake. It wasn't my style. When I said a few moments ago that what happened at Marrick should be forgotten, I meant *all* of it. The whole episode. I cannot imagine what I was thinking of to get so involved with you and your concerns.'

There was a short silence. Then he said, 'I won't accept this! I know there's something between us that not even you can ignore.'

'I can and will!'

The carriage was turning into Charles Street. John took her chin in his hand and drew it round. His lips close to hers, he said softly, 'Kiss me, and then tell me you can!'

This man needed a lesson, thought Caroline with a spurt of anger. How dare he think he has only to speak sweetly, cajole me with a kiss, and I'll come running! She looked into his eyes and he bent his head and kissed her. With the best will in the world her response was not quite as controlled as she would have wished. The devil was right, she thought with habitual self-mockery. There was something quite powerful between them. But if it *killed* her she would ignore it!

'You see?' he said in tones of satisfaction. 'Doesn't that prove it?'

Caroline leaned back, her green eyes glowing in the light of the flambeaux as they drew up to the house. 'Oh, John!' she breathed softly. 'That was wonderful! In fact...in fact, it was very nearly the nicest kiss I've had since coming to London.'

John complacent smile was transformed into angry

astonishment. The sight amused her so much that she was laughing as they got out of the carriage.

She was still laughing as they walked up to the door, and he gave her another furious look. But after a moment she pulled herself together to bid him goodnight, and he shook his head and smiled reluctantly in response. 'I'd forgotten your tricks,' he said in a resigned voice. 'No quarter given. But you haven't put me off, Caroline. I promise you I shall win!'

'I wouldn't wager too much on your chances if I were you, Lord Coverdale. That is, if you have marriage in mind. If I *was* looking for a husband, there are more than a few gentlemen in London who could be serious rivals. Even discounting those who are only attracted by my fortune. Goodnight.'

When John called at Charles Street the next afternoon he was once again perfectly self-possessed. Harriet was with him, and responded very affectionately to Caroline's greeting. Lady Danby sat back and listened with interest to Harriet's artless account of what had been happening at Marrick since Caroline's departure, and began to suspect that Caroline had been rather less than frank with her about her activities in Yorkshire. She was intrigued by Lord Coverdale's attitude to her friend, too. There was no doubt that he was interested in her. But he was also clearly on his guard, and after a few minutes Lady Danby came to the conclusion that there was much more between her guest and Lord Coverdale than either would admit. How delightful it would be if Ivo's Colonel had found the woman of his choice in Caroline Duval! She would make a wonderful Marchioness! Lady Danby began to think out ways of promoting the match…

Unfortunately, her happy plotting was interrupted by

the arrival of Sir Anthony Grainger. Sir Anthony had a decided air of fashion, and prided himself on being acquainted with anyone worth knowing in London. His family was an ancient one, and his estate in Kent was large, though somewhat run down. His first wife had brought him a fortune, but rumour had it that his expenditure so outstripped his income that his funds were now beginning to run out. If he was to keep the standard of living he had set for himself, said the gossips, he had an urgent need to find a second wife as well endowed as the first. But if Sir Anthony was worried it did not show in his manner.

'My dear Lady Danby,' he said in his fashionable drawl, bending low over his hostess's hand. 'I have no need to ask after your health—I can see you are flourishing! Your stay in the country obviously agreed with you.'

'Thank you, Sir Anthony,' said Lady Danby with something of a snap.

'And Mrs Duval! Lovely as ever!'

Caroline was conscious of something like a snort from the man standing next to her. She said hastily, 'You are always very kind, sir. May I present you to Lord Coverdale and his daughter, Lady Harriet Ancroft?'

'Grainger,' said John with a curt nod.

'I already have the pleasure of Lord Coverdale's acquaintance, Mrs Duval. But not that of his charming daughter…Lady Harriet?'

Harriet coloured at the admiration in Sir Anthony's light blue eyes, but after a quick glance at Caroline she smiled politely and gave him a perfectly judged curtsy. Caroline glanced at John and they shared a brief moment of pride.

'How may I help you, Sir Anthony?' said Lady Danby briskly.

'I fear my mission is in vain. I was hoping to invite Mrs Duval for a drive, but I see she is occupied this afternoon. May I hope for better luck tomorrow?'

Before Caroline could speak, John said, 'Unfortunately Mrs Duval has just promised to take my daughter to… to…'

'Hampton Court,' said Lady Danby.

'Ah, yes! I knew it was one of the palaces, but couldn't remember which,' said John blandly.

'Did you really, Mrs Duval?' exclaimed Harriet. 'I didn't know. Oh, thank you! I've wanted to go there ever since I heard of the maze. I long to see it!'

Caroline gave first John, then Lady Danby a very straight look, then smiled apologetically at Sir Anthony. 'Perhaps the day after?' she said.

In the face of Lady Danby's support Sir Anthony could hardly say he was undeceived by Lord Coverdale's manoeuvre. He put a good face on it and arranged with Caroline to meet her in two days' time, and shortly afterwards took a somewhat cool leave of his hostess.

'What do you think you're doing?' demanded Caroline as soon as Sir Anthony had gone.

'Trying to save you from yourself!' said John. 'I'm surprised you want to spend your time on that second-rater!'

'When I want your interference I'll ask for it!' she began hotly. She stopped and looked at Lady Danby, who was observing this exchange with interest. Caroline took a breath and after a pause said thoughtfully, 'Why didn't I think of it before? Of course, I could ask Sir Anthony to escort us! To…to…Hampton Court!'

'I shall be your escort,' said John. 'I'm not letting a well-known fortune hunter loose on my daughter! Or anyone else I care for.'

'Was I wrong?' asked Harriet anxiously. 'Do you not wish to go after all, Mrs Duval?'

Caroline went over and took her arm. 'Of course I do!'

'Then I should like Papa to come, too.' She smiled innocently into Caroline's eyes. 'You and I, and Papa.'

Caroline turned somewhat desperately to Lady Danby. 'Wouldn't you like to come, too, ma'am? The drive should be a pleasant one.'

Lady Danby could have laughed aloud at the renewed anxiety on Harriet's face. Lady Harriet Ancroft was not quite the mouse she seemed! The little minx was apparently as eager as she was to promote a match between these two! She would wager a substantial amount that at some point in the expedition the girl would see to it that Caroline and her father were left *à deux*. Of *course* she didn't want anyone else along to play chaperon. So she said obligingly, 'It's kind of you to ask, my dear Caro, but I'm already engaged.' She added innocently, 'I could come on the drive the next afternoon with you and Sir Anthony, if you wish?'

Lady Danby was perfectly correct. Harriet disappeared into the maze at Hampton Court with an airy wave of the hand and, unknown to the two she left behind, armed with a plan of its layout. She had no intention of accidentally finding her way out too soon. The other two sat down to wait on a bench under a large oak tree. The spot was quiet, removed from the busy pathways of the park.

'Did you plan this, Lord Coverdale?' asked Caroline calmly.

John began to chuckle. 'I wish I had! But the credit lies with my daughter alone. With a little help from your hostess.'

'I can't imagine what they hope to gain from it.'

'I'd have thought that was obvious! To leave us to have a talk. It was clearly impossible yesterday.'

Caroline considered him with her habitual expression of secret amusement. 'And what does Lord Coverdale wish to say? I do so hope he is not about to remind me again of what a dissolute creature I am!'

He became serious at once. 'Please, Caroline! I beg you! I've thought hard about what you said the other night. I'd like to talk to you more about it. Don't you think you owe it to me?'

'In what way?'

'Because our acquaintance has been such an extraordinary one! We both know so much about one another, in spite of the barriers we have both put up against the rest of the world. We can't simply deny that knowledge exists.'

'I can and will!'

'I say you cannot. The events of that journey north did away with pretence, you know they did. You say you can't forgive yourself for becoming involved, but you could no more help getting involved than I could. In Buckden you witnessed my most private feelings, feelings I had kept hidden for years. You were there at High Hutton when I discovered that Gabriella, whose memory I had venerated for years, hadn't been worth a single moment's grief. On that terrible evening at Marrick, you experienced the very worst of my nature. You have seen me as no other creature in this world has seen me, the best, and the worst of me. Don't you think you owe me a chance to plead my case? Can't you drop those defences of yours with me in return?'

Her expression changed. She looked down at her hands. 'Very well. I'll be serious. For a while I thought I *could* abandon my defences with you. Up to the moment you showed me how little you really thought of me.'

'When I attacked you?'

'No. When you believed all those things Edmund had written about me. I knew how you must be hurting, how angry you must be about Gabriella. And I had come down that evening ready to comfort you in any way I could. Freely. In *any* way. You wouldn't have had to coerce me, I was prepared to offer you whatever kind of comfort you wanted.' She looked at him then, the green eyes for once dark and unguarded, and he could see through to the truth in them.

'And I threw it away,' he said heavily.

'I saw that you really believed I could have seduced Robbie Coburn. I had thought you different, that you would know that to be impossible. But you believed it, just like all the others. That was the moment I decided I had made a mistake.'

There was a short silence. Then he said, 'Tell me. At one point—before the ball at Marrick—I was almost sure I wanted to marry you. I thought we could even learn to love one another. If I had asked you then, before we went to High Hutton, what would you have said?'

She jumped up and started walking away. 'Why are we talking of this? It's in the past! And best left there!'

He caught up with her. 'Is it really too late, Caroline? If I ask you to marry me now, could you bring yourself to agree?'

She stopped short. 'No! I would not!'

'You don't love me? Not in the slightest?'

'That's not the question! Whether I love you or not doesn't matter. I don't trust you!'

'Would you marry anyone else?'

'No, of course not!'

'So there is some feeling there for me! Caroline, I promise you, if it's the last thing I do, I'll teach you to trust me again.'

She looked at him then, her expression openly derisive. 'And how will you begin to do that, Colonel Ancroft? Even supposing I let you near enough to try!'

In the carriage on the homeward journey Harriet chattered gaily about the people she had met in the maze. But from time to time she looked anxiously at the two people she loved best. To judge by their faces, their afternoon talk didn't seem to have done much good. And her concern increased during the days that followed.

Caroline went out with Sir Anthony the next afternoon, and quite frequently after that. In the evenings, too, she seemed to be encouraging him, allowing him more than the conventional number of dances, and flirting with him outrageously in the interval. Soon odds were being offered in the London clubs that Sir Anthony had at last succeeded in finding his second rich wife.

Lady Danby was seriously worried. Caroline was deaf to pleas and warnings alike, and her assurances that she had no intention of ever marrying Sir Anthony were little consolation. When Lord Coverdale called one afternoon, only to find Caroline out with Sir Anthony yet again, Lady Danby invited him to sit down and talk to her. She wasted no time in coming to the point.

'Lord Coverdale, am I right to suspect that you have an interest in Mrs Duval?'

John stiffened. 'I fail to see—'

'This is not the time for conventional politeness! I have become very fond of her myself, and at the moment am considerably worried about her! She is running a quite extraordinary risk. Sir Anthony Grainger—'

'I know something of his character, ma'am.'

'You need not be afraid she will marry him!'

'I am not. At the moment Mrs Duval is determined to marry no one. When she changes her mind, it will be to marry me.'

'Excellent!'

He smiled and said wryly, 'I am glad you approve, Lady Danby. As you've probably guessed, there's something of a history between Mrs Duval and myself, which makes matters complicated, but in the end I hope to persuade her. Meanwhile, I'm aware of the risks she runs with Grainger, but if she will not listen to you, then she will certainly not listen to me.'

'She has raised Sir Anthony's hopes too high, and indeed, society, too, expects an announcement soon. Caroline hasn't realised what it will do to him when she rejects him—as we know she will. The loss of a rich bride will be nothing compared with the loss of face he will suffer. And that is something Sir Anthony Grainger's pride won't tolerate. He'll seek some sort of revenge, I know he will.'

'I agree. It's also worth remembering that almost the only thing which keeps Sir Anthony's creditors at bay is the prospect of his marriage to a very wealthy woman. For this reason I do try to keep an unobtrusive eye on them both, but for God's sake don't tell Caroline this!'

Lady Danby was happier after this conversation. Lord Coverdale's hopes that Caroline would marry him heartened her. She had already suspected that Caroline was running away from something, and now she knew what it was. Caroline was clearly more attracted to Lord Coverdale than she would admit, and she was afraid. Her stubborn resolve not to marry was being tested to its limits, and her persistent cultivation of Sir Anthony was no more than a desperate attempt to break that attraction. What puzzled Lady Danby was why she should wish to do so!

She decided to tackle her guest one day, and broke one of her house rules and entered Caroline's room without being asked. Caroline was surprised but invited her to sit down.

'My dear, can't you tell me what is behind all this?' Lady Danby asked when they were settled. 'I don't believe you would behave as you are doing without a very good reason.'

Caroline stiffened but said coolly, 'I'm not sure what you mean.'

'Why, your constant appearances in the company of Sir Anthony Grainger.'

'Are you trying to warn me yet again?'

'Against Sir Anthony? I know better than to try. But I am now concerned for *you*. If you carry on encouraging Sir Anthony without eventually becoming engaged to him, you risk being ostracised from Society—not because the *ton* approve of the man himself, but they approve even less of an outright flirt. A jilt. There, I've been frank with you. I hope you appreciate my motive. And now I'll repeat my question. Why are you doing it? Is it because you're running away from a different engagement?'

'What do you mean?' asked Caroline sharply.

'Caroline, I've seen a good few love affairs in my time, including the one between Ivo and Jossie this last year. That had its moments of drama, I assure you! So I am not without experience in these matters. I suspect that you are in love. Not with Anthony Grainger, but with John Ancroft. Now tell me I'm an interfering old woman!'

Caroline was silent for a good few minutes. Then she

said, 'I do love John Ancroft, yes. But I won't marry him!'

'So he *has* asked you?'

'Yes.'

'Then why? Apart from the fact that he must be one of London's most eligible bachelors, he is a fine man! You've said you love him. Why on earth won't you marry him?'

'If I loved him less I should be more likely to consider marrying him! I was hurt quite badly once before by a man I thought I adored, Lady Danby. I won't risk it again.'

'How old were you that first time?'

'Seventeen.'

'Then you are being quite extraordinarily foolish. Seventeen is no age to throw away all the richness that marriage and the love of a decent man can bring. Marry him, Caroline!'

'I won't! I thought he knew me, but he betrayed me!'

'Did he go off with another woman?'

'No! But he believed that I had seduced another man!'

'He was probably wild with jealousy at the time. Caroline, you're too sensible to condemn a good man for one mistake. They're too rare to waste.'

Caroline was silent, and Lady Danby left her alone to think over what she had said.

This conversation had its effect, though the end result was not one which would please Lady Danby. At first Caroline stubbornly dismissed her advice. Lady Danby didn't know the full story. She was wrong in her assumptions. John had not been jealous, his behaviour had been far from that of a decent man... There was no reason to listen to any of it! But she was more influenced by Lady Danby's words than she wanted to admit, and when she found herself wondering whether she *had* judged John too harshly and started to imagine what marriage to him would be like, she panicked. Instead of softening towards John, she pushed the thoughts angrily away, and flirted all the more outrageously with Sir Anthony.

An end had to come. Eventually the time came when Sir Anthony decided he could safely declare himself. During an afternoon drive in his phaeton he offered Mrs Duval his hand, his heart, and his ancient name.

Chapter Fourteen

To do her justice, Caroline had never intended her affair with Sir Anthony to get as far as an actual offer. She thought he had accepted the fact that she was not interested in marriage, and would therefore not risk making one. But she saw now that she had made a mistake. His ardour, or more probably the pressure of his financial commitments, had driven him to disregard her many warnings and she was faced with the embarrassing task of refusing him.

'You do me a great honour, Sir Anthony,' she said slowly. 'I truly hadn't realised that you intended to spring this on me so suddenly…'

'Oh come, my dear!' he said. 'You needn't play feminine games. You're not a blushing débutante. I've had a great deal of encouragement from you in the past few weeks. Don't pretend you're surprised.'

'But I am! I thought I had made it clear that I had no intention of marrying again.'

'I know you said so. But I couldn't possibly take such a ridiculous notion seriously. And I still don't. As my wife, you will have a position in the world that no widow could aspire to. My name is one of the proudest in England.'

'I...I'm sorry if you feel you've been deceived, but I can't accept your very flattering offer. I assure you that, when I told you I would never marry again, I meant every word.'

'But the whole of London expects you to marry me!'

'Then the whole of London will be disappointed!'

He drew in a breath. His face was normally pale, but now it was ashen. For a moment she was frightened, as he gave her a glittering stare, and the fingers holding his whip tightened. But after a moment's visible effort, he smiled ruefully and said, 'I can't deny this is a blow. I've been too hasty, I see. I thought we knew each other well enough for me to hope... No matter. Perhaps I will persuade you to change your mind later.'

'I am quite sure you won't, Sir Anthony. I repeat. I will never marry again.'

'But you—' he began again angrily. Then he stopped short, and smiled again. 'You will have to forgive me. Of course, I must accept what you say. For the moment, at least.' He looked at her and added lightly, 'What an awkward situation! I dare say you would prefer me to take you back to Charles Street?'

'Thank you,' said Caroline, feeling very uncomfortable, and wondering about that first reaction of his. She was sure it had been one not of disappointment, but of fury. The blow to his pride had been immense. But as they drove back he resumed the light-hearted, urbane manner that she had always enjoyed and she was reassured. As they drew to a halt in Charles Street he spoke more seriously again.

'I trust my impulsive actions haven't destroyed our

friendship, Caroline. I've enjoyed your company more than I can say during these past weeks.'

'As I have enjoyed yours. But I think it would be wiser to—'

'Please!'

She looked at him. He seemed quite calm, but his hands were trembling. He saw her glance at them and smiled ruefully. 'You can't blame me for feeling somewhat disappointed that the most beautiful woman in London has turned me down. If you will grant me your occasional company I shall promise not to importune you again. Not till you show me you have changed your mind.'

Somewhat reluctantly she said, 'Very well. As long as you understand, Sir Anthony, that my decision won't change. And, in fairness to both of us, I think we should see rather less of each other.'

'Of course! Good! Good!' He spoke almost disjointedly, and after seeing her down from the phaeton he drove off again without saying anything more.

The gossips soon observed the change in Mrs Duval's behaviour. She seemed to be perfectly friendly with Sir Anthony Grainger, but spent altogether less time with him. The odds on an engagement between them lengthened considerably, and Sir Anthony came in for a fair number of sly digs. He took it all in surprisingly good part. Caroline was impressed and said so to Lady Danby.

'Beware the smile on the face of the tiger,' said that good lady. 'Leopards don't change their spots!'

'I suppose you'll tell me next to watch out for the snake in the grass,' laughed Caroline. 'Well, before you bring out any more of your menagerie, I shall tell you that I shall be as prudent as you could wish. Though I really don't think there's any need. Sir Anthony was surprisingly disappointed, but took my decision very well, and his behaviour since has been exemplary.'

'Ha!' was all Lady Danby could find to say.

The Calthorpes arrived in London and Lady Danby invited them to an evening party. Caroline was introduced to a tall, hazel-eyed man with a most attractive smile. His wife was also tall, dark-haired, and at first sight only moderately good-looking. But when she smiled, which was often, her whole face lit up, the unusual golden-brown eyes glowed and she was suddenly beautiful. It was obvious that they and Lord Coverdale were very good friends, and Caroline remembered that Adam Calthorpe was the man in whom John had confided when they were both wounded in Spain.

John seemed somewhat preoccupied, and spent some time talking quietly to Lady Danby on the other side of the room. At last Caroline couldn't resist going over to ask him if there was anything wrong.

'Wrong? Why should there be?' he asked.

'Don't fob me off, John. I'd like to help if you have a problem. Harriet looks well enough—in fact she gets prettier every time I see her—but is she happy?'

'Perfectly! Especially now that Kate is here to see to her.'

It was unworthy, Caroline told herself, to feel a pang of jealousy. It had always been intended that Lady Calthorpe would sponsor Harriet during the season. In any case she herself was hardly suitable!

John went on, 'Kate has arranged to take Harriet to Lady Danby's dressmaker tomorrow.'

'*Modiste*, John. *Modiste.* Dressmakers don't live in Bruton Street.'

'You know her?'

'Madame Rosa made the dress I'm wearing tonight.'

'In that case, I can have no doubt that Harriet will be well served. You look very lovely in that dress.'

'Good God! Is that a compliment? A genuine, undiluted compliment? This is a rare event.'

He smiled. 'I often think them. I'm not always sure how you'll receive them, so I say nothing.'

Caroline was disarmed. 'A woman is always pleased to hear she is looking her best, sir! But this doesn't put me off. What were you saying to Lady Danby that made you both so serious?'

'I…I was reassuring her. About Harriet's dressmaker. *Modiste!*'

He refused to say any more. Caroline was not satisfied, but when she saw the Calthorpes regarding the two of them with keen interest she had to let the matter drop.

In fact, John had been telling Lady Danby that Sir Anthony's affairs were now in a desperate state. The word in the clubs was that his creditors were closing in on him.

'What happens if he can't pay?' asked Lady Danby.

'If he can't fob them off, and I doubt very much that he can, he will go to prison. Unless he flees the country first.'

'Let's hope he decides to run,' she said. 'We'll be well rid of him.'

'My concern is what he might do before it comes to that. Caroline is a very rich woman.'

'You know he has already asked her and she refused?'

'How on earth should I know that?'

'I'm sure I don't know, Lord Coverdale, but it has happened.'

'So, Grainger now knows she won't marry him, does he?'

'I told you she wouldn't.'

'So you did—and I agreed. Does she realise that she's now at risk? I've told you before, Grainger can be a very dangerous man when cornered.'

'Oh, come! You're being too melodramatic. What can he possibly do?'

'I don't know, but I don't trust him. He still sees Caroline, doesn't he? And she can be a touch foolhardy, wouldn't you say? Scornful of risks?'

She stared at him, then said, 'I'll try to keep an eye on her. It won't be easy.'

'Make sure she keeps Bellerby with her when she goes out.'

'Of course!'

The next afternoon Caroline was walking back along Piccadilly from Hatchard's bookshop when Sir Anthony Grainger drew up beside her.

'Good afternoon!' he called. 'May I take you up?' Caroline hesitated and he added, 'I wish to consult you. Come with me for a short drive in the park and then I promise to deliver you safe and sound to Charles Street in good time to change for dinner.'

She made up her mind. 'Very well!'

It took a minute or two for Sir Anthony to give the reins to his groom and jump down, and Joseph, who had escorted her to the bookshop, took the opportunity to protest. 'It's all right, Joseph!' she said. 'What can anyone do to me in broad daylight, on one of the busiest thoroughfares in London? I really don't think I need you!'

Sir Anthony appeared at her side. 'Ready?' he asked with a smile.

Joseph was still doubtful He stood watching them drive away with a frown on his face.

* * *

'Surly devil, your groom!'

'Joseph is a very faithful servant, Sir Anthony. But I don't think he likes you!'

'The likes or dislikes of a servant are of small consequence!' he said. 'Are you comfortable?'

'Thank you, yes. What was it you wanted to ask me?'

'I've been interested for some time in moving to Jamaica. I understand that life is comparatively cheap there, and, as you've probably heard, it may shortly become necessary for me to leave England. A friend of mine has sent me some views of a certain property on Jamaica. They are very beautiful, but since I have never been there I have no idea whether they are authentic. Could you have a look at them for me?'

'Of course. Where is the property? In Kingston itself?'

'Just outside. Will you come with me now to see these pictures?'

'I...er...I'm not sure... That is—'

'My dear Caroline! I'm asking you out of friendship. I have promised not to ask anything more until you are ready to listen. Surely we can deal sensibly with this?'

'I just wish Joseph was—'

'Shall we return for him? Or, I have a better idea! I could send for him as soon as we arrive. Would that do? Would you come with me if I promised to do that?' He smiled at her so indulgently that she felt she was being too prudish for words.

'Yes,' she said. 'That would do very well. Where are these pictures? In Curzon Street?'

'No, I have them in my other house.'

Caroline hesitated. 'Your other house?'

'It's in Kensington, just a short drive through the park, as I said. The whole excursion shouldn't take long.'

Caroline knew Kensington, which was a pretty little

village not far out of the centre, and a fashionable place to live. She was reassured. 'Where did you say the place in Jamaica is?' she asked as they set off at a good pace through Hyde Park. 'Outside Kingston? Do you have its name?'

'You shall see,' he said. 'I think you will agree that it is extremely beautiful.'

Meanwhile Lady Danby was busy with a houseful of guests. Just after Caroline had left for Hatchard's bookshop, Ivo and Jossie Trenchard had finally arrived in London. A message had been sent to let Lord Coverdale know, and he, Harriet, and the Calthorpes had come round immediately. The reunion between the three veterans of Waterloo was complete, and the house was buzzing with excited questions, exclamations and greetings.

When Joseph arrived on the scene he had difficulty in reaching Lord Coverdale, but as soon as John heard that Mrs Duval's groom was outside he made some hasty excuses and hurried out to see him.

'What is it?'

'He's taken her, Colonel! And I don't trust him to bring her back safe.'

John didn't waste time asking who 'he' was. 'What the devil are you doing here?' he asked angrily. 'Why aren't you with her?'

'She said she didn't need me—he were only taking her for a drive round the park.'

'The fool! I could wring her neck!'

'Best do that after she's safe, Colonel,' Joseph said stolidly. 'I wasted some time going to look for you at Mount Street first. They've been gone half an hour already.'

'Go round to the stables. Get some horses. It might all

be above board, Joseph, in which case we shall meet them in the park. If not... We shall pay a visit to Curzon Street. I'll make my excuses.'

John went back into the room and began to explain why he had to leave so suddenly.

'Hold on, Colonel! Is someone in trouble?'

'I don't know, Ivo.'

'It's Mrs Duval,' said Lady Danby, sounding very worried. 'We think she may be in some danger.'

'It's probably nothing at all, ma'am,' John said encouragingly. 'Grainger could hardly abduct her in broad daylight.'

'Grainger!' exclaimed Ivo. 'That villain! He's capable of anything! I'm coming with you. I'd enjoy a ride in the park, especially if it means I can spike Grainger's guns.'

'I'm coming, too,' said Adam. 'If gossip is to be believed, Grainger's a desperate man at present. I don't think Mrs Duval understands how dangerous he can be.'

John turned to the manservant in the door. 'Get two more horses. Fresh ones. These gentlemen are coming with me.'

A minute or two later the three men left the ladies behind and joined Joseph Bellerby outside.

'Well!' said Jossie Trenchard. 'Will one of you please tell me who this Mrs Duval is? She sounds a complete nitwit to me! Why is everyone so concerned about her?'

Lady Danby exchanged a glance with Kate Calthorpe. 'She comes from Jamaica. A widow. She's staying with me at present.'

'There's something you're not telling me, Godmother! Out with it!'

'We think that the Colonel may be...may be interested in her,' said Kate. 'You'd like her, Jossie. She's certainly not a nitwit.'

'Colonel Ancroft! In *love*? I can't believe it—I've obviously stayed away too long! But wait! Mrs Duval isn't by any chance an *elderly* widow, is she? Did she go north with the Colonel last July?'

'Yes,' said Lady Danby. 'At least, she was in the north. With the Colonel. But she's far from elderly.'

'She's a beauty,' said Kate. 'And Lady Harriet is very fond of her, too. I do hope they find her soon.'

'I wonder…' said Jossie, her sea-green eyes glowing. 'I wonder…' She saw the anxiety on her godmother's face. 'You needn't worry,' she said confidently. 'Those three men dealt with Napoleon. They're not going to let a piece of vermin like Sir Anthony Grainger beat them. But I can't wait to see the Colonel's "elderly widow".'

'She isn't elderly, Jossie. I've just told you.'

'She was when the Colonel first met her.' But when the other two asked her what she meant, Jossie only laughed. 'Don't you remember, Godmama? Ivo told us about her last year.'

The four men found no trace of Sir Anthony's carriage in the park. 'Then it's Curzon Street,' said Ivo.

'Mount Street first. To fetch some pistols. It won't take long.' John led the way to his house, where they armed themselves. Then they went round to Grainger's house in Curzon Street. A band of creditors was waiting outside the front door. John made his way through them and hammered on the door. It was opened by a harassed manservant. 'I've told you,' he said, 'Sir Anthony is not at home!' He made to shut the door, but John put his foot in it.

'In that case, where is he? I'm not one of his creditors. I shan't dun him. Just tell me where I can find him. In fact, I have a guinea or two right here. For you, if you can tell me where to find your master.' The man eyed the gold held in front of him. He drew John into the hall and whispered, 'He went for a drive in the park, but he has a house on the road to Kensington. Grainger Lodge. He might have gone there to avoid this lot.'

'Thank you!' John passed over the money and pushed his way out again.

'He's not there,' he shouted. 'You're wasting your time. Come on, Ivo, Adam. We'll come another day.'

As soon as they were out of sight of the horde, John said tersely, 'Kensington. Grainger Lodge. Come *on*!'

They galloped off again in the direction of the park.

Grainger Lodge lay on the Bath Road some way out of Kensington Village itself. It was quite a substantial house, set in a small park, but somewhat isolated. Remembering the picturesque village street and the pretty houses crowded together, which she had seen before, it was not quite what Caroline had imagined. There was also a remarkable lack of staff, a surly-looking fellow keeping the door the only visible servant. Caroline stopped at the door and turned to her companion. 'Who will fetch Joseph Bellerby?' she demanded.

'I promise to send my groom as soon as you give me the word. He could be back with your servant in half an hour or so.' Sir Anthony laughed. 'Surely you can trust me to restrain myself for such a short time?'

'I'll make sure you do! I'll be frank with you, Sir Anthony. This is not at all what I expected. I don't like the absence of other people around. And I think I've been unwise to accompany you to this house when my friends have no idea where I am. I think I should like you to take me back!'

Sir Anthony looked at her with surprised reproach. 'My

dear girl, don't be so foolish! What have I done to give you such distrust of me? I thought we were still friends, Caroline. And I was so looking forward to having your opinion.'

Caroline eyed him thoughtfully. It was true, he had behaved very well over the last few weeks. It couldn't have been easy for him. She had hurt him once. Perhaps, after all, she owed him something. 'Very well. But I want you to send for Joseph immediately!'

'It shall be done.' He went back to his groom and said a few words. The man nodded and led the horses away. 'Now, let me show you this picture.'

'I thought you said they were views.'

'There is only one that matters. You will be astonished how lovely it is! Come this way! It's in the saloon. The light is better there.' He led the way through to a large, airy room that overlooked the back of the house. At any other time Caroline would have been full of admiration for its outlook. But her eyes were fixed on an easel that stood by one of the windows, placed to get maximum light. The picture on it was draped in a cloth.

'Would you like to draw aside the cloth, Caroline?' The anticipation in his smile made her uneasy.

'No, you do it,' she said. He stepped up and removed the drapery. Caroline caught her breath. The painting on the easel was not a landscape. It was a nude portrait of her, one of a number of such pictures painted in New Orleans, most of which her grandfather had bought up and burnt. After a moment's silence she asked curtly, 'Where did you get this?'

'Beautiful, isn't it? As a view of Jamaica it could hardly be surpassed.'

'Where did you get it?'

'My cousin Edmund sent it. You realise, of course, that

it's a copy, a copy of the one in a certain house in Kingston. I understand men over there pay large sums of money to see the original. Do you think they might do the same here for this copy? Or shall I keep it for my own delectation?'

'*Your* cousin Edmund?'

'And yours. Edmund Willoughby's father married a Grainger—my father's sister.'

Caroline turned to him, the picture forgotten for the moment. '*You* were the one who helped him in his attempts to steal the chalice!'

'Poor Edmund! He didn't do very well in spite of all my efforts. Still, he did send me this after he got back. However, I'm not yet sure what I should do with it. What do you suggest?'

Caroline was herself again. 'You can do what you damned well like with it, Sir Anthony! As a piece of art it isn't worth the canvas it's painted on. A very poor copy!'

'So you wouldn't mind if I displayed it? Not even if it proved embarrassing to your friends?'

Caroline hesitated. Then she said, 'What do you want?'

'That's better! I want what I've always wanted from you. Marriage.'

'I can't believe you love me.'

The mask dropped for a moment from Sir Anthony's face. 'Please!' he exclaimed with contempt. 'Let's not deal in fantasy. If I weren't in the direst necessity I wouldn't for one moment consider marrying the whore who posed for that picture, or was guilty of some of the other antics Edmund told me about. Till now I have been proud of my family name. But alas! I need your fortune. Necessity forces undesirable bedfellows on us all!'

'How right you are! Let me be quite clear on this. You

are threatening to publish this picture unless I marry you. Your…honourable name doesn't object to blackmail?'

'I tried to persuade you first, remember.'

'And I gave you my answer. It is still the same.'

'You deceived me,' he said with sudden passion. 'You led me to believe you would marry me!'

'I did not!'

'You made me a laughing-stock! And you're going to pay for that! One way or another, you'll pay! And I promise you! Unless you agree to marry me—immediately—the world will see that picture!'

'You may be prepared to marry a whore for her money. But I refuse to marry a liar and a cheat, a fraud, and a loser! You haven't the nerve to show that painting, Sir Anthony! My friends would soon have you despatched and you know it!'

Her words stung him. He snarled, 'I doubt your friends will be so anxious to defend you when they see that picture and hear of the tricks you got up to before you came to England. As soon as those stories get out—and they will—there isn't a soul in London who would have anything to do with you!'

'You're wrong! There's one who knows everything you know about me, and more, too, and he would marry me tomorrow if I agreed. No, you can do your worst! I'm not afraid of a cockroach such as you!'

He went white. A new, more vicious, tone entered his voice as he said, 'Are you too stupid to understand? You haven't a choice. If neither persuasion nor blackmail will work, there are other ways of convincing you, not all of them as pleasant! You said yourself that your friends don't know where you are. We are quite alone here, except for my men at the doors, and they won't interfere.

There's no way for you to escape. Oh no, Caroline, I assure you, you'll be happy in the end to marry me!'

'I'd rather kill you first!' Even as Caroline hurled this defiance at him she was cursing her stupidity in coming here so unprotected. She didn't even have her pistol...

The blow from his fist on the side of her head was so completely unexpected that she staggered and almost fell.

'How?' he asked softly, advancing towards her. 'How will you kill me, Caroline?' He aimed another blow, but she managed to dodge it and ran round the other side of the table in the centre of the room. His whip lay where he had left it on the table. Snatching it up, she let fly with it. It caught him full in the face. He gave a shout of pain, but quickly recovered and grabbed the end of the whip, jerking it out of her hand.

'Something else to add to the score,' he said thickly, wiping a trickle of blood from his cheek. 'It will be a pleasure to teach you a lesson.'

Caroline picked up a heavy candlestick that stood on the console nearby. 'You'll have to catch me first,' she said.

'I will, my dear, I will,' Sir Anthony said, coming slowly round the end of the table. 'Eventually.'

Keeping her eye on him, Caroline edged away towards a side table. On it was a favourite weapon. She picked up the decanter in her free hand and smashed it against the wall. A stream of red wine splashed over her dress like blood. 'You won't find it easy,' she said fiercely, holding the jagged edges towards him.

'No?' With a sudden flick of his wrist he sent the whip snaking across to wind itself round her wrist. He gave it a vicious tug and the decanter dropped from a hand that was suddenly nerveless. Beside herself with pain and fury, she threw the candlestick at him. It caught him on his shoulder, but didn't stop him. With a shout of triumph he rushed towards her and threw her against the table.

'Now who's master?' he gloated, pinning her beneath him and forcing cruel kisses on her.

The feel of his body pressed hard against hers made her feel sick, his hot breath was stifling her... Caroline fought like a demon, using all the tricks she knew, but he was stronger than she was and he knew it. He pressed her back over the table, till she thought her spine would snap. She thought briefly of John. How she wished she could have told him what she really felt about him, how much she loved him! Too late now. Her strength was failing, but she would kill herself before she gave in to this madman. Though, she thought with a last touch of irony, it looked as if Sir Anthony was crazed enough to do that for her. In his fury he appeared to have forgotten that he needed her alive! He was staring wildly, his hands round her throat, squeezing the breath out of her lungs. She felt herself growing dizzy...

John burst through the door and what he saw brought a mist of rage to his eyes. With a roar of anger he leapt through the room, took Sir Anthony by the collar and flung him away to the floor, uncaring that his quarry landed with his head hard against the leg of the side table. He pulled Caroline up and cradled her. 'Are you all right?' he asked, his voice hoarse with anxiety.

'John!' she said faintly. 'John, it's you! Oh, thank God! Thank God!'

Still holding her, John turned to face Sir Anthony, who was struggling to his feet, trying to pull a gun out of his pocket at the same time.

John drew his own pistol. 'I'm a better shot than you, Grainger,' he said levelly. 'Though there's nothing I'd like better, don't tempt me to shoot you. Put the gun down. Put it down, I say!'

Sir Anthony had little fight left in him. His sundry hurts got the better of him, and he threw the gun away and collapsed to the floor again.

John's two friends came in, looking remarkably cool for two men who had just dealt, very roughly, with Sir Anthony's henchmen. 'Pity!' said Ivo, dusting his hands. 'I see we're too late. I'd have enjoyed dealing with this one, too.'

'You can take him away,' said John. 'Where are the others?'

'Tied up in the cellar with Bellerby in charge. He might now consent to march them to the watch house. There's one just down the road. Till now he's refused to leave the house before he knew Mrs Duval was safe. What shall we do with this fellow?' Adam asked.

'I don't want him taken with the others. Take him to the cellar and leave him there for the moment. I need to think.' He turned to Caroline, who had been held close to him throughout this. 'Caroline?'

'John, I...I thought I...' Caroline burst into tears.

'Oh, my love, my darling!' John said shakily, folding her close in his arms and kissing her. 'Don't cry, I can't bear it. Caroline, my love...'

Ivo and Adam looked on with amazement at the scene before them. Was this Colonel Ancroft, the stiffest, most coldly reserved of all Wellington's officers, passionately comforting a woman, who, in spite of her distraught state, her tumbled hair, her dishevelled clothes, was one of the most attractive women they had ever seen? They could hardly believe it. But then, as the kiss showed no signs of coming to an end, the two friends recalled their manners, went over to Sir Anthony and hauled him to his feet.

Their Colonel didn't even notice them leaving, as they removed their captive, and took him to join the others in the cellar.

When they returned after a suitable interval, they were relieved to find the atmosphere slightly less intense, though Caroline was still held close to the Colonel's side.

'What's this?' asked Adam as he picked up a picture that had fallen to the floor. 'Good God!' he exclaimed, as he put it back on the easel. He threw a quick glance at Caroline, then stammered, 'Excuse me, ma'am! I didn't realise…'

John said, 'What is it?' and went to look, closely followed by Ivo.

'Good God!' they said, practically in unison. Ivo looked back at Caroline with renewed interest.

John cleared his throat. 'You'll forget you ever saw this,' he said sternly to the other two.

Lords Calthorpe and Trenchard both hastened to assure him they would, indeed they would, on their honour!

'It's a very poor forgery,' said John. 'Nothing like the original.'

'But, John, how did you know that?' asked Caroline in amazement. 'You've never seen the original!'

'Oh, yes, I have,' said John. 'Twice.'

Adam and Ivo watched with interest as Mrs Duval, who had so far not turned a hair, even while they examined her portrait, was suddenly scarlet with embarrassment. 'John!' she exclaimed. 'How could you! What will your friends think?'

'That you'll *have* to marry me now,' he said with satisfaction.

Caroline looked at him and started to laugh. She turned to Adam. 'Lord Calthorpe, I am more obliged than I can say for your help in rescuing me. If you can forget every second of the last five minutes, I should be even more obliged.'

'Readily, ma'am. On one condition.'

'Really?' said Caroline raising an eyebrow.

'That you'll put my commanding officer out of his misery. I haven't yet heard you say yes.'

Caroline's lovely smile flashed out. 'I'll do that with all my heart!' She turned to John. 'Can you forget the stupid things I've said?'

'If you'll forgive the stupid things I've done.'

'It's a bargain. I'll marry you, John.' He took her hand and kissed it, then drew her to him again. Ivo cleared his throat apologetically.

'Er… Strange as it may seem, I haven't yet been introduced to the lady at present in your arms, Colonel.' With a wicked twinkle in his eye he added, 'Though I feel I already know her quite well.'

Caroline burst out laughing again. 'I've waited so long to meet you, Lord Trenchard. I've heard so much about you and your wife. But I never thought the meeting would be quite as unconventional as this!'

'I'm honoured to make your acquaintance, Mrs Duval. May I wish you and John all happiness?'

'And I,' said Adam. 'But we still haven't settled the problem of Sir Anthony.'

'May I make a suggestion?' said Caroline.

'About Sir Anthony?'

'He said he was thinking of going to Jamaica to escape his creditors. I think it might be wise to help him on his way.'

'He certainly can't stay in England without being sent to a debtors' prison,' John said thoughtfully. 'He won't want to risk that. I think it's a good idea.'

'But that means he gets away with attacking Mrs Duval!' exclaimed Ivo.

'A court case might be…a touch embarrassing?' suggested Adam. 'Evidence, and so on… Not that I'm remembering anything, mind!'

'Quite! I think we should adopt Caroline's suggestion. I've already sent one man off to Jamaica. Sir Anthony can follow him. Betts will deal with it.'

'He can join his cousin,' said Caroline. 'Two villains together.'

They returned to Charles Street, and while Caroline escaped to her room to make herself respectable, the gentlemen gave their version of the events in Grainger Lodge. By the time she came downstairs they were waiting for her, glasses at the ready and several bottles of champagne in a cooler on the side. John handed her a glass, and smiled deep into her eyes, giving her his own private toast. Lady Danby dismissed the servants who had been busy laying refreshments out on the table, then raised her glass.

'There are so many toasts that I don't know where to begin! To Caroline and Lord Coverdale. Happiness and long life! I can't say how relieved I am that you've finally come to your senses, Caroline! And I hope Lord Coverdale realizes what a lucky man he is!'

They laughed and drank and she went on, 'Next, to Jossie and Ivo. Welcome back to England. We've missed you! And…' she paused, and gave a mischievous glance first at Kate and then at Jossie '…to the future generation! To the first young Trenchard, and the second young Calthorpe!' New exclamations and congratulations ensued, as Kate and Jossie laughed and shook their heads at Lady Danby.

Then Caroline stepped forward. 'I am so glad you are all here. And I'd like to propose a toast to our own future generation. To the first young Ancroft. To Harriet!' She held out her arms and Harriet ran to her and was roundly hugged.

Finally, John held up his hand.

'A last toast,' he said. 'To Wellington and the men of Waterloo. To all those who, like Kate's brother, our friend Tom Payne, didn't survive. And to those of us who did.'

It was a solemn moment. They stood round in a circle and raised their glasses. Lady Danby stood beside Captain Lord Trenchard and his Jossie. Major Lord Calthorpe had a comforting arm round Kate. And Colonel Ancroft, now Lord Coverdale, stood with Harriet, his daughter, on one side—and Caroline, his love, on the other.

'The Duke!' they said. 'And the men of Waterloo!'

* * * * *